A Gift for Lila Rose:

A China Adoption Love Story

By Fred Ford

PublishAmerica
Baltimore

ISBN: 1-60610-292-3
PUBLISHED BY PUBLISHAMERICA, LLLP
www.publishamerica.com
Baltimore

Printed in the United States of America

TABLE OF CONTENTS

To Babe, Mom, and Dad
My heroes

gift (n.)

1. Something that is bestowed voluntarily and without compensation.

2. The act, right, or power of giving.

3. A talent, endowment, aptitude, or inclination.

·2011·

Venita—
    Sometimes you have more in common with a person than you realize. This is my cousin's story & I would guess you may find yours within the pages. Enjoy! Hubby.

"The only true gift is a portion of thyself."
—Ralph Waldo Emerson—

OPENING CREDITS

It's magic, movies are, the only true magic I know. The big screen is like a window through which I view another man's vision, hear his voice, and appreciate an imagination different from my own. For many, the movies are entertainment, a fun way to spend leisure hours, the burden of conversation lifted from a first date, or an escape from reality. For me, movies present a real challenge: to seek my own voice, dare to be original, and one day to step on the other side of that window and, through the magic of movies, to share my vision with the world.

I lack only one thing: an inspiration....

ACT I-
THE GENESIS

Chapter 1
CREATIVE SPARKS AND ELEPHANT FARTS

The common thread that weaves through every stage of my life's unique journey is movies. And the most significant movie of my lifetime is the one I produced as a gift to my daughter Lila Rose, who my wife Babe and I adopted from China in 2004. The story of the adoption and the movie it inspired is, to date, the story of my life. The adoption taught me a deeper meaning of love and introduced me to a wondrous example of the power of prayer. It enriched my marriage and altered the course of my life in ways I never dreamed of.

As far as I can tell, the story began in 1964, the year my love affair with the movies began...

Arlington, Massachusetts
December 1964

It's Christmas day. I'm five years old and standing on the roof ledge of my house wearing my new Superman outfit. I'm ready for my first flight. My younger brother Tommy is next to me. He's Batman. Since Batman doesn't fly, I'll be flying alone. I'm not afraid of heights but I'm not so sure how this outfit will help me fly. I feel the same as I did a few minutes ago, when I was wearing pajamas. What's the problem? Maybe the roof's made of kryptonite.

Before I leap, I hear Mom.

"Boys!" she yells. "Come inside, it's cold out there."

Where'd she come from? She's wearing a funny look on her face as she waves us inside with half her body hanging out the window.

"Come on inside," she smiles. "Come on…come on." Sounds like she's singing.

Tommy and I crawl back inside. Mom slams the window shut and latches it. When she turns to us she's not smiling any more. She has one of those angry looks on her face that make her eyes water.

"Don't you ever, ever go on that roof again," she yells. "Do you understand me?"

I nod. I'm in trouble.

"It's *very* dangerous. Superman can't really fly and neither can you," she says.

How was I supposed to know? He flies on TV.

Mom leaves the room and I'm not happy about Superman's secret: he doesn't really fly. Probably can't deflect bullets off his chest either. Next thing you know Mom will tell me there's no Santa Claus.

What am I supposed to do now? I can't fly and I can't deflect bullets. My Superman outfit is nothing more than a pair of pajamas with a cape. It's okay; it's Christmas. I have a whole bunch of other new toys to play with. Besides, I can have fun teasing my sister Lorraine. She's been waiting an hour for a cake the size of a hockey puck to finish cooking in her Easy Bake Oven.

I love Christmas.

* * *

We're driving to Grammy's tonight for a holiday visit. She lives in South Boston, which we call Southie. Dad is one of Grammy's ten children so her house gets crowded on holidays, especially Christmas and St. Patrick's Day.

"Group!" Dad yells. That's the sign it's time for me and my brother and three sisters to go.

We drive from Arlington to Southie in our white Ford Falcon. As we get near Boston, I look for Johnny Walker on his billboard. We approach the tunnel near South Station, and there he is with his vest and top hat.

"Hi kids," Johnny calls. His voice sounds like Dad's, only more squeaky.

"Hi Johnny Walker, bye Johnny Walker," we say as we zoom past.

"Bye kids, have fun at Grammy's." Dad's lips never move. I know because I watched him the whole time.

We get to Grammy's and I feel shy because there are a million relatives there. I stand in line for a kiss from Grammy. She's sitting in her big chair at the dining room table as always. My aunts, uncles, and cousins are crowded into the house and Aunt Cackie is playing Christmas carols on the piano in the living room. Everyone's drinking beer, smoking cigarettes, and eating Grammy's potato salad or tomato soup cake. Grammy seems surprised at how tall I'm growing. Aren't I supposed to grow? What's the big deal?

Another thing people say is, "All you Fords look the same." It's true because I look like my brother and sisters. Except my sisters can't pee standing up since they don't have whoozees; they have little bums instead.

Grampy's not here any more. He went to Heaven in '63. I don't remember much about Grampy. He looked just like dad only shorter and with white hair. I can't remember much about him dying. Mom and Dad were visiting him for Father's Day when Grampy died.

Dad planted a baby tree in our front yard right after Grampy died. It looks like Charlie Brown's Christmas tree. I don't remember much else about Grampy. When Dad told us Grampy died it's the only time I ever saw Dad cry. That's what I remember most about Grampy dying: Dad cried—and that little baby tree planted in the front yard.

Grammy owns a color TV and I can't wait to watch it. I could watch the color all day; it makes the TV shows look different—almost like being at the movies. Our black and white TV at home just isn't the same. I go to the living room to see what's on. Uncle Billy, the world's loudest Bruins fan, is watching a hockey game and smoking Lucky Strikes.

I give Billy a hand shake and squeeze tight like Dad taught me. Billy reacts like I just squished the bones in his hand.

"Where'd you get that grip?" he says.

I turn to the color TV screen. Watching hockey is great but I'm hoping between periods Billy will change the channel and turn on some cartoons: Huckleberry Hound or Yogi Bear and Boo Boo.

Right after I plop on the couch to watch the hockey game, Uncle Paul and Aunt Joyce show up with four of my cousins. The loud noise is about to get louder. That's what happens at Grammy's; cousins and aunts and uncles come and go all day and the kissing and hugging and handshakes never stop.

Just before we leave, I get a nice bowl full of Grammy's potato salad, the greatest food I ever tasted—including Captain Crunch with Crunch Berries and Fenway Franks with Gulden's mustard.

It's dark by the time we leave. I have a headache from all the noise and singing and excitement and smoke. I kiss Grammy before I leave. I fall asleep as we drive home, missing another chance to talk to Johnny Walker.

* * *

Right after Christmas, Mom's taking us to the Regent Theater to see *Mary Poppins,* a movie by Walt Disney.

Movies are magic to me. When I'm watching a movie I don't want them to end. I'm going to be a movie star some day, singing and dancing—maybe even flying like Peter Pan. Maybe I'll make my own movie. The Regent Theater is my favorite place in the world, except home, and Grammy's house, and Wells Beach in Maine.

We walk from our house to Arlington Center. I'm walking too fast at first.

"Freddie, don't walk too fast," Mom says. "Stay together."

That's our motto outside the house: stay together. And don't talk to strangers. And watch out for people like the Boston Strangler—who finally got caught this year.

Me and Tommy walk in front of my sisters and Mom. I know the way by heart: down to Broadway and take a right and don't get near Broadway because of the speeding cars, be careful to watch out for the thorny bushes surrounding the Donovan's yard, past Palmer Street and Webster Street and Franklin Street, past the 7-11 where I slow down to think about a Slurpee, and next to 7-11 there's Toy Land where I stop to look at the Rock Em Sock Em Robots in the display window.

"Can we get them, Mom, pleeeeease?" I ask Mom.

"You have enough toys, keep walking," Mom says.

I walk past the used car dealership and the fire station in Arlington Center hoping the loud sirens won't go off suddenly and scare the crap out of me. I slow down at Woolworth's and look inside while I imagine hiding in clothing racks and searching for toys, then I turn right on Medford Street and there it is: The Regent Theater!

We stand in line while Mom pays for all of us and we walk into the lobby where I smell and hear popcorn.

"Let's go," Mom says; meaning no popcorn.

In the lobby, I see a poster of coming attractions: *It's a Mad, Mad, Mad, Mad World* which we saw last year. For days after seeing that movie, I drew pictures of the scene at the end when all the guys were in the hospital covered with bandages after falling off the fire truck ladder.

A man is standing in the lobby wearing a gray suit. He's always here. He looks like Alfred the butler only with darker hair. As I walk by, he winks at me. I don't know how to wink yet and he's scary so I keep moving.

Once inside the theater, I follow Mom into one of the rows closest to the screen and stare at the red curtain in front of the movie screen. All of a sudden, the curtain parts and the lights go off.

Cartoons play on the screen before *Mary Poppins* starts. They look so great all big and colorful, so much better than our TV where Dad says it snows on every program—even on Jackie Gleason in Miami Beach. The first cartoon is Bugs Bunny and he's trying to get away from some big hairy monster who keeps saying, "I will hug him and squeeze him and call him George."

Then Road Runner and Coyote comes on and Coyote can't catch Road Runner because he buys all his traps from ACME and they don't work. I could watch cartoons in the movie theater for the rest of my life.

Mary Poppins comes on after the cartoons. I cry at the end of the movie but don't let anyone see me. I don't know why I'm crying; it was a happy ending. I want to come back and see it again tomorrow. But I know Mom won't let me. So I'll probably act out the movie at home.

Dad buys the *Mary Poppins* album a few days later. I play it in his bedroom on Dad's record player over and over, listening to *I Love to Laugh* and *Let's Go Fly a Kite* while I act out the movie. Only I can't float in the air like Uncle Albert and Bert. I can't float and I can't fly. Remember?

* * *

The Wizard of Oz is coming on TV soon. The commercials are showing on TV. By the time the movie is shown I'm looking forward to it like Christmas morning. Watching *The Wizard of Oz* every year is a holiday in our house.

The night of the movie, I have butterflies in my stomach.

"Put your pajamas on kids," Mom says. That's the signal we're about to head upstairs to Grandma's for the movie.

I put my pajamas on and race upstairs with my sisters and brother. Grandma is smiling as always.

She has bowls of M&Ms waiting for us. I plop on the floor in front of the giant Zenith black and white TV. The movie starts when the MGM lion roars. He's not the same as the Cowardly Lion. Dad says so and Dad's the smartest man in the world so I believe him.

We watch the movie and I love it. I get scared when the big ugly trees start yelling at Dorothy and throw the shiny red apples at her and when Cowardly Lion comes bombing out of the woods. I'm scared of the flying monkeys too; sometimes I have nightmares about them.

The movie ends and I try not to cry when Dorothy says, "There's no place like home." I don't let anyone see me crying; I don't want my sisters to think I'm a sissy.

It's past bedtime. I kiss grandma and head downstairs to bed. The movie credits are still rolling.

I crawl into bed and can't sleep. I lie awake for hours thinking up ways to keep the movie going. I imagine Dorothy going back to Oz, seeing her friends again, and meeting a new friend: Me! My own version of *The Wizard of Oz* plays for hours in my head until I fall asleep.

The next day I act out scenes from the movie with my brother Tommy. I gather up a bunch of clothes and shoes; then push my bed away from the wall and crouch in the narrow space between the bed and the wall.

"Oh-wee-oh, weeeoooo-oh," we sing, trying to sound like the guards outside the witch's castle.

Tommy plays the scarecrow, wearing one of mom's floppy hats. I play the Tin Man; my hat's a funnel. We pretend we're being attacked from behind just like in the movie. I duck low in the space between the bed and wall, mess up my hair, and fling shoes and clothes in the air. When we're done, we gather the clothes and shoes and do it again and again.

Later, it's time for *Sea Hunt*. I lay stomach-down on the linoleum floor and pretend to swim, moving my arms and legs like a frog man and making the bubbling sounds of air escaping my air tank. I crawl on my belly and spit on my arms and hands as if I'm really getting wet. I enter the cave—the frightening space under my bed. I find stuff that looks a lot scarier than any of the stuff Lloyd Bridges ever found.

I can't really fly like Superman or visit Oz or swim under the ocean like Lloyd Bridges. But in my imagination, I can do anything.

So I visit my imagination all the time.

* * *

It's 1968. Grandma leaves for work a few days before St. Patrick's Day and never comes back. Mom is on the phone all day and her voice sounds funny.

"Is she okay?" she asks. "Is my mother okay?" She asks this over and over.

She gets her friend Margie to baby-sit and leaves. Mom comes home after dark. Her head is wrapped in a kerchief and her face is sadder than I ever saw it.

Grandma's sister—who we call Sister even though she's my mother's aunt—shows up later that night. I never saw anything but a smile on Sister's face; but not tonight.

The house seems different tonight. Dad tells us to play quietly in the living room. I don't play; I sit on the couch and try to listen to what the adults are saying. Still no Grandma; something strange is going on.

Margie comes over on St. Patrick's Day to baby-sit. I guess we won't be going to Southie for the St. Patrick's Day Parade. I'm going to miss all my cousins and aunts and uncles and Aunt Cackie playing the piano and running downhill on the sidewalk of Mercer Street to Grammy's house. And I'm sad I won't be seeing Grammy or her color TV. Most of all, I miss Grandma.

"We're going to Grandma's wake," Mom says. "We'll be home later."

Mom still looks sad. But I'm happy they're going to wake Grandma even though I'm not sure how they're going to wake her or whether or not Grandma's coming home after they wake her up.

Dad's good friends Jim O'Keefe, John Mulkern, and Lorrie Prudente go to the wake right after celebrating St. Patrick's Day, which means they drank a lot of beer and were probably loud. Drinking beer seems to make your hearing worse because everyone who drinks it talks louder. Dad says having a wake on St. Patrick's Day is like the old Irish wakes he used to go to in East Cambridge. I don't know what Irish wakes are. I don't even know what regular wakes are. And I don't ask.

Grandma doesn't come home after the wake. The only thing Mom or Dad says is she's in Heaven.

A few days after the wake, Mom still seems sad. Dad's at work so I'm able to play slip-and-slide with Tommy without Dad telling us to stop. Slip and slide is a game where we run down the hallway from one end of our house to the other and slide along the floor into the pile of Mom's shoes in the hall closet. My younger sister Jeanne and Alison play in the hamper and mess up all the clothes Mom folded.

All of a sudden Lorraine drops her glass and it breaks on the floor and there's grape juice and broken glass everywhere. Mom's trying to cook dinner but when she comes out of the kitchen to see the juice and the glass and the clothes all over the place and me sitting in the closet with her shoes all messed up Mom starts to cry.

"That's it; I've had it," she says really loud.

Mom doesn't cry like this too much; only when she reaches the end of her rope, whatever that means.

She walks real fast to the door and leaves to go upstairs and slams the door.

It gets real quiet and all five of us are standing still like we just got sprayed by Mr. Freeze's gun. Lorraine starts to cry and then goes into the kitchen. She usually has good ideas when things like this happen so I follow.

I go into the kitchen and Lorraine is boiling hot dogs and heating up some B&M baked beans. I get a plate and fork and knife and mustard and ketchup ready. When Lorraine's done cooking, we clean up the glass and grape juice then carry Mom's meal upstairs.

We walk into Grandma's old bedroom. Mom is drying her eyes with a tissue. Lorraine hands the plate of hot dogs and beans to Mom and I give the mustard and ketchup to her.

"We're sorry Mom," Lorraine says.

Mom takes the plate and ketchup and mustard and puts them on the night table then gathers us all into her arms and hugs us. Then she starts to cry again but different from before. I think these are happy tears, like the ones I cry at the end of *The Wizard of Oz* and *Mary Poppins*.

* * *

With Grandma gone and our family growing too big for the second floor apartment, me and Tommy move into one of the two bedrooms on the third floor. My younger sisters Alison and Jeanne take the other bedroom.

The first night in my new bedroom I hear the creak of one of the stairs leading up to the third floor. I panic. I imagine the Boston Strangler coming up the stairs real slow. I lock the door and get back in bed. The loud creak continues all night and I get about a minute of sleep.

The day after surviving my first night in the new bedroom, I'm starring in my own movie with my brother Tommy. He's a year younger than me but we almost look like twins only he's smaller. So we made up a movie called *Twin and Twinnie*. It's more like a really long TV show than a movie. It's about two boys who look just like each other but aren't really twins. The movie goes on all day. I guess it's pretty boring to anyone except the two us. What do you expect from someone who crawls along the floor spitting on himself?

Later, I play records in Dad's bedroom. I put on the Dixieland record and pretend I'm playing the trombone. My parents bought a trombone for me and I'll be taking lessons at school. I can't play it yet so I pretend. After Dixieland, I conduct the orchestra playing Bizet's *Carman*. I play it over and over and try not to scratch the record.

I like the trombone because of *The Music Man* and the song "76 Trombones." Once I start learning to play trombone at school, I practice at night; it's like music homework. I'm not good at first even though I'm playing easy songs like "Red River Valley" and "When the Saints Come Marching In." I hit a lot of flat notes, which I call elephant farts, because that's what they sound like. Not that I own an elephant.

One day at school, the music teacher Mr. Gouvier tells me he picked me to be in the school orchestra. To celebrate, Dad buys a bunch of Glen Miller records for me. I listen to Glen Miller playing "Moonlight Serenade" and I think: Is that a trombone? I could never make mine sound that good. I decide I'll be retiring the trombone soon.

Dad calls Grammy on the phone one Sunday.

"I have something I want you to hear. Listen," he says, then puts the phone in front of the horn of my trombone. I play Grammy's favorite song: "My Wild Irish Rose." I bet I'm the only person in history to ever play "My Wild Irish Rose" on the trombone over the phone to their grandmother.

That week I have to play a song in the school recital. I'm playing a duet of "Born Free" with my classmate Billy Friece. We've practiced for weeks but I'm still afraid I'll accidentally make an elephant fart.

The day of the recital, a bunch of kids are backstage tuning up. We're all nervous and everyone's playing warm-up notes of different songs. The sounds are enough to give me a nervous breakdown.

One by one, we're introduced as the audience claps. Billy and I are the next act and Mark Haroutunian is having a hard time playing "Polka Dot Polka" on his squeaky clarinet. So far, there hasn't been a single performance I'd call a tough act to follow. When it's our turn, my knees are knocking.

Mr. Gouvier says, "And now ladies and gentlemen, to play 'Born Free' on their trombones, here are Fred Ford and Billy Friece."

The audience applauds but somehow I don't hear much. I feel funny, like I'm about to crap in my pants. I stumble to the microphone, standing side-by-side with Billy. My knees are still knocking and cold sweat is pouring out of me. Mr. Gouvier raises his arms as conductor and me and Billy raise the trombones and place our lips onto the mouthpiece. For the first note, the trombone's slide is pulled close to my face by my right hand—the slide hand. For the second note I'll need to extend the slide out as far as I can reach. I know the rest by heart.

Mr. Gouvier nods and pulls his hands apart. Me and Billy pucker up and blow into our trombones and the first note comes out as clear as Snow White's complexion—a term Mr. Gouvier uses. But then, as Billy extends his slide all the way down for the second note, my attempt nearly sends me into a front somersault as if someone smacked my head from behind with a frying pan. By accident, I locked the slide in place and forgot to loosen the nut before starting the performance. Again, I feel I'm going to crap my pants—only worse than before.

Billy continues and I stop playing. Trying to be real cool like James Bond, I loosen the nut and wait for the second verse to begin. It starts and I jump in and keep playing to the end of the song.

The crowd applauds and we leave the stage. I'm so relieved I nearly start to cry.

After the concert, I'm afraid to face Mr. Gouvier. When he comes backstage I explain what happened with the locked slide.

"You handled it perfectly," he says. "I knew right away what happened, but you didn't panic and you played it cool and pulled it off. Nobody knew the difference."

My first performance in front of a live audience is over. I think it's the only trombone version of "Born Free" ever played in public. Even though I almost blew it, I want to perform again. Maybe I won't quit the trombone after all. Maybe I'll get good enough to join the Boston Pops.

My career in show biz has begun!

* * *

I'm sitting in Sunday school and bored so bad I think I'm going to die. It's bad enough I have to go to school all week and then church on Sunday, but on top of it all: *Sunday* school. My teacher is a nun who looks like Ernest Borgnine. I'm paying attention to make sure she won't get mad. Also, I don't want to spend eternity in Hell.

While teaching the class about prayer, the nun says, "In the Bible, God promises that all prayers are answered. He says, 'Ask and ye shall receive, knock and the door shall be opened'."

I decide to ask God for a Reese's Cup when class is over.

A student raises his hand and the nun calls on him.

The kid asks, "What if a kid in St. Louis asks God for the Blues to win a hockey game and at the same time a kid in Boston asks God for the Bruins to win? How can God answer both of their prayers?"

I'm thinking it's a pretty cool question. I want to hear how the nun answers.

"God answers prayers in mysterious ways, in His time, and not always in the way or the time we expect," the nun explains.

I'm not sure what mysterious means, but it seems she didn't answer the question. Maybe the game between the Blues and the Bruins will end in a tie.

I figure one tough question per class is enough, so I don't ask mine: If God created everything, who created God?

Mom always told me: God has *always been*! When I think about that, I get dizzy. I also wonder how God can be everywhere at once. Thinking about God is hard because I can't see Him, unless you count the crucifix hanging on the wall at home.

Mom and Dad read the Bible to us once in a while. I get bored and I have a hard time believing the stories. Like Moses parting the sea and Jonah jumping into the whale's mouth like Pinocchio.

I get bored in church. Of all the things Mom and Dad make me do, church is my least favorite. Also, eating spinach and going to the dentist and having globs of Dippity-Do rubbed into my hair.

Once in a while I hear a Bible verse I like. I'm in church one day and the priest is reading about a poor widow who puts two small copper coins into the treasury. Compared with the donations made by the richer people in the town, the widow's two coins don't add up to much.

When Jesus sees the donation, he says "the poor widow gave more than anyone." It's all because she gave everything she owned and not just the leftover.

I'm not sure if I'll ever have the same amount of faith as the widow but I hope when I grow up I will. The story sticks with me for days, like Turkish taffy on my teeth.

* * *

We have only one television set in our house and my three sisters always want to watch something I don't want to watch. So I don't see all the shows I want to because Mom says I need to share. The only show we all like is The Jack LaLanne Show with Jack and the organ music and his stupid white dog. When Dad gets home, it's Walter Cronkite and that's that.

Usually we don't watch TV during the day. Mom says, "It's beautiful outside, go outside and play," even if it's cold.

I play a lot in the back yard. Sometimes, I take a spoon with me and dig in the dirt.

"Don't dig too deep," Dad says, "or else you'll dig all the way to China."

Digging to China sounds like a fun idea. I'd want to visit China even though the only Chinese person I've ever seen is Odd Job from *Goldfinger* and Kato from *The Green Hornet*. And I don't want to meet either of those guys because they know karate—and Odd Job has a deadly hat.

When the weather's not good and sometimes at night I watch my favorite TV shows: *Batman, The Flintstones, Lost in Space,* and *The Man From U.N.C.L.E.* Once in a while they make a movie version of the TV show and The Regent Theater plays it for a week. *The Man From U.N.C.L.E.* movie is playing now. I take my $1 weekly allowance from Mom and run to the theater with Tommy to watch it.

I can't take my eyes off the screen for two hours. It's the best movie I've ever seen. On the way home I pretend I'm Napoleon Solo and Tommy's Illya Kuriakan. Tommy always plays the sidekick because I'm older.

When we get home, I beg Mom for another dollar so I can see the movie again tomorrow.

"Please ma, it's the best movie ever," I say.

"We'll see," Mom says, which I'm happy to hear because with Mom "we'll see" means "yes"—as long as I don't do anything stupid like try to fly off the roof in my Superman outfit.

My days at the Regent Theater and the three-story home in Arlington, Massachusetts end in the middle of my sixth grade school year in 1971. Dad's moving the family up to Salem, New Hampshire. I'm sad about moving. I'm president of my class and I have lots of friends and I'm in Boy Scouts and I have my first girlfriend: Cheryl Head.

I don't want to move even though Canobie Lake Park is in Salem near my new home. I don't know anybody in Salem. I hope Salem has a movie theater.

Chapter 2
FREDERICK FORD COPOLLA

Bellport, New York
July 1996

It's the Fourth of July and a perfect weather day; the type that ought to carry with it a $50 fine for those who choose to stay indoors. Lured outside by bright sunshine and the temporary emancipation from work obligations, the residents of eastern Long Island are busily filling the day with their favorite activities—or, for some, their favorite inactivity. My wife Babe and I drive south in our Honda Accord from our garden apartment complex to the tidy suburbs of south Bellport as we listen to The Beatles' timeless *White Album* on the car's cassette player. Our destiny is Fairway Drive, where construction of our house is scheduled to commence tomorrow. A month short of my thirty-seventh birthday, I'm about to realize the elusive dream of home ownership. Once settled into our new home, Babe and I plan to start a family. Things are good.

What's more, a new day in my life as an artist is about to dawn; for today I begin filming for my first movie!

Months ago, when the vague plans to build a house began to crystallize— thanks in large part to a mortgage commitment for a construction loan—I was inspired to commemorate the occasion by producing a movie. I bought a video camera and began to mentally concoct a loose format for a movie, though I haven't a clue how to edit video. The editing dilemma, therefore, gets crammed into the overstuffed Cross-That-Bridge-When-I-Come-To-It file in the far recesses of my brain.

What inspired me to make a movie? Easy….

...my wife Babe. After rescuing me from the self-indulgent life as a bachelor, she's affirmed every good part of me: my faith, sense of humor, and creativity. Our love is the most precious thing I know.

She thinks I can write as well as Woody Allen. Whenever we see a Woody Allen movie, she says, "You could write something like that." It's such a comfort to hear; and so breathtakingly untrue.

Nevertheless, she recognized in me a talent to create and write. So on my thirty-fifth birthday, she blessed me with ten books about writing screenplays. I read one after another, and suddenly the vague image of creating movies took on a recognizable shape.

When I finished the books, I became a veracious reader of screenplays. Between the How-To-Write books and screenplays, the lid to my imagination had been pried open and the slumbering bear within my mind emerged from hibernation. Inspired, I began to write a screenplay titled "The Burdens of Death," a murder mystery.

At the same time, I continued to write my own material for a stand-up comedy act stalled in mediocrity. Don't tell Babe that. She thinks I'm hilarious. When I opened for Mr. Kotter himself, Gabe Kaplan, at the sold out Medford Inn years ago Babe insisted I got more laughs than Kaplan.

The crowd at Medford Inn was the exception, not the rule. Many of my gigs were poorly attended and some were downright embarrassing—for example, the night I performed in front of an audience of eight at Tiny's Cow Palace, a sweltering dive in Westhampton more suited for a cock fight than a comedy show. Through it all, Babe was the common denominator, always there for support—telling me I'm as funny as Woody Allen.

I had read time and again that in order to be a successful writer I had to do two things: read a lot and write a lot. I had the first part down pat. But I had yet to develop the discipline to write with any frequency. My inexperience showed when I tried to create a screenplay. I had read over and over screenwriters should "show-don't-tell"; in other words don't be obvious. My attempts to be clever and surreptitious resulted in hours staring at a blank computer screen or, worse yet, a page or two of actual writing. The dialogue sounded contrived and ridiculous; the

29

plot as uninteresting as an essay on snoring remedies. So while I continued to wrestle with the screenplay—and clinging to the notion this would somehow help—I joined a writer's group.

In the writer's group, five pages of my screenplay were read aloud each week, along with five pages from all the other writer's screenplays. It didn't take long to verify what I already knew with blinding clarity: my screenplay sucked. When it was read aloud, I felt as though I was listening to my grandmother sing Kate Smith ballads at Karaoke.

None of it mattered to Babe. "You're going to write a great screenplay some day, hon, just stay with it," she'd say. Her unflinching belief I could rise above my career as real estate appraiser and part-time comedian to become a successful and sought after screenwriter always managed to stir my creative juices.

I was determined to keep at it until the summer we had the house built. My writing, thankfully, was interrupted by the inspiration to videotape and edit a movie about the house construction. This was the biggest event of my life up to this point, with the exception of my wedding (and, technically speaking, my birth). Accordingly, I figured a movie about the process would be a worthwhile endeavor and a unique way to preserve the event in ways cinematic. It excited me to think about making a movie, a lifelong dream that had reluctantly taken a back seat to idle thoughts, meaningless social obligations, hours spent glued to a couch watching television, and uninspired career choices.

With a projected audience of one—Babe—I was inspired to give movie-making my best shot. Without Babe, none of it would have happened.

We travel east along Head of the Neck Road, then turn right (south) onto Fairway Drive where I quickly pull to the curb. With the car stopped, I turn to Babe and mentally stammer through my pre-rehearsed explanation pertaining to the first scene to be filmed. My vision involves shooting the scene while seated on the hood of the car with the camera pointed straight ahead as the car proceeds slowly through our new neighborhood toward the site of our soon-to-be built home. I plan to use the footage with the opening credits; the audio provided by Gary Glitter's *Rock and Roll Part I.*

All potential alternative openings to the movie have been carefully considered and then tossed into my mental waste basket. The vision I hold for the movie's opening is both clear and non-negotiable; thus I am prepared to fight studio heads, producers, co-producer, and anyone else inclined to offer alternative openings. Unfortunately for me, the entire crew and cast consists of one person: my wife, for whom my negotiations always tend to favor. And so, on the first day of shooting, only one obstacle remains: convincing Babe this is a good idea—and reminding her that under the burden of my weight the hood of our car will likely suffer the insult of a permanent wok-sized dimple. By default, therefore, she has been elected to operate the camera atop the hood.

I mentally dig in for the tussle, armed with pre-rehearsed and well reasoned comebacks for the anticipated—and inevitable—backwash of objections from Babe, and fully prepared to beg if necessary. I take a strategic deep breath, face Babe, and say matter of factly, "OK, I need you to sit on the hood of the car and operate the camera. Point it straight ahead and keep as steady as you can and I'll drive down the road slowly while you videotape."

The casual tone fails; Babe reacts as though I asked her to perform a strip tease in the middle of the street.

After some inspirational coaxing, which nearly regresses into promises that I'll cook dinner for the next month, Babe reluctantly agrees. With my assistance, she crawls delicately onto the hood and positions herself in the center. I hand the video camera to her and she balances it on her right shoulder as she divides her mental focus between the scene she's about to videotape and the balance she'll need to maintain in order to avoid rolling off the hood like a bag of callously placed groceries. When all is well—or, as well as it's likely to get at any rate—I take my place behind the wheel and accelerate to a crawl down the tree-lined street as Babe videotapes. As I drive, I'm careful to keep one eye on the road and one on my voluptuous—and temporary—hood ornament.

We roll past homes of our future neighbors as if inching along in a one-vehicle parade with an audience of no one. The homes we roll past are mostly twenty to thirty year old ranch and cape cod style homes with neatly landscaped front yards. The road is spotted with mid-morning sunlight filtered the leaves of maple and poplar trees which loom above the street like clouds of butterflies. Eventually, we arrive at the site of our home just short of the road's cul-de-sac. As I slow to a stop, I avoid the urge to yell, "Cut!" I've already jeopardized my directorial debut (and marriage); no need to push the envelope.

The blazing sun bakes the freshly blacktopped road surface and the strong odor attacks my senses as I exit the car. Babe did her best to keep the camera steady but is less than thrilled with her effort.

"I'm sorry, I did my best," she says half-apologetically. "The camera's heavy and I was trying to keep my balance. I think the camera bounced around a little. I hope it's OK."

The thought of Take Two has less appeal than a visit to the proctologist. Getting Babe to sit on the hood the first time was hard enough. The footage she captured will just have to do. To my delight and surprise, I review the bouncy footage later that day and conclude that it works perfectly. Ironically, this same jostle-and-bounce filming technique has evolved into a popular and trendy method of scene-shooting for cinematographers in Hollywood— particularly in war movies where the jerky eye of the camera is used to simulate chaos. Such techniques are used to nauseating extremes (in my humble opinion) in the popular TV show *NYPD Blue*. Strictly by accident, Babe and I have become movie-making trailblazers.

The following day, a one-man crew arrives with a bulldozer to clear the site. I arrive shortly thereafter and the man glances my way indifferently as though observing a squirrel and continues his work with casual indifference to my presence and the camera pointed in his direction. I videotape off and on for a half-hour as a large section of the site is cleared of trees and brush. The heat is relentless and, though early in the morning, my work shirt is soon soaked with sweat. No matter, though, for I have an insatiable desire to see the home constructed step by step before my eyes—and the eye of the camera. I find none of it boring or insignificant and I'll endure any weather— and the moods of all subcontractors—to capture footage every day.

* * *

As the months advance, I immerse myself in the movie-making process as I view footage over and over and mentally concoct images of how the footage will flow together in movie sequences. Part of this process involves listening to various songs in search of appropriate music for the underscore, rapidly exchanging CDs in the player as I listen to one after another on my headphones; searching for just the right song for each section of the movie. I also view footage from movies and TV shows, seeking home construction scenes—like the Amish barn-building scene from *Witness*—that will somehow mingle with my home construction footage to create something entertaining, coherent, and stimulating. Why am I spending so much time on this movie, a movie that will be seen by only a handful of people, perhaps only two (me and Babe)? It all boils down to passion and everyone's passion is different. My passion is movie-making and writing. That creative passion has always been present in my mind, gagged and ignored, smothered beneath a drop cloth of meaningless activity, recurring habits, and mindless career or social obligations. Once recognized, the passion swirled in my subconscious mind twenty-four hours a day; like a vulture circling the carcass of a water buffalo.

Songs of all types are summoned for the movie's soundtrack: The Beatles' *Fixing a Hole* will accompany the pouring of the foundation; Queen's *We Will Rock You* for the sheetrock installation; James Taylor's *Steamroller* for the blacktopping of the driveway, and so on.

One night I'm wearing headphones as I sit at the table in our cramped dining room, listening to CDs, and scribbling notes into my journal like a scientist conducting a lab experiment. Meanwhile, Babe is sorting through small swaths of carpeting as she scours catalogs and generates ideas for how our new home will look: the color of the siding, style of kitchen cabinets, and such.

After two hours, Babe's heavy eyelids offer protest and she opts for bed. Meanwhile, I'm still at it. She strolls from the living room to the dining area to check on me. I don't notice her at first, entranced in my notes and music as the mental images of the movie take shape one scene at a time. All the while, I wear one of those distant smiles on my face as if I just recalled a funny incident from my past. Eventually, I notice Babe and freeze in my tracks.

"How's it going?" Babe asks.

"Good," I say as I remove my headphones. "I think I found a great song to use for the interior house painters. Did you ever hear the Herb Alpert music on *The Dating Game*?"

"Mmm, I'm not sure," she says.

I remove the headphone jacks and play *Whipped Cream* for her. I observe her face, hopeful the song will stir her juices the same way it did mine.

"Yeah, I've heard that," she says. The tone in her voice suggests the song failed to inspire a single ripple in her juices.

"I'm going to use this song with the footage of the painters," I say. I waltz around the room to the music with an imaginary paint roller in my hand, rolling to the music and nodding my smiling head as if to imply: yes, you like?

In the spirit of the bestselling book *Men are From Mars, Women are From Venus*, I have just spent two hours immersed with my CDs and had finally stumbled upon the audio diamond in the rough I was seeking; another found piece of the puzzle for my movie. Babe, on the other hand, has just completed the essential and tedious chore of sorting through catalogs in an effort to decide how our new house will look when completed. To date, my input on such decisions has been limited to one recurring response: whatever you think.

We're on different planets.

* * *

Construction is complete in mid-November. We close on the mortgage the day before Thanksgiving.

It's a frigid day as high winds delivers cold air in sharp stabs. After the closing, we scurry to the car and thaw as the violent wind whips all around us, threatening to roll our Honda Accord across the parking lot like a tumbleweed. When sufficient feeling returns to my hands and face, Babe videotapes me from the passenger seat as I explain how incredibly fortunate and happy we feel.

The years in a garden apartment, the financial struggles, two jobs, the illusive dream of homeownership struck down time and again by escalating home prices and insufficient down payment money is suddenly a part of our past. Babe and I have hoisted the flag of the American Dream triumphantly into the air. Despite the sudden and gloomy presence cast by the long shadow of a thirty-year mortgage, I feel emancipated.

* * *

Early one Saturday morning a few weeks later, I arrive at the studio doors of Video Specialties located in the crowded Main Street shopping district in Smithtown. Christmas is only a few weeks away and the row of stores along Main Street are festive with lights, decorations, and—of course—signs enticing the world to come inside and acquire everything at 30% off. I'm dressed in a long black overcoat as I haul a big duffel bag. I could easily and justifiably be mistaken for a weapons smuggler. The mixture of road salt and ice is crushed beneath the weight of my boots as I stride purposefully toward the studio.

Before entering the studio, I pause and release a visible plume of cold breath; a heavy sigh of anticipation similar to a sigh preceding a job interview. I let myself in. My arrival is greeted with a look of amused repulsion from Jeremy Radino, lead editor and co-owner of Video Specialties.

"What the hell is that?" he laughs nervously, pointing to the duffel bag.

"My lunch," I blurt, opting for self-deprecation. I rumble forward and give Jeremy a big hug and an emphatic whack or two on the back. Jeremy treats me to a quick tour of the studio as I remove my overcoat. I'm mesmerized by the monitors, recording devices, tripods, tapes, and editing stations. Somehow, the studio even *smells* of technology.

"What are these?" I ask curiously as I point to a shelf containing dozens of VHS tapes.

"Edited wedding videos," Jeremy says with a nonchalant shrug. "Some couples never pick up the tapes. They just walk away from the down payment and we never hear from them again. I have nearly five-grand sitting on that shelf."

The news staggers me. A strange wave of compassion and curiosity washes through me as I try to reason why couples would miss out—for whatever reason—on the movie version of their (supposedly) special day. Months—even years—after the wedding, the couples have mysteriously vanished while their movies, bursting with life and memories, sit lifelessly on a shelf; on display and unclaimed like puppies in a pet store window.

We sit at Jeremy's work station and he says, "OK big Fred, let's see what you've got."

I excitedly unzip the duffel bag to unveil the ingredients of my movie: several tapes containing the footage I had videotaped (and one scene Babe had videotaped from the hood of our car) of the house construction, dozens of VHS tapes of various movies I plan to grab scenes from without a hint of copyright permission, fifteen or so CDs (the songs for which I will use with similar copyright infringement), a full script of the movie I have planned, and my journal.

My eagerness to get started is unlike anything I've felt in a long time. With the gag removed from my passion, the movie ideas wiggle impatiently in my mind like a pending wedding proposal.

I sit with Jeremy for two consecutive weekends as I watch with envy at the ease with which he manipulates video and audio clips on his computer. In my mind, I see myself editing with such effortless skill some time in the future. The vision of editing my own movies attaches itself to my creative mind and quickly becomes an immovable fixture.

During consecutive weekends, I never leave Jeremy's side as I continuously issue instructions and hand CDs and VHS tapes to him. Little by little, the movie I created in my mind comes to life on the video monitor. It's cathartic and amazing; artistic sky-diving.

Each time I leave the studio, the edited scenes linger in my mind like the good-night kiss of a first date. I can't wait to get back to it. Every second I spend away from the movie is connected with a stream of restless thoughts and images that play in an endless loop in my subconscious mind. The thoughts won't relent until the movie is complete. The movie hounds me like a pack of hyenas nipping at my heals.

On the last day of editing, I explain to Jeremy that I have several credits to include at the end. He allows me to type the credits, watching with little interest as he speaks casually on the phone. But his attention is seized and he lets out a wallop of a laugh when I type my adopted stage name for the directorial credit:

Directed by
FREDERICK FORD COPOLLA

The last thing I do is record an audio voiceover for the end of the movie. I had written the voiceover during the final stages of the construction. Jeremy hooks up the microphone to the recording deck.

He presses the RECORD button and says, "Knock yourself out, Copolla," then hurriedly exits the studio for a short walk across Main Street to buy dinner at Boston Chicken. Alone with my thoughts, the microphone, and the piece of paper on which my voiceover is written, I take a deep breath and begin.

I passionately record the voiceovers into the microphone. When I'm done, I press the STOP button on the recorder and slump weakly into the chair as my creative subconscious takes its first break in six months.

Jeremy comes back with dinner and within a few hours the movie is copied to VHS tape. With the edited tape in my possession, I exit the studio. It's early evening and the crush of Christmas shoppers has subsided as the Main Street shopping day winds down. As I walk out of the studio and onto the sidewalk, I'm a different person than I was a week ago when we started. The black and white dream of making movies, at times vague and beyond my reach, is now a Technicolor rainbow sprinkled with sparkling possibilities. I experience a wave of euphoria, the type I imagine a long-distance runner feels while crossing the finish line of a marathon.

I arrive home a half-hour later weighed down with an exhaustion I never expected. The movie refused to let my mind rest for several months, its presence as distracting as Joan River's voice. Though insignificant in the grand scheme of life, I tended to the movie as though it was the master work of my creative existence. In my mind, it warranted nothing less. I committed my whole heart to the project to celebrate an important event in our marriage. Moreover, I felt the movie was a unique way to offer the best part of my creative talent to Babe. Now at the finish line, the drain of energy finally tramples me.

As I scurry through the mud room and into the kitchen, Babe is at the table with a book. She perks up as she sees me. "How'd it come out?" she asks excitedly.

"I think it's pretty good," I say, intentionally downplaying what I really think of it.

We adjourn to the living room for the formal premiere, joined by our dog Daisy, a black terrier and unwitting co-star of the movie. Daisy's participation is attributable solely to her mouth-watering anticipation of a kernel or two of dropped popcorn.

The only way Babe will fully comprehend my movie-making madness for the past six months is if she loves the movie. Despite the drain I feel, the thought of watching the movie with Babe provides a surge of adrenaline. I insert the tape into the VCR and then position myself next to the fireplace to make a brief dedication.

I hoist my glass of beer overhead and steer my dedication in the direction of Babe, "You inspire everything good in me: my creativity, my faith, my generosity, and my sense of humor. This movie would be meaningless without you and never would have been made if you hadn't inspired it. I love you. And without further adieu, ladies and gentlemen—and dogs—I give to you *Ford's Fairway: the Construction of Our Home*."

With the formal dedication out of the way, we watch the movie, a little over an hour in length. As the voiceover plays near the end of the movie, Babe cries for several minutes.

My first movie—with an audience of me and Babe—has been a sensation; a permanent contribution to our marriage. Whatever it was that triggered the palpable stir in my imagination is now taking a victory lap for inspiring such a unique movie. The success of the movie and the surge of creativity it inspired have blossomed into a new creature, one that now rummages through my creative mind in search of a new project.

* * *

I wake up the next morning burdened by an odd mix of accomplishment and loss. I feel a part of me died when the movie came to life. It's an unexpected trade-off: my first artistic hangover.

During the time I filmed and edited, the movie had taken up residency in my imagination and caused a gradual and undetectable drain of my energy. With the experience over, I crash. Every thought seems vague and unimportant, as visions of the movie drift from my mind like ribbons of smoke from the smoldering remains of a bonfire.

Despite the exhaustion, the exhilaration lingers. I can't think of anyone who has created a movie similar to the one I did. From the first scene to the last, the movie was unique. Uniqueness is OK with me so I embrace it. It's something to build on.

Of greater relevance, the edited movie evolves into the most satisfying and meaningful gift I'd ever given. Babe's reaction inspires a profound and satisfying sense of validation. After producing only one movie, I'm addicted.

In the years to follow, movie-making becomes my sole hobby—not to mention the source of innumerable frustrations. I purchase a new Windows-based computer, hardware, and software for digital video editing and then with the aid of a classroom in a book I teach myself how to edit. The problem with these books is there is no way to ask the teacher for clarification when things invariably go wrong. My editing progress, therefore, becomes slowed by a steady flow of failures and computer crashes, during which time I take Bill Gates' name in vain several thousand times. Each failure is greeted by a disturbing message that pops up on my computer screen: *You have performed an illegal operation.* So in addition to being a failure, I'm also a fugitive.

Somehow, I develop enough editing know-how to become capable. And after thousands of crashes, the purchase of three different computers, and years of dedicated effort, my knowledge of video-editing advances to the point that I can finally make movies on my own.

My first solo effort is a retirement video tribute to my good friend Billy "Willie" Wilson. After serving 20 years with the NYPD, he retired in June of 1997 and my gift to him was a movie appropriately titled "Free Willie." It takes six months to film and edit but it's worth every second, as it was enormously popular with Billy and many others. A half-year later, I gather all the video footage from past Disney vacations and produce "Disney Daze," exclusively for Babe. We watch the movie on her birthday (May 3) in 2000. She laughs and cries with the same emotion and joy as when we watched the home construction video.

By this time, I am actually getting somewhat proficient at editing and before long my speed improves. I make several more family movies, including a tribute to my parents titled "Surrounded by Love." I have my father's old 8mm movie reels from the early 1960's converted to DVD then edit the footage into a chronology of my beloved childhood, using voiceovers, music, and current-day recollections from my siblings. The editing produces in me a daily dose of deep, almost dizzying nostalgia. My parent's reaction to the movie validates my efforts in a big, big way.

With my editing skills sufficiently honed, my opportunity for a bigger challenge surfaces. My uncle Jackie, the youngest of my father's four brothers, works as an attorney for the Neighborhood Legal Services in Lynn, Massachusetts. His law firm voted to honor him with a roast to commemorate thirty-one years of service. They expect a crowd of more than three hundred.

Babe and I are visiting my parents during the Christmas holiday when Jackie stops by. He was present for the premiere showing of "Surrounded by Love" and he was very impressed. As we sit in my parent's living room catching up, he describes the roast his co-workers are planning and then says to me, "I was wondering if you'd be interested in doing a video."

DING. The bell for the first round has struck!

Days after I accept his request, I have returned to Long Island when a package from Jackie arrives by mail. The package includes his resume and a letter that details a variety of personal information. The package also includes two VHS tapes that contain hours of Jackie's home movies: staged home productions, vacations, and an episode of his Mr. Rogers's parody *Mr. O'Reardon's Southie Neighborhood*. I view the footage and become mildly amused and, unfortunately, artistically paralyzed. My imagination is stalled as the traffic jam of images, video clips, and ideas honk their horns in the central business district of my overcrowded brain. Nothing comes to me; I'm stumped. In my effort to prepare a script for the movie, I have arrived at a deserted island commonly known as Writer's Block.

In order to escape the deserted island, I re-read Jackie's letter and suddenly the movie gets its spark. Contained in his letter is Jackie's mention of the time he was interviewed by *60 Minutes* co-host Morley Safer. At the time, Jackie was representing an elderly woman who was being evicted from her house by her own children. The segment aired but Jackie's interview was dropped onto the cutting room floor. Jackie often jokes, "Maybe if they changed the name of the show to *61 Minutes* I would have made the final cut."

With that laser beam of inspiration, a mockumentary titled *The 61ˢᵗ Minute: John J. Ford's Brush With Fame* is born.

I sit at the computer for days writing a script, amending it, re-writing it, aiming to make it both funny and touching. When the script receives approval from the coordinators of the event, I get busy editing.

As always, the editing consumes me. I think about the movie day and night and edit every minute I can spare. The movie is a mock episode of *60 Minutes,* wherein the host tracks the fictitious story of an Austin Powers look-alike (my uncle Jack) in his quest to sue Mike Meyers for copyright infringement. Along the way, the law suit generates national interest, prompting *60 Minutes* to get involved.

At the end of the movie, I pay tribute to Jackie with videotaped testimonials from friends and co-workers, followed by a photo montage accompanied by Frank Sinatra's *My Way*. When I watch the edited movie from my computer for the first time, I'm alone in my studio. As the movie ends, I cry uncontrollably for several minutes. This has become a ritual that signals the end of the creative process and a return of the bittersweet combination of loss and accomplishment. I realize the part of me given away will return as something bigger and more wonderful, hopefully an inspiration for another movie. That's the thing with giving: the gift is always replaced by something bigger and better; whether it's money or blessings or a smile. Give it away and watch how it returns in abundance.

* * *

On April 26, 2003, Babe and I pull into a parking space outside Jimmy's Allenhurst, a large catering facility in Danvers, Massachusetts. Seconds later, a car pulls into the empty space next to me. The driver is none other than Uncle Jackie, wearing his traditional bow tie and smile.

"Well, how'd it come out?" he asks expectantly.

"It's pretty good," I say with quiet assurance.

An hour later, after the silent auction bids have all been made, more than three hundred guests are noisily herded into the function room, where two large video screens are erected, one to the right and one to the left of the dais at the front of the room. Farley Dalton, the MC and coordinator of the event, welcomes the audience and introduces me to start the roast.

I provide a brief introduction of the movie and then retell a funny story about Uncle Jackie, which receives merely a smattering of tepid laughter due my uncharacteristic blown punch-line. My introduction is intentionally brief and when I'm done I signal to the Audio-Visual crew and instruct them to lower the lights and roll the tape.

I had projected this moment in my mind and had imagined numerous outcomes—many disastrous. None of the movies I've produced had ever been shown to a crowd larger than a dozen or so family members. The thought of having my movie broadcast to an audience of 300 produced fear of failure I'd never previously known. As the lights dim and the movie begins I feel suffocated with nervous energy.

To my relief and utter delight, the reaction of the crowd is greater than expected: laughter, applause, and undivided attention from the second the movie projects onto the two screens. With each laugh, my insides are tickled. The favorable reaction continues throughout the entire seventeen minute production. At the end, with the photo montage playing to Sinatra's *My Way*, many of the attendees have tears in their eyes. The standing ovation that erupts at the end of the movie is long and loud. I have hit a home run and as I round the bases, I am filled with incomparable feelings of accomplishment and joy. In the midst of the ovation, Jackie seeks me out and we embrace in a tight hug.

The ovation eventually subsides and the roast continues, but my attention is held hostage by recurring thoughts of the audience's reaction. The ovation replays over and over in the theater of my mind. It was the heartiest validation I ever experienced, the equivalent of riding the twenty greatest roller coasters back-to-back.

As I sit through the rest of the roast, I realize with certainty that I have survived movie-making boot camp. I'm on my way. The talent God blessed me with has joined forces with passion to produce something worthwhile— and gaining momentum. There are movies to be made and I embrace the opportunity with determination and anticipation—yet still no direction. The direction will come, but only with the appropriate inspiration. Inspiration will unlock the vault to creativity. But where on earth will the inspiration come from?

Unknown to me at the time, the inspiration is closer than I realize. My life is on a collision course with it and nothing can prevent it from arriving. For on the *very day* I completed editing Jackie's movie, an abandoned baby only thirty-five days old, named Jiang Xiaozhong, was found in southern China. Through that abandonment, God laid the foundation for the inspiration of my lifetime: the adoption of my daughter Lila Rose.

Chapter 3
THE PRISON OF INFERTILITY

Port Jefferson, New York
December 2002

It's Christmas morning. I'm huddled with Babe on the ground of a frozen parking lot outside a medical clinic. Babe is throwing up and between heaves she's crying. Our quest to have a baby has sunk to a new low. In that moment, the dense fog surrounding infertility lifted and for the first time in five years I have clarity in my thoughts about the treatments: *enough—no more of this.*

I never saw this coming. Infertility drifted into our lives like a cloud of carbon monoxide. Its effects were uncompromising and indiscriminate. As with any other physical or emotional handicap, it was never on the radar screen the day Babe and I got married in September 1992, when the driving rain of tropical storm Danielle doused our special day with promises of fertility. We began our new lives together with lofty aspirations for fulfillment, good health, and prosperity. There was no contingency plan; no accounting for plague or misfortune—only a promise to one another in front of a congregation of family and friends that we would stay together in both sickness and in health.

* * *

Our attempts to have a baby commence five years after our wedding day, just months after being liberated from our lives as apartment dwellers and the move into our newly constructed home in November 1996. Our years enduring upstairs neighbors with fetishes to vacuum rugs at 2:00 in the morning or play toss-and-fetch with dogs the size of a bison are over. And with the removal of those hovering distractions, it is time to have a family.

44

With no hint of the pending infertility—and to be blunt about it, infertility has no duty to leave hints—our initial efforts consist of well-timed sex. The traditional recipe for baby-making requires strict adherence to timing and ovulation. Initiation for sex is taken over, therefore, by an ovulation predictor kit.

Despite our well-timed and physically satisfying interludes, the attempts fail to produce a pregnancy. And then one month casually graduates into a year with no pregnancy. As time ticks on with no results, our feelings about the lack of pregnacy mutate from casual indifference into quiet panic.

With a year of failed attempts strewn in our wake, Babe takes some initiative.

"Hon, I made an appointment with a fertility specialist," she says, as we eat dinner one night.

It's a statement, not a suggestion. It is an announcement as to the direction we will take in our effort to get Babe pregnant. Though I can't think of any reasonable objection, my initial reaction to her announcement is one of shame. I take infertility personally. I somehow reason the failure is my fault. Self-pity has a much lower success rate than infertility doctors and besides, Babe didn't solicit my input when she made the appointment. My reaction to her statement about the fertility specialist, therefore, was one of predictable surrender.

"OK," I say as I grasp Babe's hand, "whatever you think."

From my viewpoint, infertility belongs in the same category as erectile dysfunction or sexually-transmitted diseases: something that happens to other people. Unfortunately for me and Babe, our ignorance of the laws of nature provides no shelter from its effects. Suddenly, we *are* the other people. A note of desperation has been struck in the symphony of our lives. It makes me uneasy.

Babe and I develop different mindsets about pregnancy. I react to it with a take-it-as-it-comes (no pun intended) attitude. We enjoy a happy and respectful marriage, an active social life, and we have a lot be thankful for. I find it effortless to shift my thoughts from pregnancy issues to more pleasurable topics: social engagements, holidays, Friday nights, or the Sports Illustrated swimsuit edition. My real estate appraisal business, movie projects, and part-time career as a stand-up comic provide more than sufficient camouflage from the emotional assault of infertility. As for children, I'll accept them lovingly from God, just I had stated in my wedding vows. What I didn't vow, but what could be said with equal certainty, is that I will accept *lack* of children from God as well. Whatever the outcome, I believe God has a plan.

As for Babe, the biological clock is ticking loudly. She's more than thirty years old and frustrated. Her disappointment with our inability to get her pregnant manifests more regularly and in more demonstrative ways, though she always maintains a strong faith and humble disposition. As for the lack of children, that option is not even on the table. Her mind instinctively and involuntarily focuses on the infertility day and night. She has discovered little ability to push the issue to the back burner. It weighs on her mind like a 500-pound gorilla. Infertility taints virtually every good thought, its effect on her mind as crippling as the presence of a cancerous tumor.

Although we experience infertility together, our respective thoughts and struggles differ widely. In that respect, the infertility experience is one of lonely confusion. It's as though we are seated on a bench at a bus stop awaiting a bus that never arrives. As we wait, I'm telling jokes to the guy next to me as we swig a beer and pass the time. Babe, on the other hand, stares straight ahead, her eyes transfixed on nothing in particular as her mind is visited over and over with thoughts the train will never get here. As odd as this might sound, we are going through the experience alone together.

The fact millions of other couples experience infertility (some sources suggest as many as 7.3 million women had difficulty getting pregnant or reaching full-term pregnancy during the same time we experienced our difficulties) is, in fact, no comfort to either of us. We have no interest in being part of the staggering statistics.

* * *

Babe and I travel to Port Jefferson for our initial consultation. As we walk from the parking lot to the building, a cloud of defeat and shame darkens my mood. After only a year of trying, we've hoisted the white flag. It's an unwelcome feeling, one that carries frustration and resentment.

The visit also produces guilt, the by-product of my unfounded and unfortunate tendency to blame myself for the infertility. Additionally, as if the situation required more negative feelings, I am paranoid that someone might notice me as I walk with Babe into the clinic. I glance side to side and walk briskly with my head down as though entering an adult video store.

Medical offices are resolute places under any circumstance. The memory of such places is nearly always linked to a prior illness or the hope attached to the treatment. Our infertility issue is about to be added to those memories, producing a combination of desperation and optimism. We enter the quiet lobby as fear and uncertainty invade my mind. We take the elevator up one flight then enter the reception office. A quick scan of the waiting room produces a flood of happy images from the posters secured to the walls: couples nuzzled with their miracle babies, medical charts advertising medications and procedures, feel-good mottos. I feel simultaneously uplifted and depressed.

Babe checks in at the reception desk. I take a seat and grab the most tolerable magazine of the many in my vicinity and pretend to read it.

While seated, I observe something that puts infertility in perfect perspective. No matter what the statistics say, no matter how miraculous the drugs are or how optimistic the doctors appear, the one thing that most effectively communicates the devastating effects of infertility is the face of a woman going through its pain. Seated across from me in the waiting room is one such woman. As I thumb through the magazine, I steal an occasional cardplayer peek at the woman. Her face is troubled with a deep sadness that exists in a place well beyond tears; the same type of sadness that affects those who grieve the death of a spouse several months after the death. The expression she wears is crippled with troubled thoughts of quiet desperation. Days after our visit I can't shake her unintended display of emotional torture.

Eventually, the receptionist calls our name and we are summoned to the doctor's office. The meeting lasts ten minutes. Near the end of the consultation, the doctor lays out the game plan.

"We're going to check both of you out," he explains cordially. "Fred, we'll check your blood and get a complete semen analysis done. Dorothy, we'll check your blood as well, that way we can test for estrogen, progesterone, thyroid, and androgen levels."

In the week to follow, our blood and my semen are checked. There's nothing wrong with the semen. The levels of production in line with men of similar age and somehow this news alleviates some of the self-imposed guilt. I'm not completely off the hook, however, as the doctor suggests some of the sperm are sluggish. Everything is fine with Babe as well; though the doctor expressed concern that Babe's eggs have an unusually hard outer cover, thus difficult to penetrate. Based on the combination of our symptoms, I envision my sluggish sperm knocking lazily on the hard shell of Babe's eggs then quickly giving up hope and retreating to the hammock for an afternoon of golf on TV.

In the months to follow, Babe endures several additional tests. Whereas the male is tested once for blood and semen irregularities, the female is often tested multiple times. If any potential cause of infertility is detected, more rigorous testing results. The tests create periodic opportunities for Babe to ponder with greater intensity the condition that never leaves her mind in the first place.

The first medication prescribed is Clomid. It is inexpensive, as fertility drugs go, and is easily taken—orally and not injected. Two cycles using Clomid produces no pregnancy and causes Babe to develop cysts on her ovaries.

Next!

The second medication prescribed is Follistim, a follicle-stimulating hormone intended to stimulate ovulation. It's an injected medication and such injections are typically administered at home by the patient or her spouse. Guess who will be doing the injections? Shortly after we agree to go this route, we visit the medical clinic for a mid-day shot administering seminar.

"I'll need you to pay strict attention to the details," the female technician warns sternly, "as any slip-up could cause discomfort or infection." Her face has the unsettling appearance of a constipated bulldog. Oddly, her scowl goes very nicely with the foreboding tone in her voice and the ancillary warnings about infection.

As I observe her movements, careful to avoid any mention that I overwhelmingly failed both biology and chemistry in high school, the technician adroitly demonstrates the proper way to mix the medication, sterilize the area where the needle will be injected, gather the medication into the syringe, remove the air from the needle, and inject the medication. The shots are administered into a stomach prop that rests of the table like a recently extracted cow liver. The technician finishes the demonstration and stares in my direction with rehearsed confidence. Somehow, this short demonstration is supposed to qualify me to administer shots.

"Pick up the syringe and give it a try," she says encouragingly.

I clumsily gather the medication, my sizable hands wrapped around the syringe like an oven mitt around a thermometer. With the medication adequately gathered, I remove air from the needles with a couple of expert flicks from my middle finger, and then point the needle in the direction of the stomach prop.

"Okay, you're going to feel a little pinch," I say playfully.

"Please! This is nothing to joke about," the technician chides.

No kidding.

In the months to follow, I administer the injections for several cycles. Our daily routine is interrupted with the uneasy procedure of sticking needles into Babe's stomach, mindful that a slip-up on my part could result in pain or infection. It's no fun for either of us. What's worse, no pregnancy results.

As the infertility persists, the frustration and questions mount. When the Follistim medication is exhausted, we decide to consult a second fertility specialist, recommended by a friend of Babe's. Once the word's out, your infertility becomes the personal challenge of the many well-intentioned friends and relatives in your life.

In addition to impatience about Babe's pregnancy, I have become resentful of the business aspect of fertility doctors. To be certain, there have been some wonderful and miraculous breakthroughs in the treatment of infertility. Couples who experience infertility nowadays are afforded more options than ever before. There are, however, no guarantees—regardless of what doctors say.

We stroll into the doctor's private office and take a seat.

"So, are we having a little trouble getting pregnant?" the doctor asks aloud, a phony smile smeared on his face. His tone carries the feigned alacrity of a TV game show host introducing the new contestants to the studio audience. I'm overcome with an irresistibly strong urge to punch his smarmy face.

"Well, *we* are, I don't know about you," I say in a voice pregnant with sarcasm. My attempt at humor falls to the floor like a droplet of blood and creates a moment of uneasy silence between the three of us.

The meeting lasts only a few minutes. The doctor indicates he wants to do a laparoscopy to Babe. Laparoscopy sounds to me like a type of dance performed by strippers in the back room of a topless bar. Nonetheless, I'll agree to just about anything. Near the end of the interview, he makes one final proclamation.

"Let's hold off on In vetro for now. We'll consider that a last resort."

He failed to ask if we would consider In vetro fertilization. If he had, I would have explained the moral dilemma In vetro presents for me. In any event, we agree to the laparoscopy and leave. When I get to the car, I'm angry. Babe's reaction is different. Rather than anger, she feels hopelessness.

"Let's just forget about the treatments for a while," she says as we drive home.

I'm surprised yet relieved to hear suggestion.

"Fine by me," I say. Seconds after our short exchange sinks in, I reach over and grab Babe's hand and say, "It's going to happen, just keep the faith."

We stop the treatments for several months, during which time we re-introduce the ovulation predictor kits and sex. My delight with the methods is more than offset with the bitterness of the results: no pregnancy.

* * *

Our next course of action is acupuncture. Once again, through someone's referral, we visit a doctor with a great track record. Up to this point in my life, I had equated acupuncture with voodoo. The mention of it conjures up images of an episode of *Gilligan's Island* when all the castaways were mysteriously feeling sharp stabs of pain, the result of voodoo doctors sticking pins into miniature dolls resembling each castaway.

I'm not aware of anyone who has successfully been treated by an acupuncturist. I'm quite confident the acupuncturist will be able to provide an impressive list. Furthermore, our referral source is reliable. So despite our ignorance about acupuncture, our optimism for pregnancy is resuscitated. We decide to give it a try.

Our initial consultation with the acupuncturist—for the sake of story let's call him Dr. Christie—is both unconventional and amusing.

We creep into his poorly lit office and detect the strong and alarming fragrance of incense. I'm struck by the small size of the waiting room, which is eerily devoid of both receptionist and patients. Babe and I exchange confused glances as we strain our eyes to read wall posters and attempt to do something useful—like locate a bell to ring to announce our arrival. The initial moments of our visit carry the same intrigue as the opening scene of a low-budget horror movie. A moment later, the affable Dr. Christie emerges mysteriously from behind a door.

"You must be Fred and Dorothy," he announces with zest as he thrusts his right hand in my direction. He's an eccentric guy, alarmingly upbeat. He was originally from England; hence he speaks with a refreshing English accent similar to the Beatles.

He leads us to a room with no lights on and the blinds drawn, the only illumination cast by several lit candles scattered throughout the room. Soft new-age music floats from the stereo speakers. I feel as though I've entered a monk's monastery.

"Please, have a seat," the doctor invites as he points to side by side, high-back leather chairs.

Babe and I sit gingerly. I half-expect Dr. Christie to break out a bong (the other half of my expectation awaits a black cat to jump from the shadows). Instead, he sits calmly across from us, grabs a legal pad to take notes, and then nestles cozily into his chair as he smiles and stares at us, glancing from me to Babe and then back; sizing us up for several seconds without speaking a word. This exercise triggers an uncomfortable silence, which produces in me an irresistible urge to laugh.

"So, tell me what you're feeling about trying to get your wife pregnant," he coaxes.

"Well, confusion…frustration…anger," I reply.

"Anger, interesting," he mutters as he scribbles busily onto his legal pad, the smile on his face overtaken by a sudden look of consternation.

The consultation continues in this fashion, as Dr. Christie asks exploratory questions and attentively listens with wide-eyed wonder, as if the answers are being delivered by the Dalai Lama.

The wide eyes and the eerie smile, along with the flickering candle light that dances on his face give Dr. Christie the distinctive presence of a mad scientist.

Eventually, he proposes some treatments and, as you might imagine, offers a great deal of optimism.

"Let's start next week. We'll go twice a week initially and then see how you're progressing." He claps his hands together and rubs them as if preparing for a feast. The smile returns and quickly inspires a faint cause for optimism. The treatments start shortly after the initial consultation and last for several months.

During one visit, I'm seated near the foot of the table where Babe is being treated. Dr. Christie pokes and prods various parts of Babe's body then slowly inserts long pins, some nearly the size of knitting needles. Several minutes later, my view of Babe conjures up an image a bull at the end of the bullfight, motionless with dozens of pins sticking out of her.

"OK, just lie still and I'll be back in a few minutes," the doctor instructs soothingly, and leaves the room.

As I stare at Babe, a wave of deep and compassionate sadness washes through me. I leave my chair, walk to the side of the treatment table, and kneel quietly next to her. Babe's eyes are closed.

"You OK?" I ask.

She opens her eyes and nods.

"I love you," I say.

"I love you too."

It's a tough moment for me and one of many tough moments for Babe.

Weeks later, after one of the acupuncture treatments, Babe is due for her period. On the arrival date, Babe says, "Hon, I don't feel bloated, no cramps or anything."

I'm psyched. Three more days pass and still no signs of a period.

This is it; finally, she's pregnant.

The period arrives four days late like a certified letter from the IRS. Babe comes home from work and I see the pain on her face. She falls into my arms and cries. Teased into a false sense of optimism, the late-arriving period merely amplifies our disappointment.

"It's going to be OK, Babe. Just keep praying. It's going to happen," I say desperately and encouragingly.

My words only cause her to sob with more intensity. She's unable to embrace the words, as her hormones perform their unbalancing act.

* * *

Saturday morning, Babe is readying herself for a baby shower and I set off for work. For the time being, baby showers produce desperate, suffocating pain for Babe. They leave her feeling emotionally crippled; like a wheelchair-bound child watching other children play soccer.

As she showers, the emotional pain suddenly drops Babe to her knees like a punch to her solar plexis. She crumples helplessly to the floor of the tub and curls into the fetal position as warm water washes over her. She cries and sobs in hiccups for several minutes. She eventually composes herself, dresses, and attends the baby shower with a smile on her face; the mask for her pain. To the rest of world, Babe is the same as always: sweet, lovable, happy, and unaffected. If only they knew.

To combat these unfortunate—and inevitable—feelings, Babe often purchases baby powder and baby lotion from the supermarket. Once home from shopping, she applies a little lotion or powder to her skin, then closes her eyes and absorbs the scent of the lotion as she visualizes Lila. She performs these creative visualizations often to combat self-pity, thereby fanning the flames for her burning desire to have a baby.

A week after Babe endures her friend's baby shower, our quest for a baby changes direction again.

"I think I want to stop the acupuncture," Babe says, almost apologetically.

Coupled with the baby shower, the late-arriving period has produced pain Babe cannot bear. We include God in every stage of treatment, though both Babe and I have become impatient with God's answer. Over time, my well-intentioned—and occasionally well-placed—words of encouragement sound hollow and trite. Their effect wears off more quickly; in fact at times don't even penetrate at all. The why-me moments, unfortunately and uncharacteristically, arrive with more frequency, the questions with more intensity. And time ticks on…

After giving up on acupuncture, we become more aggressive. We opt for Artificial Insemination (AI). This is a fairly common and safe procedure, wherein the practitioner inserts specially treated sperm through the cervix into the woman's uterus. This procedure is performed around the time of ovulation and requires the male donor to provide sperm in a much more impersonal way: into a plastic cup. Shortly after the cup is soiled, it is quickly transported to the medical office like a tube of blueprints relay-raced to Mike Brady.

At this point in our battle against infertility, I welcome some comic relief. The plastic cup thing carries a comedic element. Babe is scheduled to visit the clinic this morning and needs me to make my donation into the cup. An awkward moment arrives as Babe hands the cup to me.

"Go get 'em tiger," she jokes playfully. I'm happy to see her sense of humor.

I take the cup and bolt upstairs to the master bathroom. I stare at the empty cup during our initial confrontation and I can manage only one thought, strictly for my own amusement: *Come here often?*

During my self administered sperm extraction, my mind instinctively creates a movie scene. I picture Babe drumming her fingers impatiently and loudly on the kitchen table—interspliced with alternating scenes of a clock slowly advancing and close-ups of my beet-red, taut, perspiring face. The music accompaniment to the scene, naturally, is Carly Simon's *Anticipation.*

My vision quickly disintegrates when I conclude my business, after which I hustle down the stairs to the kitchen. Babe is seated at the table with a look of amusement on her face.

I hold up the cup and say, "Yo Adrian, I did it!"

I hand the cup to her and she says, "Wow hon, that was quick."

I suppose expediency, in this instance, is preferred. Nevertheless, I don't quite know whether to take her comment as a compliment or an indictment. Whatever, I did my part. Babe speeds off to courier the sperm to the medical office and the amusement of the situation, thankfully, outweighs the feelings of despair.

Weeks later, Babe's period arrives like a gout attack. At this point, both of us are contemplating, with growing dread, the realistic possibility we will never have children. Those thoughts are consuming Babe.

* * *

We decide to take a respite from all treatments in the fall of 2002 in order to ease some pressure off our brains and alleviate the month-to-month drama from our lives.

During the years of failed attempts to impregnate my wife, our sanctuary is our annual trip to Walt Disney World. The 2002 trip takes place in October. We experience a classic, mid-day Florida downpour on our drive from Orlando Airport to the resort, and optimistically view the rain as a sign of pending fertility—ignoring the fact similar rain on our wedding day has yet to come to fruition. During the vacation, we make several attempts to get Babe pregnant. The—ahem—*climax* of one such attempt is accompanied by the simultaneous grand finale of a fireworks display at the Magic Kingdom. The loud explosions fill the night air at just the right moment, as laughter fills our room.

"That's a sign, it has to be," Babe muses in a breathless voice. I agree.

During our visit, we spend a few hours with a sales representative to learn more about the Disney timeshare, marketed as Disney's Vacation Club. The model units are located in the Disney Boardwalk area, where a team of well-rehearsed and well-groomed sale agents wait to casually pounce on their next guest. We arrive and end up in the office one of the handsome male sales representatives.

Minutes into his presentation, in an attempt to gauge our needs, he asks, "Do you have any children?"

"We're working on our first," I admit solemnly.

He holds up four fingers. "My wife's pregnant with our fourth," he muses dreamily, then shakes his head and smiles, seemingly astounded at his own virility. In order to ensure the dagger is completely inserted into my wife's heart, he continues, "I *look* at my wife and she gets pregnant."

So that's what I'm doing wrong!

We decide against the Vacation Club for a number or reasons. The salesperson's comments didn't help.

Babe's period arrives shortly after we get home from the vacation. Our nightmare is reborn, more gruesome than ever. We both felt the Disney Magic would produce a pregnancy so this failure is particularly painful. Infertility is kicking our ass.

"I don't want to be sixty years old having never heard a child call me mommy," Babe manages through tears.

Her comment leaves me with a loss for words. My ability to comfort her is buried beneath the weight of hopelessness. I step forward and give her a hug. It's the only thing I can think of.

* * *

The adoption process begins the exact moment the fertility treatments officially end on Christmas morning 2002. On that morning, Babe and I travel to the fertility clinic. We've decided to try Artificial Insemination again so I spend the early part of the morning rendez-vousing with the plastic cup.

Our scheduled visit coincides with Babe's ovulation, which falls on December 25. Among its other annoyances, infertility takes no holidays. Like it or not, the treatment needs to happen today.

Babe doesn't feel well and slowly reclines her chair as we drive.

"You OK?" I ask.

"I feel a little nauseous."

I drive north and the streets are quiet with many homes lit up with Christmas and Channukah decorations. I feel unsettled and depressed. Despite the lights and decorations, it doesn't feel like Christmas to me.

We enter the parking lot to find it mostly abandoned, with only one other car in the lot. Obviously, it is owned by the unfortunate soul who had to make the same sacrifice on this blessed holiday to administer the procedure to my wife. The procedure takes only a few minutes but when Babe emerges from the treatment room, she looks as though she just witnessed a child get run over by a truck. We receive our instructions, hastily finish the paperwork, and leave. Babe is muffling sobs beneath her tightly closed lips.

As we exit the building, Babe moans, "I don't feel good. I think I'm going to be sick."

I have my arm around her and we shuffle gingerly across the deserted parking lot to our Jeep Grand Cherokee. As we reach the car, she drops to her knees and vomits. The only comfort I can offer is a hug from behind and some steady arms for stability. We stay on the ground for several minutes, oblivious to the cold or the absurdity of spending our holiday tangled together on the frozen pavement of a parking lot.

And so on Christmas morning, with my arms wrapped around Babe as a we huddle on the ground in the parking lot of a medical office building, our fertility treatments come to an unceremonious end, the taste of failure as bitter as the chill in the air.

Fortunately, God has another plan.

ACT II-
THE
INSPIRATION

Chapter 4
THE THOUSAND MILE JOURNEY BEGINS

"A thousand mile journey begins by taking the first step."
—Chinese proverb—

"I need to talk to you about something," Babe says resolutely. The words and the somber look on her face suggest trouble.

I hastily ransack my subconscience in search of an infraction; a missed date of importance, an unintended slight, any potential transgression I can think of. Heavan knows, there's quite a potential list. Finding no infraction during the brisk inventory of my mental rolodex, I take a seat at the kitchen table across from Babe and ask, "Everything OK?"

"My mom told me about an adoption workshop on Saturday in West Islip. I was wondering if you wanted to go."

Trouble isn't brewing after all; I'm relieved. I stare at Babe and all I can see is the emotional pain attached to the years of infertility treatments. That pain has robbed her beautiful face of a smile too often. I'm indifferent about of adoption. Whenever the topic of adoption was raised over the past few years, I brushed it aside quickly with a generic let's-see-what-happens response. The topic never graduated into a serious discussion. At this point, however, adoption represents possibly our only viable option to become parents. What's more, I'll do anything to protect Babe from additional suffering.

"OK, let's go," I say.

Now it's her turn for relief. "Thanks hon," she says and sighs. Tears well up in her eyes as she forces a smile.

In the days leading up to the meeting, I selfishly hope it will be cancelled or, even more improbably, Babe will change her mind. The more I contemplate the matter, the more I view adoption as raising someone else's child. I'm simply not interested.

Saturday arrives and the meeting hasn't been cancelled. With strong reservations, I accompany Babe to the car. During the drive to West Islip in our black Grand Cherokee, the only objection I can muster is a casual disclaimer.

"I'm making no promises. I'll be open-minded about this, but I really don't know how I feel about adoption."

Babe grabs my hand and says, "Thanks for doing this."

It's a misty morning and light rain is falling. Few words are spoken as we drive. Soft music from the radio and intermittent squeaks of windshield wipers are lost in the background of our respective thoughts and fears.

We arrive at the library. The rain has stopped and a light fog has settled in. Suddenly, the day posseses an eerie, surreal atmosphere. As we enter the library, I feel as though we're being transported through a dark tunnel to a place in a parallel universe.

We're the first to arrive and we follow posted signs to a conference room, where thirty or so folding chairs are neatly arranged in the center. At the front of the cluster of chairs is a bulletin board with numerous displays about international adoption. We walk over and casually peruse some of the displays as we exchange hushed small talk about being the first ones to arrive. Eventually, we take a seat in the last row (at my insistence). Minutes later, the representative from the adoption agency strides into the room and fans rain from her umbrella.

"Hi, I'm Cathy Dinowski from New Beginnings," she announces as she walks to us and shakes our hands.

Cathy possesses the calm and pleasant demeanor of everyone's favorite aunt and I immediately feel at ease with her. Five other couples eventually filter into the meeting. I'm anxious to get this underway—and over with. As I await the start of the meeting, I feel obligated to tell the world I'm not interested in adoption. So I fold my arms across my chest and grimly force a resolute smirk onto my face.

Cathy begins the meeting with a pleasant welcome. She speaks with concise, intentionally measured words and when she needs to seize our attention, she spices her presentatoin with an exaggerated facial expression or sudden body movement. The information—and her method of delivering it—is both engaging and intriguing. I'm so engaged, in fact, I eventually sit up straight and unfold my arms.

Of all the adoption programs discussed, I find the China program particularly intriguing.

"In China, most families are allowed only one child per household and the preference of many parents is for a male child. This has resulted in the widespread and routine abandonment of baby girls, as well as selective abortions," Cathy says.

As she speaks, an assistant distributes brochures to the attendees. I feel disturbed by the information and when I see the beautiful faces of the many Chinese baby girls as they smile at me from the printed handout, I'm haunted.

"They'll realize one day they were given up because they are females," Cathy discloses sadly.

As she speaks, something inside of me changes. God plants a seed in my heart. That's about as simply and honestly as I can describe it: my baby Lila Rose is born to my heart that moment.

A question and answer period follows Cathy's presentation.

"Do you have to travel to China for the adoption?" barks a woman seated on the other side of the room.

"For China, yes," says Cathy, "for Korea and some other countries, the baby is brought to the United States."

In my mind I think the information will squash the possibility of a China adoption. Babe would rather dine on live worms than fly.

"When couples travel to China, do you recommend they take their real children with them?" asks a man near the front.

Cathy pauses and a wry smile spreads onto her face. She allows a few seconds of silence to filter through the audience before she answers, "Did you hear what you just said—your *real* children. That is sometimes the mind set of prospective parents looking into adoption. I must tell you, adopted children are just as real as biological children."

Her response strikes a nerve and inspires some introspection. She then explains the biological children issue is a personal one and she encourages parents to speak frankly with the child and permit them to get involved with the decision to travel.

At the end of the seminar, a little more than an hour in length, we take some literature and thank Cathy before we leave. The information is still sinking in as we walk from the library to the parking lot. My legs feel a bit wobbly as I try to process the barrage of foreign thoughts and feelings that invade my mind in rapid streams. As we reach the car, I feel as though I'm coming out of emotional anesthesia. Babe and I get into the car and quietly drive off without a word to each other.

At one point during our drive home I interrupt the contemplative silence and ask, "Well, what do you think?"

"I would do it in a second," she says.

It's the type of remark that drops like a seed into the subconscious and slowly germinates there in the months to follow. For many reasons, the comment startles me. To begin with, Babe typically ponders issues carefully before she makes up her mind. Secondly, she hates to fly. She has always wanted a baby girl and I assume she wants to go to China.

An uncomfortable silence follows; then the inevitable return question.

"What about you?" Babe says.

"It was interesting," I admit. "I never knew about the one-child policy in China. It's…really interesting." I'm doing my damndest to dodge the question.

"Do you think you'd ever adopt?" she asks hopefully, her not so subtle strategy to combat my dodging.

"I need to think about it, hon. I don't know."

Silence returns. Minutes later, with both of us mesmorized by deep thought, Babe breaks the silence.

"When Cathy said one day they'll realize they were given up because they were females I felt like someone stabbed me in the heart," Babe murmurs as she stares straight ahead, tears pooled in her eyes.

To her credit, Babe never pressures me in the days to follow, though I sense a mule of anxiety kicking in her stomach. She allows me time to contemplate my feelings about adoption. But her voice—"I would do it in a second"—replays over and over in my mind, louder and with greater impact with each subsequent echo. No amount of soul-searching on my part will alter the urgency created by her surprising admission.

There's a scene in *Pulp Fiction* that provides a fair analogy of how I view my decision about adoption. Near the beginning of the movie Samuel Jackson's hit-man character has just busted through the door of a seedy apartment and shocked a group of young men, who had apparently ripped off Jackson's boss. Jackson and his side-kick (played by John Travolta) have arrived to exact some revenge. With tension running high and the group of young men essentially shitting their pants with fear, Jackson calmly helps himself to a bite of a Kahuna burger. While he chomps contentedly on the burger, he explains how much he loves hamburgers and then confesses, "Me, I can't usually get them because my girlfriend's a vegetarian," he pauses and shrugs, then continues almost as an aside, "which pretty much makes me a vegetarian too."

As I contemplate the prospect of becoming an adoptive parent, I relate to the Jackson character. Babe wants to adopt, which pretty much means I'll be agreeing to adopt too.

Of greater significance, however, I feel transformed by the meeting. Regardless of the weight of Babe's words, I too have strong feelings about adoption. Initially I feel confusion. But the more I contemplate it, the more I sense the presence of that seed in my heart. As I search for answers, I feel pulled toward adoption by a force greater than my own will. I take comfort in the thought that adoption may well be the answer to the hundreds of prayers I've spoken over the past several years.

I continue to give the issue thought and prayer over the next several days. Being a real estate appraiser, I have ample time alone with my thoughts as I travel around various parts of Long Island. During one of my visits to the Hamptons in eastern Long Island, I take a detour to the south shore to visit an ocean beach in Montauk. I sit by myself for several minutes and seek answers. A medley of summer sounds—the roll of the surf, a toddler's giddy shriek, the raucous complaint of a sea gull overhead—is muffled beneath the wind that whistles through the empty crib in my soul. I'm conflicted by my feelings toward adoption. I'm scared, but I reason that is normal for any prospective first-time parent, adoptive or otherwise. I leave the beach with no answers; only a cold reminder of how small I really am. The decision to adopt, on the other hand, is big; the biggest decision I've ever had to make. If I agree to adopt, my decision will completely rearrange a life I am perfectly content with. Once I say yes, there's no turning back. The finality of such a decision is daunting.

* * *

A few days later, Babe and I go out to dinner at The Oar House, a waterfront restaurant and marina in nearby Patchogue, one those places in Long Island that appear to have been named by the arbitrarily arranged letters of a losing hand in Scrabble. The canal dances with sparkling light from the setting sun as many enjoy cocktails on their moored boats and the outdoor dining area while Ed Travers and his two-man band perform Jimmy Buffet's *Pencil Thin Moustache*.

At my request—fearful that the lack of breeze will threaten a mosquito-free dinner—the hostess leads us to a table indoors. Earlier in the day, I committed my heart to adoption. I also made a related decision: now that I have committed, I will never, under any circumstances, say *anything* to my wife that resembles "this was all your idea." I am committing to this voluntarily; for better or worse.

I can't think of a dramatic way to inform Babe of my decision, so during a lull in an unrelated conversation, I simply say, "So you want to go to China?"

Her eyes well with tears and she nearly leaps from her seat as she drops her fork and grabs my hand, then says, "Really?! China?!"

"Well, yeah, that's where you want to go, right?"

"Either China or Korea. In the Korean program, the child is brought to the U.S."

For some reason, I instinctively thought Babe was drawn to the Chinese baby girls. She always wanted a baby girl and most of the pamphlets we looked at on the day of the workshop were of Chinese babies.

"It's going to be a long flight," I say as I smile. "You sure you want to go?"

I've released Babe from prison. She lurches from her seat, ambles around to my side of the table, and lunges into my arms for a big hug and kiss.

"Thanks hon." She's crying. "Do you mind if I call Nikki and my mom?"

"Of course not," I say assuringly.

She kisses me a few more times and leaves the table to call her sister-in-law and mother. Meanwhile, I sip a Cosmopolitan and daydream about the future. Our lives are about to be rearranged and I'm still uneasy about adoption. The process has barely begun and already it's *the* major issue in our lives. Though I've committed my heart to adoption, and I'm confident it's God's will for our lives, I can't help but ask myself one question over and over: What have I gotten myself into?

Life-changing moments occur all the time, often when you least expect it. Sometimes a spoken word makes a big difference: an unexpected compliment, some well-timed advice, a sermon, or a line from a movie. And so, while we enjoy a casual dinner, my life and marriage are changed forever with the casual utterance of seven words: So you want to go to China?

We finish dinner and move to the bar for after-dinner drinks. Several drunken patrons are thoughtfully screaming at the television and calling for manager Bobby Valentine's head because the Mets just blew a three-run lead in the ninth. This, of course, leads me to ponder: how many runs did Bobby Valentine give up?

After we get our drinks we toast. In the past five years, Babe's mood has rarely been more lively or joy-filled. She's a frisky as a kitten. Minutes after our toast and some breezy smalltalk, she asks, "How do you like the name Lila Rose?"

"Lila Rose? Sounds poetic," I say philosophically.

"Lila is my great grandmother's name and everyone in my family loved her."

The name, I admit to myself, has a lyrical ring to it. Drawing on the Hollywood influence I've been hypnotized by since childhood, I break into song as one of the members of the barbershop quartet on *The Music Man:* "Lila Rose I'm home again Rose…"

* * *

The following day Babe phones New Beginnings to initiate the process. While she's on the phone, I am struck with a Frederick Ford Coppola inspiration: make a documentary about the adoption. Given my past history of movie-making, it seems perfectly fitting to produce a movie as my very first gift to Lila.

"They're sending out the paperwork tomorrow," Babe says with a smile as she hangs up the receiver.

"When you were on the phone I had a thought," I announce.

"Oh-oh." Years of experience have trained Babe to beware of those rare moments when I announce I've had a thought.

I ignore her and say, "I'm going to make a movie about the adoption, to give to Lila when she turns sixteen."

Babe is touched. "That's a *great* idea."

"I'll give it the old Frederick Ford Copolla treatment."

"Can I make one music suggestion?" Babe asks eagerly.

"But of course."

"Somewhere in the movie, you have to use 'At Last' by Etta James. I heard it the other day and it became my song to Lila."

"Lila Rose Comes Home at Last," I say slowly, pensively. The movie title is born.

The initial stack of paperwork arrives a few days later weighing as much as an issue of *Good Housekeeping*. There is nothing complicated about it, but the sheer volume of forms and applications is cumbersome. In addition to standardized forms, we are each required to write biographies and we need to complete a letter requesting permission to adopt. The letter is to be addressed to Mr. Lu Ying, Director General for the China Center of Adoption Affairs. We've already been granted permission to adopt by God; thus the formality of a letter to Mr. Ying seems to be a secondary consideration. New Beginnings, however, warns us that the letter is of utmost importance. As such, they provide careful guidelines and strong suggestions.

Our letter is as follows:

Dear Mr. Ying:

We respectfully submit this letter for the purpose of asking permission to adopt a child from your country. We thank you in advance for your time and consideration in reading this letter. My name is Fred Ford. I was born August 6, 1959 in Boston, Massachusetts to Joan (Delaney) and Gerard Ford. My parents are both Irish. My wife's name is Dorothy (maiden name Krakaur). She was born May 3, 1966 in Long Island, New York.

Her parents (Hewlett and Dorothy) are a mix of nationalities, including Polish, Russian, Jewish, and Czechoslovakian.

My wife and I were married on September 26, 1992. In our hearts, we wanted to have 2 or 3 children, though we wanted to wait a few years. We waited and then commenced with attempts to have a biological child. Our efforts are ongoing.

We have prayed constantly, seeking God's will and an answer to our most heartfelt desire to have children. I think we would be ideal parents due to the strength of our marriage, our deep faith, our commitment to family, and our personal values. Over the past year, we have given some thought to adoption. It motivated us to attend a meeting sponsored by New Beginnings. That meeting changed our lives.

During the meeting, the coordinator went into great detail about the need for parents for thousands of foster children in various countries. Many couples who had adopted were in attendance and my wife and I were moved by their testimonials, particularly concerning the unique plight facing the girls of China. As the meeting proceeded, I felt as if God planted a seed in my heart. The seed has blossomed ever since and I'm sure it is my daughter. By the time the meeting was over, I think both my wife and I had decided we wanted to adopt a young girl from China. In some ways, I think China selected us, too.

Accordingly, we submit this letter. We formally pledge, with all our heartfelt intentions and with our promise to God that we will NEVER abandon or abuse the adopted child. We will devote our lives to raising and educating the child until she reaches adulthood (and beyond). We will love her unconditionally and give her all the same rights and privileges as if she was our biological child. Our parents and siblings feel the same way, anxious to have Lila Rose (the name we selected) join our family. As I mentioned previously, we feel she is now a seed planted in our hearts. When the seed grows into our own baby, I will cherish and love her with all my heart and soul.

Frederick and Dorothy Ford

Our biographies—which have been intentionally and cleverly edited to omit any mention of personality flaws, emotional instabilities, family dysfunction, bad eating habits, past driving tickets, 30-day late payments on our credit reports, or any other attribute that might paint us in a less favorable light than Barbie and Ken—are boastfully forwarded to New Beginnings along with the first wave of completed paperwork, and a copy is also forwarded to a social worker who will get in touch with us to set-up a home visit. One of the many pre-requisites of adoption is successful completion of a home study. The fact a social worker could potentially obstruct our adoption generates a mental image of a scowling battle-ax with the ability to extract confessions from war criminals. In short, I imagine a cross between Mrs. Doubtfire and Sherlock Holmes.

New Beginnings reveals inconspicuously little about the home study. If anything, they downplay it. Babe makes the appointment and both of us burst into fits of panic. The pending visit from the social worker triggers a critical self-examination of our lives and our home. It creates instant paranoia. Suddenly, I view every object in our house as blatant evidence of our dubious character.

The wine rack, for instance. It sits harmlessly in the corner of our dining room and I stroll past it ten times a day without so much as a second glance. Suddenly, the wine rack calls out to me in the fiendish voice of Satan accompanied by the ominous echoes of a cathedral pipe organ. Its presence creates conflict and questions: What if we empty the wine rack of all the wine bottles; would this help? Or give the impression we are lushes who can't manage to keep enough wine on hand to satisfy our thirst? What if we fill the wine rack to capacity; would it be transformed into merely a piece of furniture? Or give the impression that we are lushes who stock the wine rack daily to keep up with our insatiable thirst? Some of the bottles are dusty. Should we dust and let the world know how clean we were? Should we leave the dust thereby creating the illusion that we never touch the stuff?

And what about the rest of the house? Are there too many sharp objects lying around? What about the electrical outlets; should we cover them? It's comical, yet at the same time the feelings of inadequacy are undeniable. Once placed under a microscope, our lives appear as untidy as Oscar Madison's bedroom.

Ultimately, we decide to simply go with the flow. For good reason, we feel well qualified to be parents. Our home is warm and inviting, our marriage solid, and despite the critical way we are currently viewing ourselves, there are no frightening outgrowths or scars disfiguring either of us.

"Let's forget any pretense, just be honest and straightforward," I suggest. "We're driving ourselves crazy trying to be Mr. and Mrs. Perfect."

The day arrives for the home study. I pace and Babe tries to find additional ways to tidy up a house that hasn't seen a speck of dust in forty-eight hours. The entire place is shining like a sultan's opal. The doorbell rings and the sound of it stiffens my spine and practically sends me leaping out of my shoes.

Babe gingerly opens the front door to reveal a peppy, middle-aged woman wearing a warm smile. She's not the battle-axe I dreaded but on the other hand I don't suspect she'll be crowned Miss America any time soon.

"Ellen," she says and extends her hand for a hearty handshake.

She's pleasant in appearance, dressed conservatively and professionally. She glances about as we stroll from the foyer through the living room and into the kitchen, where the aroma of freshly brewed coffee hangs in the air like an unanswered question.

Once seated at the kitchen table, Babe asks, "Would you like something to eat Ellen, a sandwich, some pastries?"

"Sure, I'll have a sandwich, I'm starving," Ellen admits lustily.

Apparently Ellen doesn't realize Babe's question is a smoke screen for the underlying purpose of her hospitality: to demonstrate her ability to entertain guests in the same dandy fashion as Aunt Bee from Mayberry.

As the smalltalk continues, I try to gauge Ellen's face, wary of any look of disgust, or even mild disapproval as she glances about the room. I am overly suspicious as I try to read her thoughts, a bit paranoid about the potential consequences of her visit.

"I read your biographies," she says excitedly. "Fred, I love the part where you describe having cool, hard sand squished between your toes as you walked along the ocean shoreline near dusk. I loved that description."

"Thanks," I say politely. This opens a window of opportunity to speak about New England and my family and why I moved to Long Island in 1984. I'm quickly warming up to Ellen and the tension has begun to subside. Suddenly, Ellen feels to me like a new neighbor who stopped by to get acquainted. I'm nearly ready to suggest a round of martinis.

Shaken not stirred, Ellen?

The casual question and answer session terminates and we then treat Ellen to a tour of our house. It's never been more immaculate. Even my Fred Flintstone doll is properly positioned and sitting upright.

At the end of the tour, we return to the kitchen. Ellen reaches into her big carrying bag as panic returns like a bad memory. I think to myself: oh-oh, time for the other shoe to drop.

To my delight, she merely pulls out some paperwork and explains that we will need to schedule a follow-up appointment upon our return from China. My wife glances in my direction with a face dripped with relief.

The visit ends, Ellen leaves, and I release a deep sigh that alters the barometric pressure in the room. The wine rack, to my delight and relief, is never mentioned. Naturally, that fact inspires me to open and consume a bottle of wine. Make that two. Symbolically, this is a big hurdle out of the way. Paranoia dissolves. And then, it's time to...

....hurry up and wait.

* * *

The burden of the fertility treatments has been replaced by the angst of the adoption process. The daily grind seems unbearably tedious, as the sands of the hourglass drip. Owing to my rather—ahem—husky build and *slight* beer belly, I have fallen into the habit of joking that *I* am carrying the baby. This always produces a laugh in those who are hearing the joke for the first time, and always continues to whiddle away at Babe's patience with each passing mention.

As I drive to work one day, I have the car radio tuned to News Radio 1010 and hear an announcement that turns my stomach upside down.

The announcer describes a breaking news story about The World Health Organization, who issued a travel ban to China because of a mysterious flu-like illness that has broken out. Apparently, not much is known about the disease though it is linked to several deaths and reports of hundreds more stricken with its symptoms. The illness is feared to become a major pandemic and there is no time table as to the travel ban will be lifted. He ends the news story with words that enter my soul like the death of a family member: Chinese officials issued a statement that all international adoptions from China have been suspended.

All international adoptions from China have been suspended—the phrase begins to sink its talons into my brain. I'm so shaken I pull over to the side of the road to compose myself. My hands are trembling uncontrollably and the only thing I can think to do is say a prayer as I mumble over and over, "This *cannot* be happening."

I get to work and sidestep any meaningful conversation with my secretary. There's plenty to do, as always. At that moment, however, real estate appraisals are irrelevant. I have momentarily lost the ability to concentrate on anything except the new story, which buzzes in my ear like a cloud of hornets. The frenzy of the office—which I ordinarily handle with simple reflex—is suddenly unbearable.

"I need a few minutes alone in my office. I'll return calls later," I say for all to hear.

I close the door to my office loudly enough to send a second message: don't bother me. Stacks of appraisal files are all over my desk awaiting my review or signature. A half-dozen Post-It notes dangle from my computer monitor. I easily ignore them and log onto my computer to search the Internet for stories related to the radio report. Eventually, I find more specifics.

It's called S.A.R.S.: Sudden Acute Respiratory Syndrome. Little is known about it, though it is feared to become a significant threat to public health. The outbreak is most prominent in—where else?—China. This isn't good.

I grab the phone to make an impossibly difficult phone call to Babe.

"Hon, I heard some bad news about China on the radio this morning," I say somberly.

"I saw something on *Good Morning America*; but I caught the tail end of the report. What's happening?"

"China has suspended all international adoptions."

As the word "suspended" spills from my mouth, I feel as though I've just fired a random gun shot into a crowd. My comment detonates an atom bomb of grief from Babe and the silence I hear from the other end of the phone tells the entire story: she is devastated.

When our phone conversation ends, Babe hastily phones New Beginnings and gets Cathy Dinowski on the phone.

"What are you hearing about the adoptions?" Babe pleads.

"We're proceeding as planned. We don't know any more than what the news is reporting but if we hear something we'll be sure to get in touch with you."

It's an honest enough answer, yet it carries no certainty. It leaves us treading water in a pool at night with no lights on and no evidence where the side of the pool is; only an assurance the side of the pool does, in fact, exist.

We are possibly looking at an extended delay. At worse, God forbid, our adoption from China will be cancelled. This is one of the many times prayer creates a sturdy bridge over troubled water. We're helpless to do anything else about SARS and we feel secure with the notion God has selected a baby in China especially for us—and vice versa. So we pray and wait.

Weeks later, the SARS outbreak is contained and the travel ban to China is lifted. When I here the news, I feel as if the jury has just read aloud "NOT GUILTY" at a trial threatening to send me to decades of prison time for a crime I didn't commit.

Thank you God.

* * *

We're at a workshop at New Beginnings office in Mineola, about an hour's drive from our house. As usual, Cathy Dinowski presides. Next to Cathy sits a resolute looking woman who wears an agonizing scowl on her face; the same type you might see on a prison warden. Six couples are crowded into a small conference room. I recognize the faces; I've seen them at prior workshops.

The workshop is designed to provide relevant information about our upcoming visit to China: travel expenses, what to expect with Chinese culture, jet lag, and so on. Cathy speaks briefly about the expenses and the cash we'll need for the donation to the orphanage.

"Very important," she says emphatically. "Your cash donation must be clean bills, no folds, no dog-eared corners. When you go to your bank to get the cash, insist on new bills. When you travel, keep the cash in a place where it won't get folded or wrinkled. The Chinese can deny your adoption if the bills are marked or folded."

The adoption just got creepy.

Cathy goes on to describe currency conversion, Panda phones (cell phones), and electrical outlet adapters we'll need purchase.

"If you plan to use a blow-dryer or battery charger, you're going to need one of these," she says, and holds up the adapter. "The electrical outlets are different in China so none of your traditional plugs will work."

"You'll need to carry several tips to give to notaries and other officials; nothing special or expensive. I must tell you," Cathy glances side to side and hesitates, setting us up for the punchline, "the Chinese love chocolate."

After Cathy concludes, she introduces the social worker with the troubled face., who then delivers a firm lecture on the respect we need to show Chinese customs and culture. Her speech triggers some thoughts about the documentary I have planned. Are there restrictions on video cameras?

During the question-and-answer period, I say, "I'm making a documentary about the adoption and was wondering if there are any videotaping restrictions In China, either legal or implied."

"You should avoid being obvious at all times," the woman barks. "Limit the amount of videotaping of the children in China. Many of the toddlers walk around with holes in the backside of their pants, covered by a flap. This allows the child to do their 'duty' right in the middle of the street or sidewalk. It would be unadvisable to videotape such things."

Her admonition arrives swiftly and unexpectedly—like a wrap across the knuckles from a nun's ruler.

I quickly decide to ignore her advice, even if the use of my video camera causes me to appear obvious. If something of intrigue hooks my curiosity, I'm videotaping. Besides, I'm a white man about the size of a sumo wrestler who frequently tells jokes and laughs loudly at my own jokes. I won't need a video-camera to make me look obvious in China.

*　*　*

We're visiting Disney World and we decide to attend a performance of the Cirque de Soleil. I'm told by many that it's wonderfully entertaining, yet I have no idea what it's about and I expect something akin to Barnum and Bailey's.

To my astonishment, the Cirque de Soleil is an assault on my senses. The music is loud and sensuous, the colors extravagant and bright; multiple performers dance, jump, flip, and cart wheel across the vast stage; props, cages, and unicycles appear out of the floor seemingly out of no where. It's like a technicolor dream.

At one point, four young Chinese girls sprint onto the stage and perform a series of juggling moves mixed with gymnastics as they toss objects high in the air then perform back flips and position themselves to catch the descending objects with strings pulled taut between their hands. Their performance is flawlessly breath-taking, and the audience roars their approval as the young girls bow and curtsy at the conclusion of their performance. I glance sideways at Babe and notice tears stream down her face.

The trip flies by. Once home from vacation the days drag, accompanied by the suffocating emptiness of impatience.

*   *   *

We're seated at the table and Babe pushes food around her plate.

"Everything OK?" I ask earnestly.

She places her fork on the plate. "Sometimes I feel the day's never going to get here."

"I know. The waiting isn't easy. But in God's time we'll have Lila."

My comment fails to inspire a reaction. Maybe I've used the "God's time" line one time too many. But beyond my impatience and my own version of how things ought to happen is an assurance from God that everything will turn out for the best. Time and again through my life, I've exercised my faith in difficult circumstances and from the bleachers of hindsight I've watched the situation play out in my favor every time; not always how I envisioned it but always for best. There is no replacing faith in God; it's the the most important thing I own.

"Sometimes I lose a little faith," she says. "Sometimes I wonder if God hears our prayers."

Her comment seizes my attention. I reach across the table and grab her hand and squeeze tightly.

"In my sophomore year of college, I was driving from the Jacksonville Airport back to St. Augustine when something happened that changed my prayer life."

"What's that?"

"It was early morning and I decided to keep the radio off and pray aloud. So I drove for about ten minutes along Route 95 and had a conversation with God. Anyone driving past me must have wondered who on earth I was talking to. All of sudden, I felt a palpable wave of doubt. I stopped praying. I got a strong feeling I was wasting both my time and my breath. I began to wonder who God was and why I bother to pray. I actually said aloud, 'who am I talking to? What difference does it make?' As I uttered those words I approached a sharp bend in the road. While negotiating the bend, I noticed a billboard off to the side of the road. The billboard was white with two giant words painted in black: GOD LISTENS."

Babe's eyes open wide.

"I'm not exaggerating; that is exactly how it happened. When it happened to me I got a chill up my spine. Ever since that day, I believe God listens," I say intensely. "And I know God's heard every one of our prayers for a daughter."

Babe sighs and tries to reconcile my story with her own feelings of impatience. I have her undivided attention and I feel I need to drive the point home again—louder and with more certainty than ever.

I squeeze her hand even tighter and look her in the eyes and say, "If we believe in God—and we do—then we *have* to believe He hears our prayers. Not just some, not just the ones He wants to hear; but *all* of them. And if we believe He hears our prayers, we *have* to believe He will answer. Otherwise, why pray? Why believe?"

She nods slowly as my words slowly penetrate. My instinct tells me to drive the point home one more time.

"God has heard our prayers, hon. And He will answer; In *His* time. In God's time we'll have our baby."

I speak the sentence as if proclaiming a passage from the Bible.

Babe smiles and squeezes my hands as though grabbing the words.

Two weeks later, at long last, God's time arrives.

Chapter 5
LILA ROSE

"Honey, we have a daughter." Babe doesn't merely speak the words; she proclaims them triumphantly through a voice choked with tears.

On the other end of the phone, neck-deep in paperwork, I feel emancipated. The joy I feel for my wife could fill a thousand empty hearts.

"I just got off the phone with Pauline from New Beginnings. They're sending the dossier by overnight mail," Babe sings.

"I'm so happy, hon. It's God's time." Near the end of the sentence, the words become choked as I start to cry.

The desperation, frustration, doubts, and emotional pain of infertility are gone. The torturous and relentless anxiety we suffered through is suddenly a footnote to the story. The good guys have prevailed; victory is within our grasp.

At work the following day, the nervous excitement about the package reduces Babe's daily routine to trivia. She systematically completes her duties as graphic artist, engulfed by a feeling she is merely going through the motions.

As she awaits delivery of the package, on the verge of seeing Lila's face for the first time, fear and anxiety resurface like the imperishable antagonist in a horror movie. The final fears are inspired by the package itself: what if it slips out of the driver's hands? What if it gets delivered to the wrong address? What if the package rips? Or burns? Or gets lost?

The face of the doubts has been altered over the years. At times it appears vulnerable to prayer and positive thoughts; other times it seems as impenetrable as Fort Knox. But the deep-seeded emotions and negative feelings they perpetually generate have been constant for many years, replaying vivid memories of difficult days, lonely hours, and baby showers that threatened to crush Babe's soul. And now, on the verge of conquering those fears once and for all, only one fear remained: the safe delivery of the package.

Around noon, her fears are permanently and thankfully put to rest. The package arrives intact. For ten seconds, the Fed Ex driver unwittingly plays the role of stork. Babe's sigh—deep and overdue—removes the weight of an elephant from her shoulders.

Though bursting with anticipation and tempted to open the package and get just one peak, Babe agrees to wait until I get home from work so we can open the package and experience this magical moment together.

After work, I arrive at home filled with nervous excitement and examine the package. As I handle it, I am, for the first time in the entire process, insatiably curious about Lila's physical appearance—even fearful. To date, her appearance was never an issue. Tucked away on the back burner of my mind, I suppose the curiosity was always there; lingering quietly awaiting its turn to affect me but, to date, playing second fiddle to the anxiety and fear that this day would never arrive. But now, as I prepare to see Lila at last, I can think of nothing else. Will she be a pretty baby? Or have some deformity? What will her eyes look like? How much hair will she have? Will she have big ears? I am suddenly strangled with fear.

I set up the tripod and video camera and direct the lens toward my wife, who is now seated at our kitchen table. To her right is my empty chair. The Fed-Ex envelope rests expectantly on the table in front of her.

With the camera and tripod set up and a fresh tape ready to record history, I press the "RECORD" button and walk briskly out from behind the camera to the seat adjacent to Babe.

Before I begin the formal speech into the camera, I turn to Babe and ask, "You ready for this?"

She smiles with tears pooled in her eyes, draws a deep breath, and says, "Yes."

As I face the camera I narrate: "This morning we received this package from New Beginnings. And we're about to open it up and see Lila for the first time."

My hands are shaking and my heart is beating at three times its normal rate. I feel claustrophobic and my breathing is short and rapid. A rare form of emotional and mental chaos arrives, brought about by strong conflict in virtually every pulse of thought or feeling. It is the type of conflict that can only be resolved by time; the inevitable graduation from present to future of a moment anticipated for years. In stand-up comedy, that moment arrives with both suffocating fear and breathless relief when the MC announces your name and introduces you to the audience. In adoption, that same unmanageable mix of feelings arrives when you see your daughter's face for the first time.

I rip open the package and hastily remove the contents. The first thing I see is a letter paper-clipped to the rest of the thick stack of documents. I flip the letter over and Babe and I simultaneously view a photo of Lila.

"Oh my God, she's beautiful," Babe gasps.

I can't believe my eyes. She's the most beautiful baby I've ever seen. Seconds after I see the photo, I think to myself: *if anyone ever touches this baby, they'll wish they were never born.* My animal instinct alarms me as I fight back tears and emotions I can barely control.

We stare at the photo for several seconds through moist eyes. This baby, our gift from God, comes to life in my heart as I stare with wonder at her photo. The seed has blossomed. Her sad, beautiful, round brown eyes plead for love and attention.

"My eyes look more Asian than hers do," Babe jokes, making reference to Lila's big brown eyes and Babe's almond shaped eyes.

The video camera continues to record as we forget its presence, hypnotized by Lila's photo. I dig through the paperwork and uncover a second photo, then a third and fourth. With each photo, the process begins anew as we study every detail of Lila's face, hands, and feet while we try to imagine holding and touching her. Babe repeats over and over, "She's so beautiful." I am so enamored by the photos I fail to notice Lila is not smiling in any of them. That fact will later be subtly pointed out by my mother when she receives the email photos.

The only disturbing thing contained in the package is the abandonment certificate, which is issued in China in lieu of a birth certificate when babies are abandoned. The certificate is three pages, the first written in Chinese with a thumbnail photo of a month old Lila in the lower left corner. I stare at the photo for several seconds with tears in my eyes. The second page of the certificate is an English translation. As I read it, I feel hollow and helpless. The certificate reads:

This is to certify that, according to the certificate records on file supplied by the Social Welfare Institute of Guigang City, Guangxi Zhuang Autonomous Region, Jiang Xiaozhong (female, born on March 14, 2003) was found abandoned beside Nanshan Roundabout, Guigang City, Guangxi on April 19, 2003 by somebody unidentified, who reported to Jiangnan Police Station subordinated to Guigang Public Security Bureau, then a policeman of the said station picked the baby up and took her to the Social Welfare Institute of Guigang City, Guangxi Zhuang Autonomous Region on the same day, by which Jiang Xiaozhong was taken in and fostered. Her biological parents were unable to be found up to present although the investigation had been conducted.

When I finish, I'm stricken with deep sadness. I feel violated, as if I had just learned my car had been stolen. A wave of nausea washes through my stomach.

I stare again at one of the photos and think: how could *anyone* abandon this baby?

To date, this is Lila's legacy, the only evidence of her existence: an abandonment certificate. Lila's biological parents cared for her for more than a month before abandoning her. They had fed her, hugged her, looked at her, bonded with her, changed her diapers, and kissed her beautiful face. And then they *abandoned* her, as if she were a stack of junk mail. Abandoning newborns, particularly females, is common and, from what I've learned, socially acceptable in China. I've even read some Chinese women feel a sense of obligation to society after they abandon their babies. After I read the abandonment document, I grab for the photos again and again as I stare into Lila's face and think to myself: *Those days are over forever, my beautiful baby; you'll never be abandoned again.*

As we continue to admire our treasured photos, I feel mystically transported somewhere off the earth into a private adoption viewing room somewhere in another galaxy; everything familiar has ceased to exist. The experience is so unique I barely recognize any of the feelings it produces.

The package also includes an invoice for $3,450, the latest in a long line of adoption expenses. The payments are minor inconveniences at this point, particularly after seeing photos of Lila for the first time. I expect to become more impatient after seeing the photos. Surprisingly, the opposite occurs. Seeing her face produces the calm of winter woods in New Hampshire. It gives the dream clarity; like the transition from blueprint to new home.

The following day, I scan the photos of Lila and email them to friends and family members. I make several hard copies of the photos and place them throughout the house and onto the dashboard of our two cars. I frequently stare at the photo taped to my computer monitor for minutes at a time and whisper to my daughter, "I love you honey. I'm going to be the best father you could ever hope for."

We have the first buds of the harvest we've reaped through many years of prayers and faith. I thank God numerous times in the weeks following receipt of the dossier. As always, God's answer to our prayer is grander and more wonderful than anything I could have imagined.

In His time, Babe, we'll have our baby. The words of encouragement, which God inspired in me and, in turn, I offered to Babe time and again, have finally come true. After years of waiting, we have our daughter.

* * *

Shortly after we receive the photos, we travel to Newport, Rhode Island for a long weekend I had booked months ago as a Christmas gift for Babe. Little did I know at the time, our visit would coincide with Lila's first birthday. Given the enjoyable history Babe and I share from prior Newport visits, including the celebration of our fifth wedding anniversary in 1997, it seems to be a perfect place to celebrate Lila's first birthday.

It's a beautiful March afternoon as we drive exultantly over the Narragansett Bridge, the yachts, sailboats, and waterfront restaurants of Newport suddenly visible from across the bay. The town is bathed in sunlight and the bay is sparkling. We drive through town and relish the familiar shops, restaurants, and other sites and then proceed to Ocean Drive and cruise slowly along the winding road past the stately old homes and mansions. I've reserved a room at Castle Hill Resort, situated on a waterfront bluff atop a forty-acre peninsula at the west end of Ocean Drive.

Our room is one of the four rooms in a Swiss-style chalet, located about a hundred yards and slightly downhill to the right of the main mansion. The room has a gas fireplace and big fluffy bed. It's perfect—except the "two-person" bathtub which taunts me with a painful reminder I'm due for another diet.

After we check in, I make arrangements to dine at The White Horse Tavern, one of our favorite restaurants in Newport, for the occasion of Lila's first birthday.

Before we leave for the restaurant, we visit the handsome bar in the main mansion. I purchase a couple of martinis and we walk outside and settle into one of several high-back wooden lawn chairs that face the bay. Once settled into our chairs, we stretch our legs and ease our minds to a Newport sunset.

An hour later, we stride joyfully into the White Horse Tavern, one of the oldest buildings in Newport and home to some great ghost stories from the bartender upstairs. The building is a two-story structure with white clapboard exterior and a small parking lot in the rear.

As we enter the small foyer, I detect the inviting fragrance of a fire burning in the big stone fireplace in the main dining area. The lights are low, except the well lit hostess station. The maitre de approaches and confirms our reservation, then leads us across the old, creaking hardwood floors to our table in front of the fireplace. Once seated, Babe casually removes a framed photo of Lila and places it atop the white linen draped over our small table.

The dining room is not as crowded as I expected it would be. Based on some low grumblings I overhear from adjoining tables I suspect the decline in popularity may well be the result of the deteriorating service. On prior visits, we found it difficult to get a reservation.

"The place is empty," I say in a low voice to Babe as I peruse the wine list.

"That's fine by me. Look at the table we got," Babe says.

The waiter comes by the table. "Good evening folks," he says cheerfully, "are you dining with us for the first time?" It seems to be the question on the mind of waiters and waitresses in every restaurant located in tourist destinations.

"No," I say, "we've been here twice before. And last night I had a very satisfying dream about your beef Wellington."

He smiles. "The best on the east coast. Care for a cocktail?"

A drunk diner from across the room yells to our waiter, "Hey, when you get a second can you come over here?"

I turn to see the man bears a frighteningly similar resemblance to W. C. Fields.

"No cocktails," I say, "we're getting a bottle of wine. Give us a few minutes."

"Very well," the waiter says politely and heads to the drunk's table.

Babe and I remain quiet as we covertly eavesdrop on the conversing pulsing from the drunk's table. He complains about his overcooked steak and slow service and too many ice cubes in his scotch.

Undeterred, we later enjoy our meal of beef Wellington and a vintage bottle of Cain 5, which washes over my pallet like liquid velvet. At the end of the meal, I motion for the waiter.

He arrives and I say, "I need a favor. Would it be possible to get a piece of cake with one candle on it?"

"By all means," he says and disappears.

A minute later he arrives, places the cake on the table, and lights the candle as he asks, "Are you celebrating a special anniversary?"

I can't even look at Babe. "Sort of," I say with a trembling voice.

"Cheers," the waiter says, and leaves.

Babe and I hold hands and stare at the framed photo of Lila. The flickering candle dances light onto her face as she stares out blankly at us. We decide not to sing happy birthday; we want to avoid the attention. Both of us have tears in our eyes.

"Happy birthday Lila," I say. "Happy birthday, my beautiful baby."

* * *

The following day, we videotape for the documentary. Initially, we attempt to film outdoors. But heavy wind and dropping temperature forces us indoors. Once inside our room, the warmth engulfs us like a hug from Hagrid. After we compose ourselves and reconstruct our windblown hair, I set up the tripod and secure the wireless microphone to the front of my wife's sweater.

Earlier in the week, Babe wrote a love letter to Lila. She decides to use her camera face time to read the letter. I videotape and she reads.

"I have carried you in my heart for a very long time. And at last, my love has come along." Babe's voice cracks and the first of many tears escape. She pauses to compose herself. "I didn't get too far without crying."

"It's OK," I say. "I can edit out parts we don't need. Just read it at whatever pace you need and pause if you need to. We have all day."

She clears her throat and picks up where she left off.

"God has shown us your beautiful face. As your mom, I promise to be here for you always. I promise to fill your life with laughter and make your heart sing the way you did ours when we first laid eyes on you. I promise to fill your home with warmth and love so you feel safe and secure whenever you are there. I promise to be a mom that you are proud of, and to love you, my beautiful daughter, unconditionally. I promise to always listen to you lovingly."

"You're doing great, hon," I say, "but you need to look up at the camera every once in a while." My directorial nature refuses to lie still.

"OK," she says. When she begins anew, she intentionally alternates her glances from the camera to the letter and continues to do so for the balance of the reading.

"When we are faced with difficult times, I promise that we will get through them together and use them to make us better people. I promise to encourage you to follow your heart the way your father and I have patiently followed ours; which has finally led us to you. Because of our enduring faith, God has blessed us immensely. You are a gift from up above. You are a pot of gold at the end of the rainbow," she says and looks up at the camera and smiles, tears in her eyes. "And we can't wait to hold you in our arms, at last. Happy birthday, my beautiful, beautiful daughter."

As she says the last lines, tears stream down her face. I think it's the most beautiful love letter I've ever heard.

When it's my turn to speak, I read some of the touching emails friends and family have sent in response to the email and photo I sent to everyone. The emails range from hearty congratulations, to compliments on Lila's beauty, to emotional outbursts and admissions of tears of joy.

When I'm done, I look at the camera and say, "And the only other thing I can say as we move this video along, is…let's go to China."

Yes, lets.

Chapter 6
KEVORKIAN, JET LAG, AND GREAT WALLS

It's departure day, May 5, 2004. Babe and I pack for our trip as we contemplate the turbulence and mystery and miracles of the week to come. Within the hour, Babe and I will exit our house in Bellport and leave behind the familiarity and freedom of our childless marriage. At one time an unreachable dream, our thousand mile journey to become parents is only steps away.

Babe asks, "How do you feel?"

"Bittersweet," I admit, almost apologetically.

The word leaves my mouth carrying the weight of negativity. We are about to realize a dream of having a baby, the pot of gold at the end of a thousand-mile rainbow sprinkled with prayers, tears, sweat, blood, heartache and, at long last, joy. Nevertheless, I have enjoyed our married life to this point and I sense that life rapidly slipping into my past as we prepare for departure; thus "bittersweet" is the word that jumps to mind.

I walk downstairs and into our big kitchen where early morning sun streaks through the rear windows, spotlighting our dog Daisy. She paces around with a curious look on her face. She's detected the luggage and has been through the vacation drill before, so she senses we'll be gone for a few days. I bend down and Daisy wags her tail and scoots over to me for a hug. As I pat her I say forebodingly, "Your days as Princess are numbered."

She licks my face, oblivious to her pending demotion. I hope her transition from princess to dog will be effortless—though I doubt.

As we prepare for the trip, the house seems eerily still. I feel as though I'm wandering inside an old photograph. Upon our return from China, the house will never be the same again, yet I can't quite visualize the extent of the pending disorder or the effect it will have on me and Babe. I haven't allowed my mind to fully wrap itself around parenthood, opting instead to focus on the first meeting with Lila and the flood of emotions the meeting will deliver. Both adoption and parenthood carry heaping portions of The Unknown, of that I'm certain.

Babe packs enough clothes to get us through six months on a deserted island. Our luggage weighs more than me. She's never been one to play it safe when packing, a trait she inherited from her brother Lance who once packed barbells so he could keep up with his workouts while vacationing—which to me makes as much sense as packing a piano to keep up with the lessons. In addition to clothes, she packs toys, diapers, hats, and shoes for Lila. Packing Lila's stuff turns into an emotional experience for Babe.

I walk into Lila's room and Babe stands frozen with her back to me, her gaze fixed on the brightly colored clothes in Lila's open closet. Thanks to the baby shower and the generosity of family and friends—not to mention Babe's occasional shopping sprees—Lila's closet hasn't a single vacancy. Her room is as perfect as a Christmas snow storm.

I slip behind Babe and drape my arms around her from behind then kiss her neck softly. She wonders aloud, "What is it going to feel like to show Lila her room for the first time?" She has tears in her eyes.

Our moment of contemplation is terminated by a ring of the doorbell. One of Babe's co-workers has arrived to transport us to the airport.

We load the luggage into our Honda Pilot and bid farewell to Daisy. With Babe waiting in the car, I re-enter the house for a final reconnaissance as I mumble to myself, "Keys, wallet, passport, money, camera, video camera, books, glasses."

Satisfied I have everything, I open the front door. I feel as though I'm passing from one life to another. Life as I've known it is about to change—quickly and drastically. Just before I exit, I glance back into our house and look up at the framed picture—a print of DaVinci's *The Creation of Adam*—on the wall above the foyer. A feeling of peace arrives; I smile and thank God for His many blessings. Seconds later, my old life disengages itself and slips away into the Sea of Memory.

An hour and a half of stop-and-go traffic along the Southern State Parkway finally gets us to Kennedy International Airport in Queens, where we plan to meet up with several couples who will travel with us and adopt babies of their own. We met many of the couples during any of the various workshops we completed with New Beginnings. Babe and I are extra early. We check in at the Air China terminal, where our driver's licenses and passports are scrutinized and then travel up the escalator one level to the food court that overlooks the check-in area. At this hour, most restaurants are closed, leaving us few options for breakfast. We scan the food court briefly and, at Babe's suggestion, make our way to an empty seven-stool bar adjacent to the Wok N' Roll restaurant. On flying days, Babe typically seeks the counsel of one or two glasses of wine prior to the flight—regardless of the time of day. With a slight twist of my arm, I agree to join her!

As we sip our respective drinks—Babe's a white wine, mine a Bloody Mary—Babe grabs the video camera and points it to me so I can record my thoughts for the documentary.

"When we were kids growing up in Arlington, we used to use spoons in the back yard and pretend like we were going to dig all the way to China," I say. Babe laughs as she videotapes. "Fortunately, thanks to modern technology, we have an easier way to get there."

Minutes later, I carry our empty cups to a waste basket adjacent to a condiment station where I detect some plastic forks and spoons. For nostalgia's sake, I grab a spoon in slip it into my coat pocket.

Babe and I proceed to the terminal where we sit and review paperwork. The seating area of the terminal is populated exclusively with Chinese people—unless you count the maintenance worker. Within a half-hour, at various intervals, the other couples arrive and we noisily re-acquaint and exchange photos and medical charts pertaining to our daughters.

Our travel group consists of four other couples from Long Island: Tom and Colleen; George and Shirley; Kitty and Rob; Danny and Karen (who are accompanied by their biological three-year old daughter Emily).

The excited exchange of photos is interrupted by a tall guy, about 6'3," who looks like he's on his way to a barbecue. He wears shorts, flip-flops, and a tee-shirt.

"New Beginnings?" he asks and points to the group.

Aside from George, Shirley, and Danny (who are all of Chinese descent), our group consists of Caucasians. Picking us out as the group from New Beginnings, therefore, carries the same deductive genius as picking out a pumpkin among a basket full of jelly beans.

"Hey, big Rob," Kitty says. She recognizes the tall guy. Kitty and her husband, also named Rob, are adopting a second baby from China. Kitty turns to the rest of us for the introduction. "Everyone, this is Rob. He traveled with us the last time we adopted."

Big Rob is also adopting for a second time and coincidentally he traveled to China with Kitty's group last time. At 5'8," Kitty's husband Rob is about a half-foot shorter than Big Rob, which naturally earns him the nickname Little Rob. There are no other Freds on the trip. Nevertheless, I'm Big Fred.

Big Rob explains he just arrived via red-eye flight from Tampa. New Beginnings has a Florida office and Rob is the only one from that area scheduled to visit China so he's been placed in our travel group.

I rise from my chair and extend my hand in Rob's direction. "Is your wife here?" I ask.

"She's home with my other daughter. She can't fly."

I quickly conclude Big Rob has some Big Balls to travel by himself to adopt from China. Babe thinks so too.

"Wow, Rob, you have *some* courage," Babe says admiringly.

Rob shrugs. "No big deal," he says. His answer is honest and humble, yet as difficult to embrace as a porcupine. Making this trip alone would be a *huge* deal and I'm confident I could never manage it.

Less than an hour later, we board an Air China plane to begin our odyssey.

* * *

Babe and I get to our assigned seats and cram our carry-on bags in the overhead bin. I take the window seat and Babe takes the middle. A few minutes after we settle in, a man arrives to take the aisle seat. He strongly resembles the infamous Dr. Kevorkian of assisted suicide notoriety. He nods our way, grunts, and straps his seatbelt. He seems nervous and harried. Facing more than a half-day confined to our plane seats, I'm certain to learn more about this character before flight's end.

The plane is scheduled to take off at about 2:00 p.m. Eastern Standard time. It's Wednesday. In China, it's 2 a.m. on Thursday. In other words, it's already tomorrow. Once we're in the air, therefore, is it Wednesday or Thursday? I'm confused. When we land in China fourteen hours later, it will be 4:00 p.m., twelve hours ahead of the time it would have been had we stayed in New York. I'll lose half a day of my life and a night's sleep and have nothing to show for it except a sore ass and cramped legs. This whole thing is beginning to sound like an Abbott and Costello routine.

On the up side, I have two books and plenty of time to read, a luxury I'm rarely afforded. Of greater importance, I have Babe. Flight attendants will stop by from time to time to bring food and drinks. For the next fourteen hours, therefore, everything I need is within reach of my seat. On the down side, the only lavatories on the plane are the size of Old Mother Hubbard's cupboard. For a man my size, using plane bathrooms is the physical equivalent of playing Twister in the trunk of a Buick. All things considered, the up side outweighs the down.

After a short wait and a few announcements, the plane speeds noisily down the runway and lifts off the tarmac. As the plane tilts upward for its initial ascent, Babe grabs my hand and gives it the death grip. Her squeeze is part YAY and part HOLY CRAP! On the whole, she seems a whole lot more at ease flying than she usually does.

"You OK?" I ask.

"I really am." She smiles.

When the plane reaches cruising altitude, the male flight attendant takes our drink orders. Babe orders white wine and I order a beer. The beer arrives a few minutes later in an unrecognizable can: blue and white with words written mostly in Chinese. I pour part of the contents into my little plastic cup and then hold the cup toward Babe for a toast.

"It's been a long time coming," I say.

She lifts her plastic glass of wine and taps my plastic beer glass with a clinkless clink as she toasts joyfully, "To Lila Rose."

A big flat screen television is mounted to the center panel in front of the first row of seats in our section. At the moment, the screen exhibits a flat map of the world and a cartoon plane representing the one in which we're flying. The plane moves an inch or so every ten minutes to adjust our new position over the world. From time to time, I catch myself staring at the map and reading the displayed flight information (altitude, elapsed time of flight, distance from Beijing, and so on). About an hour into the flight, the tedious map disappears and is replaced by the in-flight movie: *Mrs. Doubtfire*. I locate a pair of cheap earphones and secure them awkwardly onto my head, providing another reminder that in most categories, including those pertaining to head size, the term "One Size Fits All" has not applied to me since sixth grade. I insert the plug into the jack on my armrest. The audio signal comes through the earphones clearly. The movie is broadcast with Chinese voiceovers and English subtitles. There's something arresting about watching a familiar movie this way. I feel as though I'm watching *Mrs. Doubtfire Meets Godzilla.* I give up on the movie within ten minutes and open my book, a James Patterson novel that will likely provide just the type of breezy read and implausible story I'm seeking at 26,000 feet above sea level—trapped somewhere between today and tomorrow.

Babe listens to her Ipod and types notes into her Palm Pilot. Over the past few weeks, she programmed a few hours of songs into the Ipod.

An hour into the flight, I take a break from reading and glance over at Babe. I'm thrilled to see her so perfectly content, excited, and at ease flying. The fact we're going to get Lila has taken the edge off her fears in ways white wine never came close to.

I grab the camera and videotape her. She smiles and makes faces into the lens. Then I videotape my can of beer, some Air China pillows, the movie screen, the clouds outside, and anything else in the vicinity—except Kevorkian. When videotaping for a documentary, the rule of thumb is: too much is better than not enough—just like food at a barbecue. Nothing is insignificant so I film everything.

* * *

We're four hours into the flight. I've finished the book but my eyelids are as heavy as rolls of quarters so I decide to delay the start of Book Two.

Our neighbor, Dr. Kevorkian, is wearing headphones as he reads from a Learning Mandarin 101 tutorial. This crash course on his soon to be native tongue will presumably allow for his seamless assimilation into Chinese society. Based on his frightening appearance, his assimilation may require more than a command of Chinese language. Suddenly, he blurts aloud, "Oon-die!"

With the headphones on, he can't monitor his own voice. In the minutes to follow, he continues to shout indecipherable Chinese words and phrases every thirty seconds. This, in turn, attracts a steady flow of glances in our direction from others on the plane, as if we're traveling with, for example, a crying baby. I interpret the annoyed glances as our dress rehearsal for dealing with future eye daggers hurled in our direction.

As if to rescue me from the verbal flotsam, Babe removes the Ipod and says, "Here, take this for a while."

"Are you sure you want to give this up? With no headphones on, you're about to hear Chinese 101 from Kevorkian," I say in a half-whisper.

Babe muffles a laugh. "I'll be fine," she says. "I'm going to try to sleep."

I take the Ipod, secure it to my head, and press PLAY as Babe leans back and closes her eyes. I glance in Babe's direction. Her face is as calm and placid as a meadow covered by blanket of freshly fallen snow. I'm hit with a wave of compassionate joy. As the wave travels through me, I hear the first of the many songs Babe has programmed into the Ipod: Van Morrison's *Into the Mystic*. I listen to the song and watch my beautiful wife; her eyes closed, her mind and soul transported to a meeting with Lila, a baby she feared she might never have. As I watch her, I feel as though I'm viewing a music video created especially for this moment as I hear Morrison's voice: "We were born before the wind...."

From the time I produced the house construction video years ago, I have developed a habit of listening to songs for their potential use in movies I'm producing. Sometimes I'll listen to a group of CDs for hours in search of the perfect song to accompany edited footage. Other times, as with *Into the Mystic*, the song finds me. For Lila's movie, I envision *Into the Mystic* as the underscore to the footage I am currently videotaping aboard the plane, as well as the footage I'll soon videotape in Beijing Airport.

Later, as I listen to the music, I'm mostly oblivious to anything happening around me as I Etta James's *At Last* streams into my brain. I say "mostly oblivious" because certain things will invariably get my attention—like a meteorite. The sudden appearance of a zebra on the wing of the airplane is another fine example. But more troubling than either of those unlikely occurrences is the fact Kevorkian has struck up a conversation with Babe and seems animated in his attempts to persuade her to his point of view.

I casually move the left earphone from my ear to my cheek so I can eavesdrop. As I do, Babe says, "We're getting our daughter."

"Are you? Terrific. Congratulations. So many people are adopting these days," he says.

"What brings *you* to China?" she asks with feigned interest.

If our plane ride was broadcast in a TV show, the theme music to *The Twilight Zone* would have begun at this very moment.

"I'm moving to China for a better life," he begins. "I want to avoid the deluge in America."

"Deluge?" It's unclear if Babe doesn't know what deluge means or— God forbid—she is seeking clarification of his statement.

Kevorkian reaches into his carry-on bag and produces a CD copy of his self-published and self-illustrated book. The illustrations alone are enough to catapult the average person into the aisle of the plane in search of a parachute. The illustrations resemble the horrifying images contained in graphic sci-fi comic books.

"Publishing in America is monopolized by New York Jews," he explains. "I couldn't get anyone to publish my book, so I self published."

"Oh," says Babe. Her comeback contains one too many words for my tastes.

"Here," he says, and excitedly hands the CD to Babe.

She accepts the gift and looks it over front to back as though examining a dead animal. As she cautiously fondles her newly acquired literary weapon of mass destruction, she nudges me and I pretend I just emerged from anesthesia.

"Oh, I nodded off," I mumble as I feign exhaustion with a theatrical yawn.

"John's giving us a free copy of his book," Babe explains.

John?

"Great," I say, and take the CD from Babe. "Alarming images," I add.

"Funny you say *alarming*. The book's message is a real *wake-up call*," he jokes. At this point, Kevorkian is drooling slightly, adding an amusing level of absurdity to our conversation.

"Well, thanks. I'll give it a read some time," I say. I'm hoping, for the sake of our brief and involuntary time together, the insincerity of my remark won't be detected.

"John was a New York City cab driver," Babe says.

Well, that explains things.

"*Was* a cab driver," he adds loudly, "and now moving to China for a better life."

"Have you ever been to China?" I ask.

He shakes his head. "Never."

Oh good, the communist oppression should be just the tonic you're looking for.

"Well, good luck," I say and place the headphone of the Ipod over my ears. The first song I hear as I restart the Ipod is *I Can See Clearly Now.* Go figure.

I glance out the window at the puffy clouds below and try to divorce the image of drooling Kevorkian so I can once again focus my thoughts on Lila.

* * *

Seven hours into the flight, I feel I've been on the plane a month. My legs are cramped, I'm restless, and my eyes are burning. Babe has the Ipod again and she seems to be asleep. It's still light outside and has been the entire flight. It's as if our plane is chasing the sunrise around the world. I need some sleep so I lower the window cover and turn off the overhead light. I grab the Air China pillow—which is about the size of a paperback novel—and place it between my head and the window cover. Several restless and uncomfortable minutes later, assisted by a deep exhaustion, I doze off.

A short while later, Babe and I awake at about the same time. Kevorkian has vacated. In my groggy waking state, I instinctively imagine he changed seats or, better yet, jumped. My wishful thinking is upended seconds later when Kevorkian suddenly re-appears and bends toward me and Babe holding two Styrofoam cups and asks, "Would you like some tea?"

His bony face is illuminated only by the small overhead light above his seat. The only effects missing in this scene from a horror movie are multiple flashes of lightening on his face and the accompanying clasps of thunder—and possibly a few loud and incongruous notes from a pipe organ.

"No thanks," I manage as I slump back into my awkward sleeping position. Babe and I both fall in and out of restless sleep for the next several hours.

* * *

The much needed jolt of adrenaline arrives by way of the public address system in the fourteenth hour of our flight.

"Ladies and gentleman, we are beginning our descent into Beijing Airport," the pilot announces.

I grab Babe's hand tightly, turn, and smile at her. My happiness for her is stronger than any other emotion I feel. When the plane's wheels touch down in Beijing several minutes later, I videotape the landing.

We have arrived on the other side of the world.

I need to pee badly but decide to wait until we deboard. After we exit the plane, we catch up with the other members of the group. Tom holds an 8" x 11" placard from New Beginnings that reads: WELCOME FAMILIES.

"Before we do anything, I have to use the boy's room," I announce. Big Rob joins me.

The video camera is permanently attached to my hand and will be for the remainder of the visit. I can't be certain if the odd glances cast in my direction are a result of my size, my Caucasian appearance, or the fact I'm carrying a video camera into the bathroom. To be honest, I don't care. All I want to do is relieve myself.

When I'm done with my business, I walk to the trio of sinks located along one wall. Seconds later, big Rob arrives.

"You ought to videotape those things," he says and nudges his head in the direction of the stalls.

I glance over and notice there is no toilet bowl, just a hole in the floor.

"Where's the bowl?" I ask.

"*That's* a public toilet in China," Rob says.

"You're *kidding* me," I say.

Rob laughs. "Nope."

I look around nervously as though preparing to steal jewelry from a case and then turn my video camera on and videotape the hole in the floor. Mr. Obvious has arrived.

Rob and I rejoin the group and we proceed from the terminal to Customs. The walls are populated by advertisements for Nokia phones, Nike footwear, and Chinese beer. The products and logos are recognizable but most of the writing is in Chinese.

We arrive at Customs where a big sign is erected: FOREIGNERS. The blatant reminder is one of many that assault my senses in the first few minutes of my visit, as Chinese conversations filled the air like verbal confetti.

George and Shirley are Asian and suddenly I'm grateful for their presence. Not only are they a delightful and agreeable couple, but they both speak fluent Chinese. This will unquestionably come in handy on those occasions when I need to ask Chinese sales clerks important questions, like, "Do you carry this in a bigger size?"

I'm exhausted but the new sites stimulate my mind and invigorate me. Babe is all smiles; she's fresh. She's ready for this. I'm not quite sure if I am. In any event, I'm in full video production mode.

We get through Customs with no hassles, though the officials scrutinize the paperwork with resolute diligence as though examining a packaged bomb.

We take an escalator down to baggage claim where a sea of Chinese people occupy virtually every square inch of space. The only non-Chinese person I detect is Kevorkian, who appears panic stricken as if he has just lost sight of his three-year old child. I nudge Babe and point in his direction.

"I give him forty-eight hours," I say.

We're supposed to meet a Chinese woman who works for New Beginnings and will be our tour guide, interpreter, and coordinator, among other things. Shortly after arrival at baggage claim, Kitty and Rob recognize a short Chinese woman wearing glasses and broad grin on her face, her hair pulled back in a tight bun like a black tennis ball.

"Gui Lan!" Kitty says and hugs the Chinese woman.

"Hello Kitty, hello Rob," Gui Lan sings, "Welcome."

We take turns introducing ourselves and I am engaged. Gui Lan comes across as gregarious, sincere, and upbeat. After she greets all of us, she gathers the members of our group into a loose huddle for the first of many daily announcements.

"Our bus is arriving shortly. We'll take it to the hotel and later we'll go to dinner," she says and smiles broadly, glancing side to side to gauge everyone's reaction, "I am so happy to see all of you. Your flight was good?"

"Most memorable," I say with a dash of sarcasm.

Minutes later we pile onto our Partridge Family bus and take off for the hotel. Gui Lan issues curt instructions in Chinese to the bus driver who, in turn, frantically loads the ton of luggage into the storage compartment of the bus before we drive off.

* * *

As the bus exits the airport, Gui Lan stands adjacent to the driver and faces us. She continues her welcome speech and maintains her balance despite having both hands wrapped around the bus's microphone.

She repeats the itinerary then entertains us with a song. Her voice is melodious and soothing and she takes great care to sing with passion and grace, as if she's appearing on a Chinese version of *The Lawrence Welk Show*. I have no clue what song she is singing, as the lyrics are Chinese. I hastily grab my camera and videotape her performance. It's an amusing moment; totally unexpected. As I videotape Gui Lan I mentally insert subtitles:

The wheels on the bus go round and round, round and round, round and round, the wheels on the bus go round and round, all through the town.

As we drive, I videotape. Everything is unfamiliar therefore even the most common objects are fascinating. The commuter bus traveling next to us, for example, is jammed with passengers who witlessly stare out the window with faces devoid of emotion or smiles, like a room full of Chinese mannequins. As the bus zooms past us on the left side, I notice the rear of the bus is covered by a big advertisement for Kentucky Fried Chicken.

We arrive at the Jiangou Hotel, check in, and disperse to our rooms. The exhaustion has deepened. The excitement of the initial exposure to China has worn off quickly. As Babe showers, I turn on the television and surf the channels in search of anything American—to no avail. The limited choices—music videos, news, soap operas—are all in Chinese with no sub-titles. I leave the TV on for background chatter as I unpack.

Later, our group meets in the lobby of the hotel and we walk three blocks to a local restaurant. During our short walk, I notice a MacDonald's restaurant and a Starbucks Coffee shop within a block of our hotel. The familiar corporate logos are as comforting as they are out of place.

"The restaurant is on the opposite side of the street," Gui Lan says, "We'll take the tunnel."

So here I am in a country of a billion or so Chinese people. To this point in my life, my daily interaction with people of Chinese descent is limited to nine people (not counting employees of Chinese restaurants, dry cleaning establishments, or really stoned people). Of the nine, seven of them—the Nusenbaum family—live in the house next door to ours in Bellport. They are wonderful and respectful neighbors and I've enjoyed their homemade spring rolls every Christmas for the past five years. Then there's Helen Moy, my 8th grade science teacher; a brilliant, graceful, and even-tempered woman and a better than average teacher. King Wong was a student-athlete who played basketball for Flagler College during my freshman and sophomore years at Flager in the late 1970's. I can't say a bad thing about any of these wonderful Chinese people—though King could have used a little work on his jump shot.

Despite my favorable experience with the nine Chinese people in my life to date, my overall feeling toward the Chinese is one of intimidation. The xenophobia I've developed over the years is owed to TV shows like *Kung Fu* and any of the various martial arts movies that became popular in the 1960's and 1970's. The only non-threatening Chinese character I can recall from movies and TV is the soft spoken Mrs. Livingston from *The Courtship of Eddie's Father*. Now that I'm in China, those stereotypical fears are unfortunately dominating my thoughts. I'm not exactly expecting some barefoot guy to challenge me to snatch the pebble from his hand, but I'm vaguely suspicious that most Chinese could cripple me with one well executed karate chop.

Gui Lan leads us through a pedestrian tunnel which passes under the highway. The New Yorker in me is wary of this option. My fears are quickly alleviated. Beijing is a bustling and fairly westernized city filled with average men and women who are essentially the same as me—only smaller and slightly different in appearance (and not a blonde in sight). They walk, bike, or drive motorcycles and cars, doing their daily business. None of their citizens wear black belts, walk barefoot, carry boiling cauldrons between their forearms, or wield numbchucks. China has oxygen, blue skies, apartment buildings, sidewalks, and pigeons, just like New York.

We arrive at the restaurant and Gui Lan takes control. She waves her arms and rattles off some instructions with the animated urgency of an auctioneer. Her short speech triggers a scattering of restaurant employees in every direction.

I turn to Babe and say, "Is it my imagination, or does she speak a lot faster when she's speaking Chinese?"

"Whatever she said, it worked," Babe says, as a friendly hostess leads us past the main dining room to an adjoining private dining room.

The room contains one round table with twelve chairs spread around the perimeter.

The round table is common in China restaurants. The center core of the table rotates right or left, allowing diners to access food from the far reaches of the opposite side of the table. This movable inner circle portion of the table is commonly known as the "lazy susan."

Tom is a late arrival at the seat next to mine. As he arrives, Gui Lan orders the food, once again in animated Chinese with hands flailing. Tom sits and gently nudges me with his elbow.

"Don't go in the bathroom; the stench is brutal." He glances cautiously side to side and continues in the hushed tone of a secret agent. "One of the waiters came out of a stall and never washed his hands before leaving the bathroom."

"Are there any toilets?" I ask hopefully.

He shakes his head, frowns, and says, "Holes in the ground."

The food arrives several minutes later, a dozen or so large dishes of various Chinese foods: chicken, duck, rice, beef, noodles, and fish. The food smells delicious and the scent of garlic is strong and easily detected. Tom turns to me and places a cupped hand over the side of his mouth. I lean an ear toward him and he says in a dire tone, "Don't eat the duck."

He then nods his head in the direction of the waiter who carried the duck dish to our table and says, as though fingering a suspect from a police line-up, "That's him."

I lean to Babe and calmly alert her which prompts her to warn the next person, and so on until the morsel of unsavory news has quietly traveled around the table. Throughout the meal, the duck dish remains staggeringly untouched.

The other food is delicious and plentiful—and unusually heavy with garlic. My delight with the food is partly attributable to the fact I haven't eaten a real meal in twenty-four hours. Our inaugural feast together has a celebratory feel to it, as we indulge in the variety of dishes and enjoy cold beer. Near the end of the meal, I detect a significant drop in my energy level. By the time we leave the restaurant, the air is cool and the sun has set. We casually stroll back to the hotel room, glancing about again at the fresh sights of Beijing, and I have just enough energy to brush my teeth and kiss Babe goodnight. I'm asleep before my head hits the pillow.

* * *

It's May 6 in China when I awake from deep slumber. I'm groggy, confused, and bloated. I slept soundly but now I'm disoriented. What time is it? What *day* is it? What am I doing here? As I make my way to the bathroom I feel as though I'm walking up a down escalator. My feet weigh a hundred pounds apiece.

After a shower, we proceed to the lobby to gather for breakfast with the others. The lobby serves multiple functions, including cocktail lounge and restaurant. Babe and I join Tom and Colleen at one of the small round tables and order coffee. Minutes later, a Chinese gentleman in a blue, pin-striped business suit sits at the table next to us and casually lights a cigarette.

"They allow smoking in restaurants?" Colleen asks incredulously in a low voice.

"It wasn't so long ago smoking was allowed in restaurants back home," I say. I look around the restaurant. Every table is equipped with an ash tray.

After breakfast, we load onto our bus for the first round of sightseeing. The seats on the bus were made to accommodate the average Chinese person. Loosely translated, that means I am likely to be in a perpetual state of modest discomfort for the next two weeks. Nevertheless, I'm eager to explore China and relax for a few days.

"Today, we are traveling to Forbidden City. Later, maybe we go to Tiananmen Square or Ming's Tombs," Gui Lan says. As usual, she's all smiles and full of pep.

The bus pulls away from our hotel and we travel through the crowded streets of Beijing, teaming with bikes and mopeds whose drivers wear helmets and tote supplies or carry backpacks; a much different rush hour than I'm accustomed to. There's a sense of urgency in every face; not a single smile. The bus driver beeps his horn continuously at the bikes and mopeds in his path. The riders casually part to the side of the road without a hint of anger or resentment; no middle fingers, no cursing. There's nothing personal about the driver's incessant horn; just another routine commute for the citizens of Beijing.

After a short drive, we arrive at the parking lot for Forbidden City and exit the bus. Lines of tourists await entry near the formal gates and many mingle about the entrance courtyard taking photos.

We enter through turnstiles as if entering Yankee Stadium. But the familiarity of the entrance is quickly displaced with a flood of foreign wonder. I'm awed at the size of the place and the array of bright colors: red, gold, yellow, and green. The extensive grounds of Forbidden City cover 720,000 square meters and contain 800 buildings—including seventeen palaces—formally occupied by royalty during the mid-Ming and the Qing Dynasties. At the time of their occupancy dating back to the 1400's, commoners were not allowed; hence the name "forbidden."

The sun shines brightly as we stroll through the vast courtyards with Gui Lan providing an ongoing verbal history lesson. Along the way, we pause to admire the palaces and bronze statues of lions and dragons (and bears, oh my).

I wield the video camera randomly, capturing footage while I remind myself I'm not here to make a documentary about Beijing. I'm here to adopt a baby and videotape the process. The quick reminder plucks me from a casual moment of nostalgic sight-seeing and replaces it with a blossoming anxiety about the upcoming meeting with Lila.

It's a hot, humid day and the sun bakes the brick floors of the various courtyards, generating enough heat to produce a feeling we're walking across a sea of hot coals. I'm physically unfit for this type of sight-seeing and I become restless with all the walking. To temper my restlessness, I play games with the video camera.

I point the camera at Kitty and say, "And there, ladies and gentleman, is the famous Forbidden Kitty."

We leave Forbidden City—to be accurate, anything but forbidden—and drive to a restaurant that features the familiar round tables, lazy susans, and assortment of Chinese food.

After lunch, we visit Ming's Tombs, which demands more walking on my sore feet and swollen ankles. The Ming's Tombs are situated on a fifteen-square mile property, replete with a ceremonial three-arched entrance gateway, courtyards, and numerous buildings and statues dated to the 15th century. As the name implies, the site contains the tombs of the thirteen Emperors of the Ming Dynasty (not to be confused with the Boston Celtics dynasty of the 1960's).

We walk along the red brick walkways past the ever-familiar scowling lion statues, all of which share a pained grimace on their faces, as though they had just swallowed the world's largest hair ball. We stroll past beautiful formal gardens and follow Gui Lan as she strides purposefully along in her flat shoes and knee-length dress. After a forty-five minute walk, we climb a steeply inclined, stone stairway to arrive at one of the mausoleums.

As we enter the mausoleum, a gush of cool air envelopes our group, bringing relief from the hot temperature outside. The concrete floor of the mausoleum is damp and the lights are turned low. Gui Lan speaks in a respectful hushed tone.

"This building contains the tomb of Emperor Zhu Di and his empresses," she explains in a half-whisper.

I'm ashamed to admit I haven't a clue who Zhu Di is. So naturally, I camouflage my ignorance with an attempt at humor.

"Any relation to Zhu Keeper?" I ask.

There's not much to look at in the mausoleum which, quite frankly, brings me as much comfort as the cool air. I have no interest in seeing a dead emperor from the 1400's and the thought of viewing dead empresses carries only a modest degree of added intrigue. We exit the mausoleum after a brief five-minute visit.

Once outside, we ascend the steep stairway and I mumble to Babe, "Do you think there's a rickshaw rental office nearby?"

"You're tired?"

"I haven't walked this much since I climbed Mount Washington twenty years ago."

As we retrace our long walk back to the bus, I decide to write a fitness book. It will be titled *How to Get In Shape and Stay That Way*. The book will contain one page of text, which will look like this:

Chapter One- How to Get in Shape and Stay That Way

Move to Beijing and become a full-time tourist.

The End

On our drive back to the hotel, we travel past Tiananmen Square but don't stop or walk around. Our visit, therefore, produces the same level of fleeting nostalgia as, let's say, a drive past the Kent State University campus.

* * *

The following day is more of the same. We eat breakfast and then climb aboard the bus to drive to the Great Wall; a twenty-minute ride from our hotel. We enter a large parking lot and once outside the bus we are able to view portions of the Great Wall on both sides of the street. Two days ago, aboard a plane flying out of New York City, I had a view of the Empire State Building. Today, I stand in full view of the Great Wall of China. In less than a week, I have witnessed in person two of the Seven Wonders of the World; pretty cool.

Some parts of the Great Wall are closed to the public. In fact, most of The Wall is in a state of total disrepair. I was surprised to hear that bit of news as heretofore I had always thought of The Wall as one of the enduring symbols of architectural superiority. The section we visit is the most popular for tourism and the most pristine and well preserved of those sections of The Wall still standing. Like many other famous sites in China, it is populated with souvenir stands.

After we exit the bus, Gui Lan organizes us and then strides toward the entrance gate as we fall in line behind her like the Von Trapp family.

Beyond the entrance gates are the souvenir and refreshment stands. Unfortunately for me, no elevator. So, like everyone else, I set out on foot to ascend The Great Wall.

Prior to my visit to China, the only "great wall" I ever visited was in left field at Fenway Park in Boston and went by the alternative name The Green Monster. The Great Wall of China is far more impressive—even if doesn't list the out-of-town scores.

Within ten minutes of our climb I start to huff and puff.

"They should rename this thing the Great Staircase of China," I say to no one in particular. I think it's a good line but no one laughs because, to be truthful, every other climber is as breathless as I am.

The steps ascend sharply from the ground level into the rolling green hills and snake upward for miles. Each step is about twelve feet wide, and the surrounding wall—or baluster—is a mix of limestone and brick. The steps are made of a hard stone, akin to slate, which appears worn from 2,000 years of passage by tourists. As a result of the wear and tear, the stones' surface is uneven and undulating, which causes some difficulty in the climb. The distance up from one step to the next is inconsistent, ranging from six inches to twelve inches or more. For some steps, therefore, I need to hoist myself rather than climb. Sightseeing has become a challenging aerobic test. The mix of physical pain and historic wonder is a common by-product of the visit to the Great Wall.

As I continue my ascent, I come across the strewn bodies of tired tourist who sit or lean helplessly against the stone railing to catch their breath. Visitors of all ages pant heavily, gasping for air. Tom stops with me at one of the intermittent landings and casually observes, "I can't believe I'm at the Great Wall of China."

His statement is so simple yet it captures my feelings so perfectly.

"This whole trip is surreal. Yesterday I'm in my cozy home in Bellport and a day later I'm halfway around the world standing on the Great Wall."

I ascend much higher than Babe, who hangs out at one of the lower landings with Karen and her daughter Emily. George and Shirley join me and Tom for our ascent and I pause occasionally to snap photos or videotape some footage for the documentary. This place that I had seen in textbooks, movies, and documentaries is now in full view of my own eyes. My unremarkable climb is now part of The Wall's extensive history. I'm overcome by a jolting dose of insignificance.

After a brief rest at yet another landing, Tom and I decide to return to earth. I walk down a few steps and my legs are rubbery and achy. The ascent requires the same muscles I've exhausted during the uphill climb; only now they have to work harder to combat gravity and fatigue, thereby preventing me from taking a full frontal summersault down the entire flight of stairs. My muscles contract and grab and I'm forced to stop with greater frequency. It reminds me of the final run of a long day on the ski slopes.

We eventually make it down and soon thereafter we're back on the bus and on to our next destination.

* * *

After lunch, we visit a genuine Jade Factory. It has become a tradition for adoptive parents to purchase a piece of jade jewelry for their baby daughters.

From the outside, the Jade Factory resembles a typical industrial building: about thirty feet tall, simple façade with big Chinese letters, and not much ornamentation. The entrance is flanked by two of the ubiquitous scowling lion statues.

Once inside, our group is hastily whisked from the entrance to a production area. A Plexiglas partition wall separates workers from tourists, not unlike the snake or monkey cage at your local zoo. The workers wear white masks over their mouth and noses as they labor diligently to create a variety of jade products.

The tour guide, a young and attractive Chinese woman, then leads our group into a small, handsome room with several display shelves containing jade items. She explains the history and various colors of jade and comments that many adoptive parents purchase jade bracelets or necklaces for their babies.

"It is also a tradition in China to rub the belly of smiling jade Buddha statue for good luck," she says. Then she points to me—the group's poster child for Buddha bellies—and coaxes me forward for a demonstration.

She continues to rattle off jade trivia as she rubs my belly, producing in me an odd level of embarrassment and childhood memories of playing Simon Says. I imagine from that point on, despite my lack of deity, the tour guide was blessed with good fortune.

After our brief tour of the assembly area and the display room, the guide ushers our group into the main attraction of the factory: a huge showroom with high ceilings and dozens of bright lights. The room is about the size of a football field. I'm awestruck. The showroom contains rows of shelves along the wall's perimeters, with each shelf populated by jade products;

rows and rows of display shelves in the middle; and numerous sales counters and jewelry display cases interspersed throughout. It is wall to wall jade products: giant ships, multi-colored globes of various size, smiling Buddha statues, jewelry, statues of animals, planes, birds; it's an assault on the eyes.

"I'm going with Colleen to look at the jewelry," Babe says. "Are you going to buy anything?"

"Do you think they sell jade beer?"

She leaves and I assume my just-looking pose as I casually peruse jade products. My hands are clasped behind my back as though strolling through a museum. I quickly discover body language doesn't translate well with Chinese salespeople; if you're breathing, you're a customer.

One after another, salespeople approach me and extend their hands in the direction of any of the various jade products, as though showcasing an item on *The Price is Right.* One guy shadows me like a police tail, ready to pounce if I stop for more than a second to look.

I shake my head continuously and avoid eye contact as I'm asked over and over if I'd like to buy something. After a while, I force a resolute glare onto my face in hopes I will be mistaken for a gangster. Nothing doing; they are relentless and suddenly I have the urge to laugh. My tour of the jade factory has turned into a comedy.

I bump into Tom, who just purchased a jade ship to display above the mantel of his fireplace at home. I decide to seek some counsel from my new friend.

"Do you know the Chinese term for 'leave me the fuck alone'?"

He laughs. "Colleen is about to buy the entire jewelry section," he says as he points in the direction of the jewelry counter where Babe and Colleen are huddled with salespeople.

I decide to pay a visit. The wry smile on my face has advanced into a quiet chuckle. Some of the salespeople add to the absurdity by tugging gently on my arm or stepping in my path. I feel as though I'm starring in a Chinese parody of *Night of the Living Dead.*

Babe notices me as I approach and makes a face intended to solicit my help; with her eyes bulged wide, her mouth upturned in a shocked semi-smile. Colleen has her outstretched hand being worked on by two young Chinese girls who attempt to force a jade bracelet onto her wrist. They labor with the serious determination and precision of brain surgeons. With the assistance of five attendants, some lubricant, and a smooth latex glove, the bracelet slips past her hand and finds a permanent, inescapable home around her wrist.

"You're going to need a stick of dynamite to get that off," I joke.

Colleen laughs and hands her credit card to the salesperson.

Babe purchases a few items, including a bracelet for her sister-in-law Nikki and a necklace for Lila. I think we're done, but the sale pitches have just begun. The salespeople grab Babe lightly by the elbow and force her from display case to display case as Babe politely says, "No thank you" over and over.

"How much for every item in the store?" I ask in jest.

Five salespeople freeze in their tracks. One actually whips out a calculator. Like everything else I've said today, my comment sailed right over their heads.

"Let's get outta here," I say to Babe through a fractured grin.

We leave the Jade Factory impressed and shell-shocked, not to mention lighter in the wallet. We now own the essential and traditional piece of jewelry for Lila—and plenty of footage and stories for the documentary.

* * *

After our visit to the jade factory, we visit one of the many state-operated department stores in this area of China. The stores are essentially Chinese Wal-Marts, carrying a variety of items. Unlike Wal-Mart, there is no tidy scheme for product displays; no "home furnishing" sections; merely an aggregation of every product imaginable, thrown together in haphazard fashion as if to disorient shoppers or inspire sudden urges to purchase both laundry detergent and snow globes. The aisles are narrow, barely wide enough for passage of two average sized Chinese people. This marketing strategy results in a layer of claustrophobia on top of the disorientation—not to mention some intimate, albeit unintended, encounters with fellow shoppers.

"We meet back at the bus in one hour," Gui Lan announces as we step off the bus.

I have no intention to purchase anything so I merely trail Babe and attempt to amuse her with my ongoing commentary, all the while hoping the Chinese salespeople somehow won't notice me. For someone my size, that is more than wishful thinking. I am having no luck being invisible. On the contrary, I stick out like a jelly doughnut in a martini.

Like the jade factory, the store is swarming with persistent salespeople. As they approach me and Babe, I decide to take a different tact. For my own personal amusement, I play the role of the serious shopper, my hands clasped behind my back like a fifth grader who has just been asked to read aloud his poem in front of the class. A salesperson approaches me as I browse a rack of kimonos and I ask sarcastically, "Do you carry this kimono in beige?"

She has no clue what I said but comprehends the word kimono so now she wants to show me every one in the store. Before long, she is tailed by three young females and the entire harem begins to follow me around, each one of them smiling and nodding, with an occasional giggle tossed in. I have become equal parts customer and side-show. Never one to back down from attention, I dance through the aisles like Ralph Kramden. The lead salesperson seems particularly amused so I grab her and whirl her around as though we're on a dance floor. I quietly hope I'm not giving America a bad name.

Eventually, I succumb to the sale pitches. A woman holds up a big yellow kimono—about the size and color of the flag of South Vietnam—and says, "Try on?"

I'm up for some good theater. "Why not," I say.

Babe positions herself to videotape the predictably sorry result as I disappear behind the beaded curtain of the dressing room. Once inside, I remove my jacket and squeeze into the kimono, its bulging seams stretched to their limit. Meanwhile, a gaggle of ten salespeople has joined my wife on the other side of the curtain, breathlessly awaiting my re-emergence.

"You ready?" I call out to Babe from behind the curtain.

"Ready," she calls back.

I swat the curtain open and step from the dressing room. The kimono is wrapped around my body like a hot dog bun around a roast beef. The unseemly fashion statement triggers a dozen amused grins and some repressed chuckles.

Embracing the spotlight, I raise both hands to my sides and twist left and right as I impersonate Chris Farley in *Tommy Boy*, singing, "Fat guy in a little coat, fat guy in a little coat."

Once Babe has the requisite footage, I remove the kimono and hand it back to the salesperson. "Too small," I say embarrassingly. She smiles back at me warmly, unable to comprehend the meaning of my objection then continues to follow me through the store for the next ten minutes in hopes to persuade me into an alternative purchase.

"Superstar," one of the salespeople says and points at me.

My impromptu performance has earned me the status of a rock star. Just call me Pot Roast.

* * *

We return to the hotel room and my clothes are soaked with sweat. I feel drained from all the walking and the jet lag isn't helping any. I turn the TV on and find a Chinese version of ESPN. It's May and I've spent three days deprived of baseball highlights and box scores. I can't recall a three-day period in my life when I endured the same combination of missing ingredients. So I settle in for Chinese Sports Center and watch a half-hour of highlights of gymnastics meets, volleyball matches, swimming races, badminton, soccer, and ping pong tournaments. The announcer signs off (at least I assume he did) and baseball is never mentioned. In my narrow view of the baseball-hot dog-apple pie-and-Chevrolet world, I find it impossible to grasp how a ping-pong match could take precedent over a baseball game between the Red Sox and the Yankees.

"I can't believe this," I protest, "a half hour of sports highlights and no baseball scores."

Babe responds with the compassion my gripe warrants: "I'm going to take a shower."

As Babe showers, I sit on the bed and my mind casually drifts from baseball to Lila. I'm excited about the adoption and I'm enjoying the sightseeing in Beijing. But beneath the surface of the enjoyment lurks fear and anxiety. It's the same blend of feelings I used to get during the last few days of summer vacation in my school years. Every activity that last week is accompanied by a blossoming dread of the loss of freedom and the rapid approach of pending obligations. To make matters worse in my current situation, I'm suddenly unsure if adoption was the right decision for me.

We meet the others in the lobby and Gui Lan excitedly announces a slight change in plans for dinner.

"Tonight, we are going to a restaurant a bit farther away to have Peking duck," she says and raises an eyebrow.

The Peking duck dinner is succulent and tasty, the most incredibly pleasing duck I've ever enjoyed, though to be honest duck is not exactly a staple of my diet. The restaurant is larger than the other one we had previously dined at, and is a much more festive place, with most tables jammed with patrons who are singing and laughing boisterously. Amidst the clamor, we laugh and gawk and enjoy some of the best Chinese food I've ever eaten.

As we walk back to the hotel, our group is approached by a young Chinese boy, about three years old. His clothes are dirty and tattered, his face sad and filthy with dirt, as he begs us for money. Being from New York, I've been exposed regularly to panhandling. But not when children are involved. I'm consumed by compassionate sadness.

George dips into his pocket and pulls out a roll of bills and is about to hand over his donation when Gui Lan frantically intercedes.

"No no no!" Gui Lan shouts as she steps between George and the children and hastily ushers George in the opposite direction.

The entire incident lasts only seconds but produces a flood of conflicting emotions, from pity to anger to confusion.

When we safely reach the hotel lobby, Gui Lan explains her actions.

"I am so sorry I forgot to tell you about this. Many people use these little children as pawns to make money. They send busses into the poorer sections of China and pick up small children to beg for money. The best to do is ignore them. Don't give them money." She is emphatic. Her announcement barely inspires a grunt from the rest of us.

When we get to the room, Babe and I revisit the incident.

"That was strange," I say.

"I can't help but think one of the children could have been Lila," Babe says sadly.

* * *

On our final full night in Beijing, Gui Lan leads us back to the restaurant closest to our hotel, the same one we had eaten at several times already. On this occasion, we are escorted to one of the small private dining rooms. After all members of our group are seated, Gui Lan rattles off some instructions in Chinese to one of the wait staff. It's time for karaoke.

Karaoke, as many of you know, is a Hawaiian word that means "Please limit your singing to the shower." It is quite popular in China and serious business, with most restaurants equipped with karaoke machines and accompanying monitors. The karaoke song book is passed around and it is thick as a Bible and contains thousands of songs.

Gui Lan opens the festivities with another of her beautiful Chinese ballads. She pours out the sweet melody in her nightingale voice, swaying gracefully with the music and leaving us all to wonder what the hell she's singing about. Not to be outdone, I volunteer to sing next, opting for *Honky Tonk Woman*. The instrumental music accompaniment starts and the tempo is much slower than the Rolling Stones version. I do my best to render a bearable version but detect some odd laughter and smiles from the wait staff. I suppose they never saw a 285 pound Mick Jagger/Fred Flintstone character sing Rolling Stones' songs before.

Later, Gui Lan grabs my wrist and pulls me up to the microphone stand for a duet.

"We will sing Edelweiss," she proclaims.

Edelweiss?! My first reaction is, "I could go for an Edel-*Bud*weiss."

Babe operates the video camera to capture the momentous performance on tape. We start the song and it instantly digresses. Gui Lan and I both wear big, fake sunflowers in our hair as we sing completely out of rhythm.

The TV monitor in the corner of the room displays the words to the song along with stock video footage of Chinese landscapes. Gui Lan stands closest to the monitor and I stand a few steps behind her, thus her back is turned to me as we sing. The first crack in our performance occurs when I bend over toward Gui Lan and lower my head to the same level as hers as I sing the line, "you look happy to see me." Gui Lan turns from the television to face me at the same moment I deliver the line and she bursts into laughter. The laughter digresses into a cough and then a mixture of laughter and coughing. She can't continue; by default, the duet becomes a solo act.

During the second verse, she leaves her microphone, shuffles over to the table, and attempts to pry George from his seat for a dance. George wants none of it so Gui Lan turns to Danny as her dance partner. As they dance, I decide to make up my own words to the song. I squat low in a sumo-wrestler stance and substitute for the words "blossom of snow may you bloom and grow, bloom and grow forever" with my own "if you rub belly you'll have good luck, have good luck forever." Meanwhile, Danny and Gui Lan waltz back and forth, cheek-to-cheek with fingers interlaced like Fred and Ginger.

The karaoke fiasco is the last light-hearted moment we'll see for quite some time. Because the following night, several hundred miles and one day closer to our daughters, we will find ourselves in southern China in a place called Nanning, about 125 miles northeast of Vietnam.

The entire tone of our visit to China is about to change in a big way.

Chapter 7
A NEW BEGINNING IN THE GREEN CITY

"My prayer was finally answered, though delayed, 'twas not denied-
The pain of love unanswered, in a moment's time subsides."
—from Alice Moore's poem *My Miracle*

"Toto, I've got the feeling we're not in Kansas any more," I say as I step off the plane in Nanning.

For the first time in our visit, I get the feeling I'm halfway around the world.

The flight time and distance from Beijing to Nanning are approximately equal to that of New York and Florida. The climate change is similar as well, as Nanning is located in the tropical climate of southern China. The air in Nanning is murky and oppressive; the humidity clings to me the second I step from the plane.

Aside from climate and geographical changes, the differences between Beijing and Nanning are stark. The airport is smaller and more antiquated, with fewer advertisements. In fact, the first recognizable sign I detect is a small one with an arrow directing the reader to the "Weak, Ill, Pregnant, and Disability Lounge."

As we approach the baggage claim, I detect a Chinese toddler as he plays near an escalator. The child giggles and screams as though the escalator is the greatest toy he's ever seen. He's wearing pants with the rear flap for easy elimination—the same one we were warned not to videotape during one of the New Beginnings workshops. Despite the previous warnings, I videotape a few seconds of the toddler.

As we walk from the terminal to the baggage claim, I have a full view of the countryside through the large wall-sized windows that line one side of the access walkway. The countryside is deep green, hilly, and vast—hazy through the veil of humid air. Literally translated, Nanning means "green city." This part of China bears no resemblance to Beijing.

We transition easily from baggage claim to our new tour bus, this one a bit more worn than the one we rode through the streets of Beijing. We load onto the bus and Gui Lan assumes her familiar position next to the driver, with the ever present microphone in her hand. A young, pretty Chinese woman stands awkwardly to Gui Lan's left.

"Everybody, this is Joy." Gui Lan says and smiles. "She will be joining us for our stay here in Nanning."

She hands the microphone to Joy.

Joy begins her speech as the bus takes off. Unfortunately, the public address system pre-dates the Ming Dynasty, thus her chipper and lengthy instructions are lost in garbled amplification. Although her English is generally well enunciated, she pronounces the word B-A-B-I-E-S as: "bye-bees." Joy mentions bye-bees often.

The bus chugs loudly along the desolate four-lane highway that leads to and from the airport. The seats are hard and uncomfortable and the shock absorbers are seemingly non-existent. Unfortunately, I am unable to steady my hand long enough to capture any video; thus I'm denied some great footage of the green hills to the right side of the road. In the distant reaches of the hills I notice some primitive tents erected: four small poles impaled into the ground with cloth stretched between the tops of each pole for rain cover. Laundry is hung on small strands of rope on either side of the tent. Families huddle together in the shade of some of the tents.

Tom, seated in front of us, turns and points toward the tent. "See that?" he says.

I nod. "Home sweet home," I say.

Tom shakes his head.

We travel past rice fields being plowed by oxen steered by workers who wear straw hats (commonly referred to as "peasant hats"). The workers are draped in light-colored, threadbare clothing. I could have traveled this road three hundred years ago and would have seen the same thing. It's surreal.

As we approach the built-up area of Nanning, I notice a lot of residents traveling on bicycles or mopeds. One of the bicycles tows a rickety two-wheeled cart that holds building supplies.

"Look hon, Fed-Ex," I say as I point to the cart.

Unknown to me at the time, many of the delivery services for this area use bicycles or mopeds to transport goods.

The closer we get to civilization the more bicycles and mopeds we see. Eventually, the streets are swarming with pedestrians, bicycles, and mopeds, on the sidewalks and streets, many within a few feet of our bus. The bus driver has little regard for the bicyclists and pedestrians. He beeps his horn and barrels brazenly ahead. I feel like our group is riding in the belly of a whale as the smaller fish scurry out of our path.

Our route to the hotel takes us through the business district of Nanning: rows of storefronts on both sides of the busy street. The storefronts measure roughly ten feet across by twenty feet deep, essentially the size of a single stall garage. The stores offer food, clothing, cell phones, and household items. The streets are overloaded with people who ride, drive, or walk; some seem to be haggling over the price of goods. The way of life seems simpler and less inviting to tourism than Beijing.

Minutes later, we arrive in the heart of the city at our destination: the Xin Du Hotel. We had been told it was the nicest place in town. Based on what I've seen during our bus ride, the label of nicest place in Nanning carries the same prestige as being voted the most handsome face in a Don Rickles look-alike contest—not exactly something to brag about. We gather our belongings from the bus and enter the air-conditioned hotel lobby, which contains a marble floor and a handsome check-in counter on the right side. Opposite the check-in counter, on the left side of the lobby, is a winding marble staircase that leads up to a mezzanine level lounge. The staircase has brass handrails decorated with blue and white balloons, with a decorative white and blue arch erected about midway up the staircase.

"What's with the balloons?" asks Tom.

"Smurf convention," I say.

Adjacent to the staircase is a handsome fountain with a small wishing well.

After check-in, we disperse to our rooms on the fifth floor. We arrive at the room and I drop the luggage then unlock the door. I take only a few steps into the room when I detect something that causes momentary paralysis. In the corner of the room sits a rickety crib with a mattress as thick as a ham sandwich.

It's time to be a parent.

Babe and I exchange glances like two paramedics who've just arrived at the scene of a fatal car accident. I plop onto one of the two beds, my eyes glued to the crib, as panic spreads through my veins. In less than twenty-four hours, a human being will occupy that lonely crib. The question I've asked myself dozens of times reappears: what have I gotten myself into?

After a brief respite, I retrieve the luggage from the hallway and inspect the rest of the room. I find the usual stuff: television, dresser, small closet, bathroom with tub and vanity, nothing out of the norm. There is, however, one notable oddity. On top of the small refrigerator rests a twenty-gallon container of bottled water and its housing unit. Wrapped around the neck of the bottle is a manufacturer's label: Pabst Blue Ribbon!

"Do you see this?" I say to Babe.

She glances up briefly, distracted, then continues to dress up the crib and fluff pillows.

Our window on the fifth floor faces the surrounding areas of Nanning: dilapidated housing projects, mid-rise hotels and office buildings, and restaurants. Beyond the built-up section, more green hills; hazy, green, and motionless as if brushed onto the landscape by Bob Ross.

After we unpack, shower, and enjoy a few glasses of Pabst, Babe and I return to the lobby to meet the others for dinner. We arrive early at the designated waiting spot near the lobby's fountain and I notice a bride and groom at the foot of the stairway. This explains the festive balloons and arch that decorate the staircase. The receiving line of wedding guests stretches from the staircase to the double doors at the lobby entrance. The air is filled with a hearty volume of laughter and the singsong voices of Chinese conversation. As each wedding guest arrives, they are handed a cigarette. As they walk past the bride, she lights the cigarette.

Gui Lan arrives shortly after we do.

"What's the deal with the cigarettes?" I ask.

"For weddings, the guests receive a cigarette and the bride lights it. This is a custom designed to wish the wedding guests, eh, good health."

Cigarettes for good health! What's the matter, they ran out of heroine?

Minutes later our group sits down for the last supper. The meal tastes wonderful but the mood is heavy; nothing like the night before when Gui Lan and I butchered *Edelweiss*.

"How bout that crib," Tom says through a mischievous grin.

"Zapped me right between the eyes," I admit somberly.

The wait—and the party—are over. Somewhere in the vicinity of our Nanning hotel room lives a little baby who will soon be known as Lila Rose Ford, the answer to many years of prayerful yearning. The following day, we will come face to face with her for the first time.

I am scared shitless.

* * *

It's Adoption Day, May 10, 2004. It is also Mother's Day. Anyone who knows Babe—especially me—views this fortuitous timing as poetic justice.

We awake after seven hours of restless tossing and turning. I don't remember sleeping for more than ten minutes.

"I can't believe this is actually happening," Babe says, as she busies herself with preparation.

The day crackles with nervous energy and I take deep breaths regularly, as if a final exam is upon me. With Babe in the shower, I videotape the room's contents, including the boxes of Godiva chocolates we brought as tips to notaries and others.

After a few minutes of filming, I stop to gather my thoughts. I don't know how to prepare for this; it is one of the many things that has to be experienced to be learned. Adoption agency workshops can't prepare you what your heart is going to feel like on Adoption Day. Nothing can.

As I wait for Babe to get ready, I gaze out the window with no particular focus, then suddenly take notice of the impoverished housing projects in the distance. When I return my gaze to the room, the first thing I see is the empty crib. I'm struck by the juxtaposition of the poor coutryside and the crib. Inspired, I turn the video camera on and zoom the lens through the window, videotape the housing projects, then slowly pull back, and eventually focus the lens on the crib. This shot will definitely make the final edit.

Babe comes out of the bathroom dressed in the clothes and shoes she had picked out months ago for the occasion: a long, camel-colored linen skirt; a pink, short-sleeved, silky top; Steve Madden alligator pumps with four-inch silver heels. Her long brown hair appears woven from silk and her beautiful face is beaming with joy.

"You're the most beautiful mom I've ever seen."

She blushes and walks over to me for a warm hug.

I shower and dress quickly then load up the cameras. Babe and I quietly busy ourselves with chores, both of us distracted with anticipation and a flood of conflicting thoughts and emotions. If our minds could speak aloud, the silence in the room would suddenly be filled with a hundred voices.

Shortly before we exit the room, I instruct Babe, "Sit on the bed. I want to videotape your final thoughts before we leave."

Babe looks into the camera. She holds back tears as she says, "We are…minutes away from getting Lila and we could not be happier. All the years of waiting patiently…it's all worth it."

She struggles to find the right words and she's overwhelmed with emotions. She ends her testimonial by saying, "I just want Lila to know how much she is *wanted*."

When it's my turn to talk, I say, "The phrase 'the honeymoon is over' typically carries a negative connotation. But that's precisely what it feels like today. The first eleven years of our marriage were the best years of my life, totally fulfilling in ways I couldn't have expected when we got married; an eleven-year honeymoon. But today, I feel the honeymoon is officially ending. And I mean that in a good way."

I keep my emotions in check but nearly lose it as I finish the speech. "Throughout our ordeal, I repeatedly assured Babe: in God's time we'll have our child. Well, I had a talk with God the other day, and He said…," I pause to compose myself then speak in a half-whisper choked with tears, "…He said it's time."

Deep in our hearts and souls we know this was our destiny: God's will for our lives. I take a deep breath, gather my cameras, clear my voice, and proclaim, "Let's do it."

When we arrive at the fountain, I turn the video camera on and walk from couple to couple, point the camera at them and say, "In one word, describe your emotions."

117

"Apprehensive," says George.

"Excited," says Kitty.

"Happy," says little Rob.

"Scared," says Big Rob.

"Finally," says Danny.

Before we depart, we get together for a group photo in front of the fountain. The bus driver snaps photos with each of our cameras and we leave for our short drive to the Civil Affairs building.

We exit the air-conditioned lobby through double doors and I'm assaulted by an oven's breath. The temperature has to be near ninety, sticky and uncomfortable. The air conditioning in the bus cools us off, though truthfully no one pays much attention.

As we travel, Tom calls out, "Hey Fred, how are those Godivas doing?"

Leave it to him to bust my balls at a time like this. In fact, the chocolates are probably as liquid as the beads of sweat that have formed on my forehead.

We arrive at the building and the bus pulls to the curb. I take several deep breaths, grab my camera bag and baby carriage, and exit. Babe is ready; beaming. I follow her inside and then the group steps into the elevator.

As the doors close and we begin our ascent, silence floods the elevator. Not the usual, temporal elevator-silence. Rather, an edgy silence; one with a pulse. The type of breathless silence that overtakes an audience as the lights extinguish seconds before the opera begins. In our case, however, the symphony to follow is unlikely to sound as soothing as *Madame Butterfly*.

We step off the elevator and follow Gui Lan and Joy into a large room that measures about twenty-five feet deep by sixty feet long. The room is empty except for several chairs placed around the perimeter. Against one wall is a small staging area flanked by two flags, one Chinese the other American. Though the room is large and mostly open, it somehow feels claustrophobic.

I have the camera ready and I'm shaking like a newborn colt. We wait only a few minutes and a young Chinese woman strides purposefully into the room through a doorway at the opposite end of the room from where we entered. She is dressed in a long and brightly colored blue dress with red and gold trim. I videotape from the moment she approaches the stage.

"Good afternoon, ladies and gentlemen," she begins, as panic invades my body.

Her short introduction contains the only words that register in my brain. As she begins the meat of her speech, my mind shuts down. My heart is thumping so loud I can't contain it. I videotape her speech, which lasts less than a minute.

At the end of the speech, she announces, "We are now going to bring the babies in. Please wait until your name is called."

I'm strangled with fear. My muscles are paralyzed and my breathing is short and rapid—I feel as though I'm suffocating.

Six Chinese women walk into the room in single file. Each woman carries a baby. I watch the procession through the lens of my video camera. The zoom lens gives me an unfair advantage. The first baby to enter the room is the one I have looked at in photos a hundred times in the past few weeks. I instantly recognize her as Lila.

Babe is panic-stricken. "Do you see her?" she asks frantically.

"That's her, the first one," I say calmly.

"Are you sure?" Babe asks, "Is that her?"

The rush of adreline overpowers me. All I want to do is get this over with, move forward, get Lila once and for all. "I'm sure," I say.

Once inside the room, the six women line up side by side and the unsuspecting babies stare at us curiously from their comfortable perch. For the babies, the experience—to this point—is probably as intriguing and harmless as a visit to the zoo. Lila's hair is pulled into a ponytail that sticks straight up from the top of her head. She's adorable.

"Colleen and Tom Truccio," the Chinese official calls out.

Colleen and Tom step forward and present their paperwork and the woman hands the baby to Colleen. Their baby instantly begins wailing; loud and horrifying cries of terror. More names are called out; chaos has arrived and its name is parenthood. I continue to videotape as our names are announced.

"Fred and Dorothy Ford."

Babe steps forward to get Lila. The woman holds Lila in her arms and approaches Babe. I had imagined a docile baby, smiling and curiously captivated by my wife's beautiful face and soft voice. I had played out this scene in my head a hundred times and in the movie of my mind the bond with Lila was instantaneous. Unfortunately, the exact opposite occurs.

Lila's face, which I've stared at so many times since we received the photos, is suddenly unfamiliar. Her glare is scornful and defiant. This is not the innocent stare of a baby; rather, the stoic glare of a battle-tested warrior. The loving and playful baby I had envisioned day after day in anticipation of this moment doesn't exist. Lila is a stranger. Her steely eyes communicate disdain, trepidation, and distrust. The rose petal lips are pressed together tightly; her smile lost in a galaxy light years from this room. The fretful wrinkles on her forehead form the letter "v" as apprehension grips her beautiful little face and fear overpowers her thoughts.

After a few seconds of the initial face-to-face meeting, the woman who holds Lila steps toward Babe and says, "Mama…mama," then hands Lila to Babe.

It happens quickly and it's awful.

Lila panics and looks backward desperately for the Chinese woman, who quickly exits the room. Lila uncomfortably wiggles and fusses in Babe's arms as she tries to pry herself loose and locate someone familiar. Eventually, seeing no options, Lila turns her stern attention to Babe and takes a mild interest in a little bear puppet that covers Babe's right hand. She dabs Lila's little nose gently with the bear and sings baby-talk. Lila turns her eyes from the bear to Babe, then back to the bear again. Before long, however, Lila's face turns sour, her mouth downturns, and the soulful, desperate tears begin. And they continue for quite a while.

Wonder mingles with horror as I view the first meeting with Lila through a camera lens. For the first minute of fatherhood, I assume the role of spectator. As I videotape, a current of compassionate sadness surges through my body over and over.

I zoom the lens into Lila's face and her mouth is wide open. Her screams are so loud and so violent she nearly chokes herself. Two tiny grains of rice are mostly dissolved but still stuck to her tiny tongue. More than any emotion I can discern, I feel sadness.

Lila's crying is distinguished by something that sounds like: "Eeeeeeee-eye."

Babe does her best to wear a happy face as she rocks Lila and says, "Shhhh, it's OK honey, it's all right."

It is anything but all right. Lila feels like a total stranger to us. As odd as that might sound, I did not expect to feel that. We had admired and stared at her photos for months now, and had become familiar with every wrinkle on her face. Each time I looked at the photo, I had fallen in love. I overlooked one important factor: while I was falling in love, Lila wasn't even aware of my existence. She's now at a terrible disadvantage and she's not taking kindly to it. In those first few minutes, the only things I feel are panic and sadness. This is difficult to watch. My first impression of Lila: she is the saddest little baby I have ever seen.

I turn off the videocamera and try to interact. My first interaction has the same level of tender love as Fay Wray's first meeting with King Kong: Lila is scared to death of me. Whenever I step within five feet of her, she begins to tremble and her crying intensifies, so badly at times that she hyperventilates. Her eyes fill with terror. I feel as though I'm watching Lila through the eye holes of one of those grotesque, rubber Halloween masks; such is the level of Lila's horror. My role, for the time being, will be filmmaker and executive assistant to Mommy.

I place the video camera in the carrying case and and remove the other camera. I take a few shots, just to document the event—though there isn't a Kodak moment in sight.

Gui Lan bounces joyfully from family to family in an attempt to facilitate a smooth transition as chaos continues to reign. The room is filled with loud cries and a mix of Chinese and American conversation; an incompatible invasion of noise I hope to never hear again.

Eventually, Babe moves to one of the seats placed along the perimeter of the room and takes a seat. I point the camera at Babe and Lila as Babe forces a weak smile. Mascara from one eye snakes down her cheek along with a stream of escaped tears. As she touches Lila gently on the cheek, Babe's hand is shaking like a rattlesnake's tail. I feel helpless.

We leave the room a half-hour later with the assurance from the foster family they will visit our hotel rooms later in the day to go over Lila's behavioral and medical chart. With babies in tow, we get into the elevator and take it to the ground floor. The silence that accomanied us a half-hour ago has vacated. We exit the building and board the bus.

Babe and Lila sit on one side of the bus and I take a seat across the aisle and take photos whenever Lila seems calm enough.

"You okay?" I ask.

She nods but I her face tells a different tale. "I just need to sit for a few minutes."

It is the most unnatural and gut-wrenching thing I've ever been through, with none of the feel good euphoria I had anticipated. Lila is devastated, traumatized, and stunned. Her whole world and everything she recognizes has evaporated in an instant with no prior warning. The familiar faces, the scents, the home, her surroundings, her toys, the sounds; all gone, ripped from her in a cruel instant. She's been whisked away by two strangers to God knows where, leaving her with a tiny heart broken in half. We can only hope the scars created by the trauma will be temporary. In the meantime, Babe and I have to deal with a baby who feels like a total stranger to both us. The job of parenthood has gotten off to a rough start.

Did you ever read a great book and then find out it was being made into a Hollywood movie? If so, when the movie was released did you rush to the movie theater with great excitement, only to be bitterly disappointed that the movie was nothing like the book? That's precisely how I felt when we got Lila. I had fallen in love with her photo over and over. I projected my relationship with her as a heart-warming and fuzzy dance: Shrek and Donkey frollicking in a park, playing peek-a-boo, giggling and rolling around the ground, as the music from *I'm a Believer* plays in the background.

After one short meeting, all such thoughts have been crushed beneath the weight of Lila's tortured soul.

Parenthood has begun and my Hollywood version of it has been shattered into a million pieces.

* * *

We return to the hotel room and neither Babe nor I have a clue what to do. The shock of the first meeting lingers like a bad scent and now we're in a hotel room improvising parenthood. It's minute by minute survivor mode.

We understood there would be struggles. In some respects, we had mentally prepared for the struggles. During one of the New Beginnings workshops, I was forewarned that babies will often reject men because of our size and deep voices. As with anything else you read or learn about, the reality doesn't quite sink in until you experience it. Reading about root canal doesn't place you in the dentist chair.

I continue to try to interact. The results are all the same: Lila rejects me every time. Any time I approach, she buries her face in Babe's chest and withdraws from me in tears as though I'm the village dragon.

"It's going to get better," I say to Babe, intending the comment more for myself than for her.

I get up from the bed and turn on the radio located on the wall panel between the two beds. A soft and depressing song featuring a flute and acoustic guitar floats from the speaker. Lila perks up a bit when she hears it, like a puppy hearing the rumble of distant thunder. The radio features no choice of stations, just the one we have on, pre-programmed with a dozen similar new age instrumentals—audio Valium. The songs seem to be having a calming effect on Lila, though they weigh heavily on my somber mood. Ironically, the music is perfectly suited as underscore music for these sad and lonely first few hours with Lila.

Lila seems ill at ease every second. Her beautiful face is masked behind fear and confusion, as if wondering when the nightmare will end. She clings to Babe as though clinging to life itself. From time to time, I videotape or take some photos. My instincts are strangled and confused. I feel only sadness for Lila. There's no relationship yet and none is in sight. Everything seems unnatural and forced.

Lila is only content when Babe cradles her in her arms and walks back and forth in the room. Any time Babe stops, Lila breaks into screams and tears of protest.

"Can you go down to the lobby and get me a Red bull or a cup of coffee?" Babe asks.

"Sure. I'll be right back," I say.

I leave the room and feel release from the claustrophobia and rejection. I take my time going downstairs to the lobby and try to reconcile my feelings as I walk. I understand my love for Lila is and always will be unconditional. Unconditional or not, what I feel for Lila doesn't seem like love at the moment; more like unconditional tolerance.

I purchase two cans of Red Bull and go back to the hotel room. As I re-enter the room, Lila quickly buries her head into Babe's bosom. I'm beginning to feel like a solar eclipse that Lila has been warned not to look at or else she'll go blind. As I approach them, I hand the Red Bull to Babe and gently touch Lila's head. She starts to cry again at the mere touch of my fingertips.

I make a conscious effort to put my own personal feelings aside no matter how this goes. So far it's not going so well.

As late afternoon approaches and Lila's eyelids get heavy—from both exhaustion and crying—Babe attempts to lower Lila into the crib. Nothing doing! Lila screams and fusses like she's being tortured. For Plan B, we place pillows around the sides and foot of one of the two beds and place Lila in the middle then cover her with a blanket. Shortly thereafter, Lila falls asleep. The day's only half-over and Lila has experienced enough trauma to last her lifetime.

With Lila asleep, Babe and I feel momentary reprieve. We curl up on the other bed and hold each other.

"It's going to be OK," I whisper comfortingly as we cuddle. "You're doing great with her."

Babe squeezes my hand but remains silent. I can only imagine what her thoughts are. Seeing how Lila has reacted to me, and knowing what type of person Babe is, I'm sure she's holding back any negative thoughts in an attempt to remain positive and focused on parenthood, with all its mysterious twists and dark alleys.

We both fall asleep with our clothes on. An unknown time elapses before a loud knock at our door shocks me out of a dead slumber. I stumble to my feet and blindly stammer to the door like Otis the Drunk. A second knock arrives loudly just seconds before I open the door. I turn the bathroom light on to illuminate the small entrance area of our room.

I open the door to find Gui Lan and a woman from the orphanage.

"Good evening Fred, may we come inside for a moment?" Gui Lan asks politely.

I open the door wider and the two of them tip-toe into the room as Babe joins us for introductions. The woman from the orphanage produces Lila's file that contains her behavioral patterns, medical history, and diet. I think to myself: *their timing couldn't have been worse.*

"I think it would be wise to turn off the air conditioning. The babies get sick easily and they are not used to the cool air," Gui Lan suggests.

I say nothing in response to her suggestion as I mentally prepare my defense of air conditioning for the inevitable discussion I will have with Babe later.

Aside from the air conditioning request, both Babe and I are intrigued by Lila's personal information. Unfortunately, my primary interest is to prevent Lila from waking up. As a result, when we are given an opportunity to ask questions, I don't. My attitude is: Lila's here and we'll deal with whatever comes.

The women leave and I go right back to the bed. Nirvana ends a few minutes later as Lila's wails slice through the room's darkness. Babe turns on both the light and the depressing music then picks Lila up and rocks her. Here we go again. This will take time and patience—and lots of both. I feel caught in a bad dream.

* * *

Later, we meet the others in the hotel dining room for another group dinner. With our group suddenly expanded by six babies, six carriages, and sixty toys, we spread out to two tables. Our arrival at the restaurant is an instant mood-killer for other diners. The babies fuss and cry as the group members exchange stories of the first few hours. It's a comfort to hear we aren't the only new parents experiencing struggles.

Lila barely eats and she cries hysterically when we try to place her in the carriage. As we leave dinner Babe carries Lila and I push the baby carriage occupied by my camera bag.

We get back in the room and we're greeted by the depressing music on the radio. The same eight or nine tracks play over and over in a pre-recorded loop and they've now become familiar.

"I want to give her a bath before putting her to bed," Babe says.

"Do you need anything?" I ask.

"Just help me with the bath," she says. Babe turns the water on in the tub and then undresses Lila, who cries. Minutes later, with a couple inches of water rippling the floor of the tub, Babe carefully places Lila into the tub.

"She has scabs on her head," Babe says distressingly as she examines Lila's scalp.

Upon touching the water, Lila's screams are other-worldly; beyond pain and outside anything I've ever heard—worse yet than the screams from earlier in the day when we first got her.

"Jesus Christ!" I yell.

"Just leave," Babe says firmly. She's tense and having an equally difficult time enduring Lila's screams and doesn't need any additional stress from me.

I leave the bathroom and pace the room as Lila's blood curdling screams vibrate through the closed bathroom door.

This is not what I expected. I flop into a chair feeling weak and useless. On top of the confusion and rejection, I feel badly I upset Babe. I know better.

After the bath, Babe walks out of the bathroom. Lila's eyes are red and her face is as sad as anything I've ever seen. She's stunned and sniffling, her breathing choppy.

"Can you get me another Red Bull?" Babe asks.

"Sure," I say. "You OK?"

"Just tired," she replies impatiently.

She's more than tired and so am I. My temporary role as Red Bull retriever will continue as long as Babe needs me. I tell myself (again): the situation will become easier. This is just temporary. I want to believe those words. I need an ounce of validation.

Sleep that night becomes a series of restless cat naps interrupted by hourly cries from Lila. We're helpless. We're stuck in the same room so we can't simply let Lila cry it out, as advised by many. Each time Lila wakes, Babe picks her up and walks back and forth with her for a half-hour or more at a time. During one of the wake-up calls, Babe reaches the point of total exhaustion.

"Can you take her for a few minutes?" Babe asks pleadingly. "I need a break."

"Sure," I say and take Lila, who screams and squirms the second she's placed in my arms. I walk back and forth in the same worn path Babe has taken a hundred times and Lila cries and reaches for Babe the entire time, pushing and squirming to get away from me, like a cat that's being held too tightly. I think to myself: *for such a small baby, she's awfully strong—and what a pair of lungs!*

Babe recoups just enough energy to begin anew and stands up and takes Lila from me. The cries stop but Lila keeps a wary eye on me as I take a seat. It takes a conscious effort on my part not to take things personally.

* * *

It's May 11 and we survived our first day with Lila. We rise early and Babe gets Lila dressed and puts her in the carriage to go to breakfast, as I try to shake my acute case of parental vertigo. Lila sits in the carriage with a face stripped of joy; stunned and afraid of what surprises lurk around the corner today. Yesterday started out very similar to this: an innocent stroll in a baby carriage. And look what happened; her life crashed all around her. It's impossible to imagine what these babies go through emotionally. I just can't fathom it.

We arrive at the smaller of the two restaurants near the hotel lobby and I detect Tom, Colleen, and their daughter Cassidy seated at a big table. We stroll over to join them. The aroma of bacon overpowers me and for some inexplicable reason I find the fragrance comforting.

"Well, how'd you make out?" I ask.

"I feel like I'm starring on *Survivor: Nanning*," Tom says.

We all laugh.

"And they're about to vote *me* off the country," I add.

Babe pulls Lila from the baby carriage and I try to collapse the legs and fold up the carriage. I find this task as difficult as nailing Jello to a wall. With some verbal direction and body language from Tom, I eventually manage to fold it up.

The restaurant is crowded with a mix of adoptive parents, babies, Chinese tourists and businessmen. I move from our table to the buffet line and load two plates full of breakfast food: eggs, bacon, sausage, toast, and fruit. By the time I return, a steaming cup of coffee awaits. Group therapy—formerly known as breakfast—has begun. Members of our group swap authentic lies about our parenting abilities as we try to comfort one another from the realities of life anew.

"So Colleen and I were talking this morning about when we're coming back for our second one," Tom says.

I nearly spit out a mouthful of eggs.

"What? You mean you're not going to adopt again Fred?" Colleen jokes.

"One and done!" I proclaim loudly.

Tom laughs for a full minute.

Babe feeds Lila, who remains sullen and quiet. Her eyes are tired and puffy and she refuses to eat anything except Cheerios. Meanwhile, the coffee surges through my bloodstream and gives me a much needed kick in the fanny. The familiarity of sharing coffee with friends is skewed by the addition of little baby girls who don't care to be among us. The feelings are foreign and relentless. Given my options, I wish I could stay here all day commiserating with Tom and Colleen, sipping coffee, and basking gloriously in a seductive mist of cooked bacon.

A couple from another adoption agency is seated next to us. Their daughter shows no emotion at all. The woman says, "She hasn't smiled or even cried much. More than anything else she seems stunned."

The father adds, "She won't even let me near her."

"When did you get her?" Babe asks.

"Two days ago," the woman says.

I'm mildly comforted that I'm not the only dad being rejected like a pimple-faced teenager seeking a prom date. I glance at Lila and my heart bleeds again. She's such a beautiful baby. She didn't do anything to deserve this. I want to hug her and tell her she's going to be OK.

After breakfast, we revisit the Civil Affairs Building to apply for passports and register the adoption. No other activities are planned; just settle in and get acquainted. With the day's formalities behind use, we pay a visit to a park within walking distance of the hotel.

We place Lila in her carriage and walk the few blocks to the park. The streets are crowded with Chinese residents. Many cast curious looks our way. I've stopped wondering why. At the moment I'm not at all curious about how Chinese residents view foreigners arriving in their country to adopt their orphans. The topic was briefly discussed during our stay in Beijing. But now, with the adoption playing out as a temporary nightmare, I have lost interest. I simply carry the video camera and push Lila in the baby carriage and patiently wait for things to get better. Simple reflex has replaced contemplation and curiosity.

The movie scenes I had envisioned for my planned documentary have all failed to materialize. I had imagined the moment we first saw Lila face-to-face would be an earth-moving, wonderful event and the edited video would be run in slow-motion through a smoky lens accompanied by Etta James' *At Last*. Strike one. My second image was a fun-loving, playful splash in the tub accompanied by Bobby Darin's *Splish Splash*. Strike two. Next up: the visit to the public park. I had envisioned some light-hearted moments of fun as I hide behind trees, walk with Lila sitting on my shoulders, discover flowers, or feed coy.

Fastball, outside corner, strike three!

We get to the park and Lila sulks during the entire visit. Her face is painted with sullen gloom, and she endures the trip with lethargy and boredom, slumped in the carriage as she timidly nibbles Cheerios from a small Tupperware container. The walk in the park is, so to speak, no walk in the park.

The park itself is beautiful, with a wide walking trail that loops around a large pond in the center. As we casually waltz through the park, we observe the formal gardens and the various ways local Chinese enjoy their moments of leisure. Some dance, others sing, a group practices martial arts, and families float along the pond in a variety of small boats, including a partially submerged miniature submarine. The pond water is a deep pea green, soothing on the eye. The weather remains tropically hot and humid.

Oddly, there are no joggers. In fact, I haven't seen a single jogger since we arrived in China several days ago. Perhaps it's taboo to jog or looked upon as anti-social. Whatever the reasons, the lack of joggers strikes me as odd—particularly since the weather is so ideal for jogging and virtually every Chinese person I've seen is physically fit.

Eventually, Lila falls asleep in the carriage. As Babe and I walk along, I take advantage of our short respite to rally my wonderful wife with some words of encouragement.

"You're the best," I say, "You're doing such a great job with her. I love you so much."

"I love you to. It's going to get better," Babe says assuringly.

I want to believe things will get better. I want so desperately for Lila to love me. At this point, however, human nature is winning the tussle for my emotions.

"How do you feel?" Babe asks.

"I feel like I'm babysitting someone else's child who hates me," I admit bluntly.

For the balance of the day, it's more of the same. All my attempts to interact with Lila are met with a trembling lip, a face filled with terror, and loud cries for mommy—even during the few seconds it takes for me to remove Lila from the carriage. She wiggles, squirms, holds out her arms in Mommy's direction, and never seems at ease until she's in the safe harbor against Babe's bosom. I keep a stiff upper lip; but I'm officially heartbroken.

When we return to the room, Babe needs to use the bathroom and hands Lila to me. Lila screams and I try to keep her calm. "Shhh, it's Ok honey. Shhh." She'll have none of it, carrying on and crying loudly. The only escape from this temporary prison sentence is the passage of time. Babe hastily completes her bathroom duty and re-emerges to restore calm.

Bathroom privileges I've taken for granted my entire life are suddenly unfathomable; like taking a relaxing shower or reading the newspaper while sitting on the toilet. It's particularly difficult and unfair to Babe, who Lila won't let out of her sight without a fuss.

At dinner that night, Gui Lan bounces from couple to couple as she interacts with the babies. Before long, she arrives to spend time with us.

"How's Lila?" she asks hopefully.

"We still haven't seen a smile," I say.

"That's because she is a proud princess," Gui Lan says. The words "proud princess" leave her mouth with the same regal splendor as the 1970's voiceover, "Ruffles have ridges." She forces a giggle and tries to get Lila to do the same, to no avail. Lila's smile is as distant and unreachable as peace in the Middle East.

Lila experiences more sleeping problems that night, accompanied by additional exhaustion for Babe and more unsuccessful attempts on my part to interact and participate. The stress becomes a 24-hour-a-day battle. At around 3:00, Lila awakens and begins crying. Babe scoops her from the bed, walks her, and rocks her gently around the room but hasn't the stamina to last very long. I take Lila from Babe and try to rock her and, as always, Lila cries. It worse this time around, however, as Lila cries so violently she begins to hyperventilate and choke. With barely a moment to sit and recuperate, Babe jumps to her feet and comes to the rescue. I scurry to the bathroom, close the door, grab a towel, bury my face deep in the towel, and scream uncontrollably for several minutes; primal screams from the deepest part of my soul. My resolve has been whittled to the size of a bed mite. Any chance to get a fresh start is crushed by lack of sleep. I have never experienced such a mix of despair and sleeplessness. Now that I've arrived in that unfortunate place, I find it very disturbing indeed.

I come out of the bathroom several minutes later, composed and ready for whatever. I sit in the chair near the foot of the bed where Babe tries to get Lila to sleep. While I was in the bathroom, Babe turned on the radio and now one of the depressing songs is playing again, adding a level of emotional torture to the latest of the impossibly difficult moments. I fix a gaze on Lila and she seems to be asleep. Babe is on the bed turned sideways from me so I can view her left profile. She leans over Lila and tries to stay perfectly quiet.

I think the moment of emotional pain has passed when I detect something that officially breaks my heart in two: a single tear dangling from the tip of Babe's nose. She has tried so hard to be strong for all of us. But the emotion and exhaustion at that moment is too much to bear. So a tear silently escaped, rolled down her cheek, and came to rest on the tip of her nose.

I quickly spring from the chair to the bed and wrap my arms around Babe as the levy breaks and we both let out sobs. Our bodies shake uncontrollably. At the moment, this seems about the same as the grief we experienced every month during Babe's period during the years of infertility. Through my tears, I whisper, "You're doing so great, hon. You're unbelievable."

I am awed at the way Babe handles the situation and our shell-shocked baby. Babe is a rock. So often during the period of infertility and the years we waited for Lila, I provided strength and support for Babe. Now, with parenthood taking on the face of a real life nightmare, Babe's strength sustains us while I'm falling apart. She is determined and seemingly tireless. In the face of this adversity, she maintains her gentle touch, her calm demeanor, and her loving patience.

"You're my hero honey," I whisper through my tears. I know it sounds melodramatic; but that's precisely what I feel.

* * *

May 12 is our third day with Lila and nothing formal is planned. The agency terms it a *rest day*. Marooned on a deserted island for six months with William Shakespeare, I couldn't have come up with a less appropriate title. Our only interaction with the others is lunch and dinner, which brings much needed companionship and beer.

I continue to disingenuously persuade myself it's going to get easier: Lila will come around, this is to be expected, and all the other clichés that have begun to resemble lies. Lila still hasn't smiled and the sudden shock she experienced three days ago hasn't thawed much.

On May 13, we resume our group sightseeing tours and take a bus ride to QingXiushan Park and then lunch. Lila exhibits little improvement. She refuses to *attempt* walking, even at the park when all the other babies walk and interact with their parents for hours. Every time Babe attempts to lower Lila to the ground, she screams as though she's being lowered into a caldron of molten lava.

I continue to take photos and capture video for the documentary, though my interest in making a movie has significantly waned. Suddenly, my heart's not in it. A movie about our adoption, I reason selfishly, will be too painful to produce and too sad to watch. For much of the time, therefore, I keep the equipment in the camera bag.

During our visit to the park, Babe caresses Lila when suddenly a group of women approach them and touch Lila lightly on her scalp.

"Lucky baby, lucky baby," they say over and over in Chinese as they huddle around Babe. I videotape the odd custom.

Later that day, we have to take care of two things. First, we pose for our family passport photo. A makeshift photography studio, consisting of a camera, tripod, a light, and bench set up in front of a white sheet is haphazardly assembled in the open foyer near the elevators. Babe secures a decorative, multi-color headband onto Lila's head and Lila claws and picks at it the entire time. Somehow, the headband stays on long enough to be included in the photo. It's our first family photograph and subsequent viewings of it remind me of the unmanageable chaos of our first few days together.

The other business involves our pre-determined donation to the orphanage. Gui Lan arranges to meet one member from each family in the hotel lobby after dinner. Based on a workshop we had previously attended, I am aware the donation is $3,000 in cash only, with strict instructions that the bills must be pristine; no folds or dog-eared corners. Once gathered by the fountain, our group proceeds to an isolated section in the far corner of one of the upper floors. The meeting produces all the characteristics of a street-level drug deal.

Two at a time, we are ushered into the low-lit room. In the center of the room is a queen sized bed, where a woman sits with her legs outstretched and her back propped against the headboard. Two men sit on folding chairs to the left side of the bed, a small table between them. All three smoke cigarettes and all three eye me suspiciously as I creep into the room with Tom and Gui Lan. I am suddenly reminded of a scene from the movie *Scarface*, where Al Pacino attempts a major drug transaction in a seedy motel room in Miami Beach.

Gui Lan begins one of her ninety-mile-an-hour Chinese conversations and as she does I covertly nudge Tom and impersonate Pacino's character, saying in a half-whisper, "Hell-lo Martha."

Unfortunately, Tom understands my *Scarface* reference and lets loose a laugh. This seems like a perfectly inappropriate arena for laughing; therefore I spend the balance of the visit biting my tongue.

One by one, we step up and sign our name, hand over the cash, then wait as they count our perfectly crisp bills. The room reeks of cigarette smoke. This doesn't feel right. I'm angry about it. The adoption has momentarily taken on the face of business deal. As the men greedily and hastily count the bills, I feel unsettled and confused. This donation business has unfortunately converted Lila into a commodity. I'm being made to feel I'm buying her. I'm not. She's a gift from God. Besides, Lila is priceless.

Gui Lan seems ill at ease with this arrangement as well. Her usual smile has eerily vacated. As soon as my pristine bills are judged acceptable, I sign my name and quickly exit the room.

As we walk back to our rooms, the mood has turned uncomfortably sullen.

I break the silence and say, "I found out what my Chinese name is."

"What is it?" a voice asks from behind me.

"Cha-ching."

I chuckle. It's a good line but nobody is laughing

* * *

Shortly after I return to the hotel room, Babe says to me in a state of total exhaustion, "I have to go to the bathroom and take a shower. You're just going to have to hold her."

Her voice is flecked with a mix of apology and resignation.

"Ok hon," I say, and take Lila from her.

As always, Lila reaches for Mommy and when Babe disappears to the bathroom, Lila screams and cries. I tune out the crying as best I can, though the volume of her crying continues to amaze me. I hold Lila and rock her as I say, "Ssshhhhh," over and over in my attempts to calm her.

While I continue to hold her, she squirms and continues to scream. Meanwhile, Babe receives a much needed respite. Despite my exhaustion and Lila's rejection, I'll continue to hold her the rest of the day if it will help Babe.

Suddenly, for reasons I can't explain, Lila stops crying. I look down to make sure she's still alive. As I do, our eyes meet and I stare into her big, brown, beautiful eyes for several seconds. It is the first time I have been able to do this without producing dreaded fear in her eyes. My heart and breath stop briefly then Lila quietly buries her head on my shoulder.

I'm shocked. I'm overjoyed. I'm crying. And, at long last, I'm daddy.

Minutes later, Babe walks out of the bathroom with a towel wrapped around her head and a bathrobe wrapped around the rest of her. She's curious about the lack of noise and tip-toes into the room with the stealth of James Bond.

When she observes Lila and me waltzing around the room with tears staining my cheeks and Lila's head buried on my shoulder with her eyes shut Babe's jaw drops open like a cartoon character who just witnessed a miracle.

She hastily grabs both cameras and takes video and photos of the momentous occasion.

This is our last night in Nanning as the following day we will fly to Guangzhou, where we will formalize the adoption at the American consulate. The mere thought of Lila's first flight sends a unappetizing wave of paralysis through my body. Babe and I continuously remind one another this is the necessary pain of the adoption, and it will get better. Love conquers all, don't you know. In fact, we have experienced some baby steps of progress already, although Lila still hasn't smiled.

* * *

The following morning, May 14, I join a representative from each family and Gui Lan in the hotel's conference room on the ground floor for yet another paperwork session. We gather at a solid oak conference table with a dozen chairs placed around the perimeter and Gui Lan methodically walks us through several pages that require information and signatures. Lila's Abandonment Certificate is contained in the paperwork. I had previously read the certificate the day the dossier arrived at our house many months ago. Members of the group are permitted a few minutes to reread the certificate and acknowledge the statement with our signature. The second reading unsettles me and I suddenly find myself distracted by thoughts of Lila's biological mother.

Babe thinks of Lila's biological mother often. I don't; and I never did. But as I review the abandonment certificate for the second time, I am filled with deep sadness as I try to fathom how Lila's biological mother must have felt after the abandonment. It was more than a month after Lila's birth, so I presume the mother had to feel *something* for her baby. What did she do or say the last moment she held Lila? How deep were the tears she cried as she walked away, knowing she would never see her baby again? For that matter, how could she allow this beautiful baby, just a month removed from her own womb, to be left in a public park all by herself, crying to no one? How often does Lila's biological mother think of Lila now? Is she visited in her dreams by images of Lila's beautiful face—a face that mirrors her own? I have some ability to empathize, but when I contemplate Lila's biological mother I simply don't possess the imagination to appreciate the depth of emotional pain she must have felt. The contemplation of it reaches so far into my soul that it leaves me haunted.

And yet there are those who suggest Chinese women often sense a fulfillment of an obligation to society when they've abandoned a female baby. That is something I will never fully embrace or comprehend.

For reasons neither I nor my wife can explain, thoughts of Lila's biological father have been virtually non-existent. Neither of us believes this was a virgin birth and we both recognize there was a man involved in at least one respect. But nearly all of our thoughts related to Lila's birth and abandonment are centered on the birth mother.

As I complete the paperwork, I receive a surge of energy. Despite the fact Lila doesn't like me I can't wait to see her again to resume the difficult process of bonding. When the paperwork is finished, I scamper to the elevator.

When I arrive at our room, Lila and Babe are on the bed.

"Hon, she *smiled*," Babe beams, as if announcing the war is over.

"You're *kidding*."

I quickly grab my camera and point it in the direction of Lila. Babe continues to make faces and do the same things she did to produce the first smile. And within seconds, Lila smiles and—FLASH—I snap the photo. Seconds later, I look at the LCD screen and drink in a photo of the happiest baby I have ever seen. I hand the camera to Babe and bury my head in a pillow and cry long and hard for several seconds. In the period of twenty-four hours, Lila has allowed me to hold her and then smiled for me and Babe. We have passed two significant milestones. The relief is enormous.

At lunch, I am finally afforded the opportunity to play the role of proud papa. The first person I show the photograph to is Gui Lan.

"The first to smile for the proud princess, I have been waiting soooo long," she sings as she admires the LCD screen for several more seconds.

During lunch, Tom and Colleen's baby Cassidy proves once again to be the big eater in the group. Cassidy is clearly the biggest baby of the group.

As we eat, Kitty says, "Fred, your daughter is beautiful."

I say, "Thanks. Yeah, she's going to be breaking hearts."

Tom chimes in, "And Cassidy is going to be breaking *legs*!"

With the smile finally coerced from Lila's beautiful face, a laugh is sure to follow. And during lunch it finally arrives. As we sit at the table and await delivery of our food, I place a cloth napkin on top of my head. Then I fake a sneeze, cup my hands in front of my nose and mouth, omit an exaggerated "Ah-choooo," and thrust my head forward. This causes the napkin to fall onto my lap. Lila smiles then laughs. So I do it again. She laughs more heartily. I repeat my silly shtick over and over, the sight of her laughing face and the sound of her little voice lifting my spirits like the first day of a three-week vacation.

Lila's poor sleeping habits persist. She wakes up several times every night filling the room with cries and screams. The night before we leave Nanning she breaks a new record, waking nearly a dozen times—more than once an hour. At one point, around 2:00 a.m., Babe finally gets her back to sleep after more than a half-hour of fussing and crying.

By this point, my exhaustion has yielded to aggravation and in my wide awake state I turn on the TV. I've watched little TV since we arrived in China. I quickly change channels with the remote and, as usual, find nothing: music videos, travel show, volleyball match—*what*?! *The Boston Red Sox*! My favorite team of all time in familiar Fenway Park is playing the Kansas City Royals. I nearly fall off the bed.

"I can't believe this," I whisper excitedly to Babe. "I haven't even seen a box score in more than a week."

The Sox are trailing the Kansas City Royals by a score of 5-0, the announcers are speaking in Chinese, and I don't care. I watch the game with the fascination of a seven year old watching his first baseball game ever.

And the Red Sox come from behind to win 6-5. Could this be the elusive harbinger of good things to come?

* * *

We are scheduled to fly today from Nanning to Guangzhou. In the morning, I visit the business center. My goal is to send an email to our sister-in-law Nikki, along with an attachment of the digital photo of Lila's first smile. From there, Nikki can forward it to others and show the photo to the rest of Babe's family.

I enter the business center and pay the fee for use of the computer, including rental of an adapter to allow a download of the photo from my memory card. A Chinese gentleman dressed in a handsome business suit escorts me to a small room that contains three cubicles equipped with computers. Two are occupied; I sit at the vacant one.

Once set up, I surf the worldwide web then log onto AOL, distractedly check my messages, then spend a half-hour typing a three-page letter to Nikki with details of the ups and downs of our journey thus far, highlighted by our recent breakthrough when Lila smiled for the first time. When I'm done typing I attach to the email a digital photo of Lila's first smile and click SEND MESSAGE.

An hourglass icon appears on the screen and sits there for several seconds, then a minute, accompanied by a cadence of my fingers impatiently drumming on the top of the desk. Several minutes later I lose my connection to AOL—and much of my remaining patience.

"Damn it," I mumble under my breath. I start anew.

I re-type the letter from memory, attach the photo, and hit SEND MESSAGE for a second time. I've now been on the computer close to an hour with nothing to show except a mountain of frustration. As I stare expectantly at the computer screen awaiting the fate of my email—with the velocity of my finger-drumming cadence increasing in direct proportion to my level of frustration—the supervisor of the business center strolls into the room and announces aloud to the three of us on the computers, "How much longer will you need?"

None of the other two computer users offer an answer, both pretending to assume the question is directed to me (even though I was the *last* of the group to take my place in front of the computer). Rather than follow suit, I break the stalemate and say, "I shouldn't be much longer, assuming this photo goes through."

"What service are you using?" he asks.

"AOL."

"Oh, AOL is very slow here. If your photo is high resolution you may not be able to send it."

My photo is high resolution so his warning strikes me like a boss's request to "come in and close the door behind you." When I turn back to my screen, I see the program has quit once again.

"I'll be just a few minutes more," I say desperately, ready to try it one more try before I give up.

I log on, type a Cliffs Notes variation of my now memorized letter, attach the digital photo, and hit SEND MESSAGE. The hourglass appears. Here we go again. I detect a deep sigh from outside the door and turn to see an impatient Caucasian man standing in the doorway with arms folded to communicate his feelings that my time is up.

Now under pressure, I close my eyes tightly and mentally speak a prayer: *Dear God, I'm sorry if this seems selfish or petty. I just want to share the photo of Lila with Babe's family. And it looks like that's not going to be possible. Nevertheless, I pray that you will supernaturally affect this computer and the attached message and allow this email to go through. Please God, help this photo get to America.*

I end the prayer and open my eyes to look at the screen. Seconds later, the email goes through successfully.

Thank you Jesus.

After lunch, we prepare for the next leg of our journey. With another plane ride looming in the shadows like a starved crocodile, the greatest fear affecting me is my anticipation of Lila's reaction to flying.

During the bus ride to the airport, I glance out the window of our bus and notice a colorful mix of grey, white, and yellow clouds gathered in the horizon. Golden rods of sunlight streak through the clouds. I videotape the clouds and sun streaks and instinctively interpret the footage as a symbol of our recent breakthroughs with Lila. In my mind I hear the notes of George Harrison's guitar at the beginning of *Here Comes the Sun*.

With the addition of babies, diapers, toys, and other souvenirs, the effort of check-in and boarding the plane has intensified. Our luggage has expanded by the approximate weight of a teenage giraffe. Thus, we now face a surcharge for exceeding the weight limit. News of the additional fees is greeted with indifference by members of our group—except the one person who has any ability to affect the outcome: Gui Lan. When she learns of the news, she angrily confronts the clerk at the check-in counter. She waves her arms and goes toe-to-toe with the guy like Earl Weaver confronting an umpire after a bad call. Within five minutes our surcharge has been waved. It's vintage Gui Lan.

We board the plane and strap in. I brace for the worse but hope for a miracle. We take off for Guangzhou, a flight of about one hour due east.

Guangzhou is a seaport, the capital of Guangdong Province in southern China. To my delight and shock, Lila reacts with the calm demeanor of the Gerber baby. She never makes a peep, content to play with her little Sesame Street figurines and chomp her Cheerios. She doesn't cry once. This is too easy. I brace myself for the other shoe to drop but it never does.

As we sit in a plane bound for Guangzhou, the book of the most difficult chapter of my married life calmly comes to an end. With my mind, heart, and soul sapped of their respective energies, we put Nanning in our rear view mirror. Hope and optimism have crept back into focus. We are on our way to Guangzhou and one giant step closer to home sweet home.

Chapter 8
THE WHITE STORK OF GUANGZHOU

"Welcome to the White Swan," Gui Lan announces over the bus microphone. The words may as well have been issued by Ricardo Montalban accompanied by a stringed orchestra playing Vivaldi's *Four Seasons*. Our arrival at the White Swan is simply magnificent.

The hotel stretches skyward twenty stories. We step into the lobby and gawk at its beauty: a handsomely decorated and spacious area of sparkling marble and mahogany sprinkled with colorful plants. From the lobby, the centerpiece of the hotel is in sight: a vaulted atrium with a gorgeous waterfall, a dazzling rainbow of flowers, and a spacious fish pond. After check-in, we walk downstairs toward the waterfall and view the restaurant and several corridors leading to rows of stores: clothing stores, bookstores, souvenir shops, candy stores, flower boutiques, and so on. Our arrival at the White Swan is like a reward for the hard work, heartache, and patience of the week that preceded our stay. Just being there gives a much needed lift.

The White Swan is affectionately referred to as the "White Stork" hotel, as most adopting couples (and babies) end up here at the tail end of their China visits. The hotel is within walking distance of the American consulate, a place we will visit in a few days to attend a swearing-in ceremony to make the adoption official. In the meantime, we have an opportunity to bounce around this lap of luxury for a few days.

Our room is on the seventh floor, with a window that faces the Pearl River.

"Look at this," I say to Babe as I admire the river view and the various ferries and fishing boats busily skirting about the river.

"Wow, what a view," she muses.

Lila glances out with vague curiosity.

"Boat," I say and point a finger toward the river.

Her curiosity ends with a recalcitrant scowl.

It's mid-afternoon by the time we get settled, so our first meal will be dinner. At this point in the trip, the group dining and the lazy susans are discontinued, as the White Swan's restaurant has a more western layout, including smaller tables set for parties of two to four. Shortly after we unpack and settle in, we proceed to the dining room, a sprawling and attractive room with multiple levels of seating. The restaurant is crowded with patrons. Along one side of the room, windows face Pearl River. The opposite side of the room faces the beautifully landscaped atrium, fish pond, and waterfall.

The hostess sits us in the center of the dining room and leaves menus on the table.

"You can choose from the menu or one price for the buffet," she states ineffectually.

"Let me check out the buffet," I say to Babe and make my way to the buffet line to take a look.

The buffet includes about ten stations: a carving station with fresh turkey, roast beef, and filet mignon; numerous trays of pasta, chicken, fish, ribs; a sushi bar with a wide assortment of rolls and sashimi; a big salad bar; dozens of varieties of breads; fresh vegetables. I've never been so sentimental about food in my life; I feel like I'm meeting celebrities.

I return to the table practically jumping out of my skin with the salivating news.

"How's it look?" Babe asks expectantly.

"They have everything: steak, sushi, veggies. When I saw spaghetti and meatballs, I nearly fell off my rickshaw."

We load a few plates with food. Lila still doesn't eat much but discovers a child's fascination with chop sticks. I videotape her as she plays and smiles. As we eat, a comfortable feeling settles over me. For the first time since our arrival in China, I feel as though the three of us are family. The feeling arrives quickly but emphatically.

Near the end of the meal, I detect a white-haired Caucasian man as he weaves through the restaurant in our direction. I catch eyes with him and he tosses a smile my way like a man tossing a coin into a street musician's tambourine. Seconds later, he stops at our table and asks, "Wanna see a photo of my wife?"

Put on the spot, I can't come up with a reasonable objection, so I merely shrug my shoulders and say, "Sure."

He removes a photo from his wallet and holds it for us to view: a beautiful, young Chinese woman of not more than thirty years old, probably half his age.

"Isn't she beautiful?" he asks.

"Yes, she is," I agree.

"I met her through a catalog," he says admiringly as he stares at the photo.

I nod as if I understand. I suddenly have no desire to talk further to him and find the brief conversation stalled in an awkward silence as he returns the photo to its place in his wallet.

"Don't worry," he says and points to Lila, "in three months she won't remember a thing."

He salutes military style and walks off. He visits no other tables and exits the restaurant. It was as if he was a messenger from God sent to deliver a message we needed to hear.

The stranger's comments trigger thoughts about my first memories as a child. I have no memories of my first three years and my father's home movies provide the only perspective of my pre-kindergarten existence. In that sense, I take comfort in the stranger's prediction. In a bigger sense, I am anxious to reach a better place with Lila.

* * *

The following day we seek out the playroom near the rear lobby entrance for the hotel. The playroom is a large open room with a soft carpeted floor and hundreds of toys of all sizes, shapes, and colors. In light of the many families with babies staying in the hotel, the playroom is enormously popular—and insufferably loud.

Lila plays giddily with a ball as she laughs no-stop. It warms my heart. I want to get some video footage but realize I forgot the camera in the room.

"I'm going back to the room to get the camera," I say to Babe.

Shortly after I let myself back into our hotel room, I locate the camera bag. I turn quickly to leave but as I glance at the aggregation of personal belongings resting on top of the dresser, I detect something that sends a chill dancing up my spine: a Barbie doll, still in its box, with Barbie cradling a Chinese baby in her arms. I stare at the toy for several seconds through watery eyes, unnerved by the emotions it stirs and curious as to how it suddenly appeared in our room. I assume it's a welcome gift from the White Swan. A bit shaken, I exit the room for my return trip to the playroom.

As I return to the playroom, I notice Lila and Babe are laughing and playing on the floor with a miniature Winnie-the-Pooh swing set. Whenever Lila laughs, a burden is lifted. Her laugh is infectious and as addictive as a container of pistachio nuts. She sounds like Boo, the little girl from *Monsters Inc.* Of greater relevance, her laugh carries a current of optimism for the future; audible reassurance.

I walk over to Lila and Babe, kneel in front of them, place my video camera on the ground, and tilt the lens up slightly to get a ground-up camera angle through the little swing set to Lila and Babe.

"What a great shot," I say admiringly to no one in particular.

Lila continues to smile and laugh. At one point, her face turns toward Babe's and the two of them catch eyes. For a split second Lila's face turns serious. The change in her mood converts lighthearted fun into a poignant moment of troubled reflection. In that one brief glance, so much is revealed. Lila's eyes seem to plead with Babe: *please tell me this isn't a dream; please tell me you'll never leave me.*

My love for Lila grows by a thousand miles in that one glimpse. There's no way to specifically convey the simple message I want so desperately to communicate to Lila: *don't worry, honey, everything is going to be all right.* I'm just going to have to prove it one minute at a time.

The formal sightseeing activity has all but ceased at this point, though not from a lack of opportunities. Guangzhou is a bustling seaport with a population of just more than 3,000,000 residents. Numerous parks and stores are within walking distance of our hotel.

One day, as the bright, warm sun coaxes us outside, we opt for an afternoon stroll with Tom, Colleen and their daughter Cassidy.

"She still eating a lot?" I ask as I point to Cassidy.

"Like a truck driver," Tom grumbles. "And guess what I found?"

"What?"

"A 7-11."

"No! Where?" I ask.

"Right around the corner from the hotel."

"Lead on, my friend. A twenty ounce coffee is calling my name."

Tom leads us to the 7-11 and when I first detect the familiar sign, I feel as though I have just stumbled upon missing car keys after a two-hour search.

We spill into the store and I glance from side to side unable to locate the coffee station. I make my way to the sale counter and lift an imaginary coffee cup to my mouth as I ask the clerk, "Coffee?"

"No coffee," she says, shaking her head.

"What?" I nearly yell.

The news stuns me. I stand in the middle of the store with mouth agape and hands on hips as if a maitre de just informed me that my reservation was given away to another party. I gaze incredulously at the clerk, who stares back at me with blank indifference as if to say, "Any other dumb questions?" After a few seconds, the shock abates and I settle for a can of Red Bull.

A few blocks from the hotel, we come upon a store that sells costume jewelry, hats, t-shirts, and other souvenirs. Outside the store is a display rack that contains several 8" x 11" portraits, including Jesus Christ and Michael Jordan.

Tom and I wander inside and quickly detect the story owner, a Chinese man with dark-rimmed glasses, hair combed straight down in pointy spikes, and teeth a comical mix of shapes and sizes. The front two teeth protrude out his mouth like side-by-side Frito's corn chips.

"It's the Nutty Professor," I mumble under my breath.

Tom suppresses a laugh. The guy comes out from behind the sales counter and walks toward us. I'm suddenly frightened.

As he approaches, he asks, "You wanna know something?"

I glance uncomfortably at Tom and then back to the man and say, "What's that?"

"All you Americans look alike."

Caught off guard, we laugh. So the guy throws the entire act at us and our visit quickly deteriorates. Tom and I can't get a word in and neither us can decide whether to laugh or ignore the guy. Given this uneasy choice, we simply leave the store. The guy follows us outside and keeps the jokes coming and then he begins barking like a dog. It's an absurd moment that keeps me laughing for several minutes.

* * *

The three planned events in Guangzhou are the medical exam, the swearing-in ceremony at the American consulate, and a trip to Six Banyan Tree Temple.

The medical exam is first. It's May 16 and our group strolls the short distance from the White Swan to the modern medical office. Once inside, we sit on benches in a small, narrow waiting room with our babies. The process moves rapidly, as each couple is ushered into a treatment area and the babies are checked head to toe by a physician. Lila is asleep in Babe's arms when we're called and once inside the treatment room she receives—quite literally—a rude awakening. The doctor handles her roughly: jabs and prods, sticks light in her eyes and ears, and places her on a scale. Lila cries and screams loudly and, with few options and no ability to assist, I helplessly videotape some of the exam.

Babe is upset by the ordeal. She glances up several times to me as if to say: is this doctor nuts?

At the end of the treatment, the doctor says through a mask covering his mouth and nose, "Baby good. Healthy baby." Then he issues a loud announcement in Chinese which I imagine must mean: NEXT.

We leave the clinic and Lila clings desperately to Babe. She's gone through so much in such a short period of time. I find it impossible to fathom what she must be feeling, what level of fear and uncertainty possess her. The transformation in my heart has gone from fear to sadness to love; yet sadness lingers, unwilling to yield to more positive emotions. I realize life is hard, but why did Lila have to learn that lesson at such a young age?

I kiss the top of her head as I wrap my arms around Babe and say, "Group hug."

Later that day, we visit the Six Banyon Tree Temple. It has a long history of about 1,400 years and contains a rich collection of cultural-relics, art exhibits, and shops—and of course the traditional Buddha statues.

We approach the tall entrance doors equipped with giant knockers. I instantly recall Gene Wilder in *Young Frankenstein*. I borrow his line and blurt, "What knockers!"

As with most of my jokes nowadays, it takes a back seat to parenting and the line goes mostly unnoticed. Once inside, our group poses for a group photo. The adults stand side by side in the back row and the babies and Gui Lan line up in the front row. Our new tour guide Ken offers to snap the photos but becomes baffled by each camera. His face contorts with a painful grimace as if he was suddenly afflicted with a half-dozen throbbing toothaches. Eventually he manages to snap two photos with each camera. When I look at the LCD screen later, I recognize the photo as an instant classic; one that will be displayed in my home forever.

As we mosey through the temple, I notice an unusual art exhibit and stop to observe for a few seconds. An artist paints with the side of his hand. He dips the hand into a container of black ink and then smears the ink onto a canvas in short, staccato karate chops, smoothing some lines and smudging others. Right before my eyes, a mountain and landscape appear. It's fascinating.

Once again, the temperature is hot; the air humid. This may be the hottest day we've seen. To date, we haven't seen a drop of rain in the nearly two weeks we've been in China.

As we browse, we come to a room filled with embroidery displays. The room is crowded. Before I tour the room to admire the embroidery, I encounter four Chinese children who gawk at me. It's not the first gawking I've been exposed to during my visit.

"Hello," I say to them.

They giggle and clutch each other. "Hel-lo," one of the kids says.

"Hello," I say again.

They laugh even harder and more chime in as they say in unison, "Hel-lo." This goes on for minutes. I'm mesmerized and, to be honest, curious why the hello exchange has struck such a fancy with them.

"Let's go little boy," Babe says to me.

The embroidery is a feast on the eyes: peacocks, landscapes, cats, and pagodas. I won't be taking any home. They're all priced at several thousand Yuan beyond my budget.

Later, we enter the courtyard at the rear of the temple and gaze at a series of ancient statues and banyon trees. A dilapidated housing project rises up over the courtyard from the adjoining property. Laundry lines are strewn with tattered clothes and mangy cats slink along the roof in search of food.

Danny nudges me and points at one of the cats on the roof.

"Not Park Avenue," I offer.

He merely shakes his head.

* * *

For dinner tonight, little Rob organizes a pizza party. Our hotel room is situated at the end of the hall, with ample room to spread out and monopolize floor space without creating an obstacle course for other hotel guests. Danny bounces from room to room to take orders.

"Meatball hero," I say. "Babe and Lila will have pizza." Of all the foreign phrases I've uttered since my arrival in China, "meatball hero" carried the greatest level of personal gratification.

An hour later, our group is sprawled out on the floor with pizza boxes and plates of calzones and heroes.

"Beer?" Rob says and holds up a cold bottle of Chinese Ying Ling beer.

"A man after my own heart," I beam, taking the cold beer from Rob.

There's not enough vacant space on the floor to accommodate someone my size—even in my best lotus position—so I remain standing as I savor the cold beer and the sights, sounds, and laughter of our group. A surge of love snakes through my soul as I embrace the simple pleasures released by this moment. I feel a swelling affection for the wonderful people who have shared our oddysey. For a moment, I drift off in a daydream that transports me back to Long Island.

"You OK?" Babe asks. I snap out of the trance.

"I'm OK," I smile, "I'm good."

During the meal, I sneak through the exit door in search of a quiet moment on the balcony, which overlooks Pearl River and the pool area of the White Swan. As I drink in the early evening scenery of Guangzhou—with its orange and blue sunset—I spot a plane as it descends toward Guangzhou Airport. As I view the plane, the opening piano notes of a Beatles' song play in my mind, followed by the lyrics, "Once there was a way…to get back homeward…"

The following morning, on May 17, we are scheduled for our swearing-in ceremony at the American consulate, about five blocks from the White Swan.

In the morning, Gui Lan knocks on our door and I answer.

"We gave at the office," I joke and Gui Lan understandably ignores my insipid attempt at humor.

"One thing to tell you. Since 9-11 no cameras are allowed in the consulate building. I'm sorry I forgot to tell you this earlier. Please don't bring your cameras."

I'm disheartened by the news. I would love to have the ceremony on video.

We exit the White Swan and push our babies in their carriages as we follow Gui Lan. As we approach the consulate, we stroll past long lines of Chinese residents who scowl at us with contempt. During our trip, we have attracted a lot of gawkers and I assume it's attributable to our ethnicity—as well as my size and mannerisms. The piercing stares we receive from those who stand in line at the consulate, however, are much different and far more unsettling. Many wait in similar lines for months in hopes to obtain a travel visa to the United States; many travel considerable distances with no guarantees of success. There's resentment and rage in their eyes; not a hint of curiosity or amusement. As we proceed toward the consulate, I catch eyes with several of those standing in line. I feel like a celebrity bypassing a long line of working stiffs waiting impatiently to gain entry to a trendy nightclub. I'm filled with an uncomfortable blend of good fortune and guilt.

Once inside the consulate building—a plain interior that resembles a Greyhound bus terminal with rows of plastic seats bolted to the floor and little to no ornamentation—the horde of parents and babies are crowded into a small room. A pleasant, avuncular man steps out of a private office and cordially addresses the gathered parents then provides a brief explanation about the ceremony. Without additional fanfare, he asks all the parents to raise their right hands and repeat after him. We repeat the oath, essentially affirming that all the statements we made on the documents to obtain Lila's immigrant visa are true. The whole visit lasts no more than ten minutes, with a majority of the time spent filing into the building and assembling in the waiting room.

When the short ceremony ends, I glance at Babe and detect a pool of tears gathered in both eyes. We smile at each other and squeeze one another's hands, then turn our eyes to Lila. It's official: Jiang Xiaozhong is now—and forever more—Lila Rose Ford.

On the way home, our group stops at a photo shop near the 7-11 (the one with no coffee) to have Lila's visa photo taken. Babe places Lila on the chair in front of the camera and then retreats so the photographer can snap a photo. Lila unleashes a series of terrifying screams. Babe and I try to calm her—to no avail. Eventually, the photographer snaps the photo with Lila in full wail.

If nothing else, the passport photo will provide a visible reminder of Lila's trauma in her first few days as Lila Ford. Some day, I'll show the photo to Lila and have a few laughs over it. Some day…

* * *

It's late afternoon and Karen visits our room with a concerned look troubling her face. Moments after entering the room, she announces apprehensively, "We may have a change of plans."

"What's up?" I say, concerned.

"Have you looked at the itinerary?"

"No, why?"

She produces the one-page itinerary and points to highlighted sections as she explains, "We are scheduled to fly from Guangzhou back to Beijing—three hours—and then less than an hour later we're expected to deboard, gather our luggage, get through customs, check in to another plane in a different section of the airport, board that plane, and fly to New York. How are we going to do that with the babies?"

Karen has introduced an excellent—and heretofore never mentioned—point. I for one have no viable response.

"Well, what other options do we have?" I ask—hastily concluding there are none.

"We're going to Gui Lan's room to see if she can do anything."

I agree to whatever the group wants. I'm homesick, exhausted, and haven't realized such a flood of emotions in my lifetime. I'll vote for whatever gets me to New York the fastest—including a Space Shuttle.

Karen and Kitty meet with Gui Lan and within an hour the itinerary has been re-arranged. Gui Lan requests one member from each family to meet at Rob and Kitty's room. I arrive early and Rob is slumped cozily in a chair as he cradles and feeds a bottle of formula to his beautiful daughter Sophia. The sight of Rob and Sophia produces in me a wave of envy. He seems to have fallen into his role as father as effortlessly as pulling on pair of socks. Sophia seems so comfortable with him. Lila and I are light years from this bond.

"Hi Fred," Rob says in a low voice, "there's cold beer in the cooler."

It has become Rob's favorite thing to say to me—and, ironically, my favorite thing to hear.

"You say the sweetest things," I say, and grab a beer.

Gui Lan and the others arrive shortly thereafter. Gui Lan carries several copies of the new itinerary and says, "I have arranged for you to fly out of Guangzhou a day early. You will check into a hotel close to the Beijing Airport and get a good night's sleep, then fly from Beijing to New York the following day."

The plan receives a unanimous and hearty approval.

"Tonight, to celebrate, we will visit a special restaurant and enjoy a pigeon dinner," she announces enthusiastically.

Her suggestion conjures up a mental image of me and three homeless people huddled in Central Park cranking a rotisserie of pigeons over an open fire. What the heck, I think to myself, I'll try anything once.

"Count us in," I chirp.

An hour before the our scheduled excursion to Boston Pigeon—or whatever the name of the restaurant is—Babe is holding Lila while she exchanges smalltalk with Kitty in the hallway in front of our room when suddenly Lila vomits, followed by tears, screams, and a fever. It's awful. This is our first exposure to that horrible and helpless feeling that arrives when your child becomes sick. I scurry recklessly to Gui Lan's room for a consultation. At the same time, I deliver the amended verdict on our attendance of the pigeon dinner.

"Count us out," I say somberly.

We do our best to comfort Lila for the rest of the night and I order room service. Lila isn't able to hold anything down but her fever eventually breaks. We feed her fluids and baby Tylenol. We will leave for Beijing the following day but the Hell on earth we go through that night makes a flight to Beijing seem like an unreachable fantasy.

What's worse, because of the S.A.R.S. outbreak from several months ago, Chinese officials have imposed a strict policy that prohibits anyone with a fever from leaving the country. All travelers who enter or exit China are screened for fevers. At the airport, we will be required to fill out and sign health declaration cards. We have less than twenty-four hours to get Lila's fever under control or we are looking at an extended stay in China. The possibility for an extended stay is about as enticing as a bathtub full of spiders.

Later that night, during one of the short time periods that Lila actually sleeps, I slip noiselessly from the room in search of a thermometer, as the one we brought with us is not working properly. I run into Tom in the hallway. He's carrying a shopping bag filled with diapers and other daily essentials.

"How was the pigeon?" I ask.

He shrugs nonchalantly and says, "Tastes like pigeon."

We both laugh. Thankfully, he has a good thermometer and I courier the device hastily to our room. An hour or so later, I begin a quiet prayer for God's intervention. I'm still pleading when exhaustion overtakes me and I fall asleep.

The following morning, Lila's fever has vacated and her playful spirit has returned. One more answered prayer in a long line of them. Several hours and one final buffet breakfast later, we are bound for the airport. The light at the end of the tunnel has finally appeared. A short stay in Beijing and our next stop will be a place I have dreamed of every day since we got here: Home.

* * *

Gui Lan will not accompany us back to Beijing. She will leave Guangzhou to return to her home and her husband. She does, however, accompany us on our short bus ride from the White Swan to the airport.

The bus takes off for the airport and Gui Lan grabs the microphone and announces, "I will stay with you right up to the boarding on the plane." She smiles comfortingly and continues, "I think it will be nice if we can sing the American *National Anthem*."

I grab my video camera and point it toward Gui Lan as she sings: "Oh say, can you see, by the dawn's early light…"

Seconds later, I am overcome with emotion and I stop videotaping while placing a hand over my eyes.

The only tense moment at the airport arrives when Lila is screened for her fever. As we wait in line, my heart beats rapidly like the Energizer Bunny's drum as my mind races arbitrarily with a slew of unsavory possibilities. I feel like the guy in *Midnight Express* approaching his plane with bricks of hashish taped to his body as he unsuccessfully attempts to get through Customs in Turkey.

When we reach the Chinese official, he hastily checks Babe's temperature and then Lila's. Shortly thereafter, he waves them through and turns to me. I practically crap my pants with relief.

Thank you, God.

We proceed to the terminal and take a seat with our babies, who all seem content to sit and play or nibble on cookies, oblivious to the turbulent twist their lives are about to take. As soon as the boarding announcement is broadcast over the intercom a stampede of Chinese people aggressively charge the gate like early holiday shoppers squeezing through the entrance doors as Macys opens for business on Black Friday. In China, there's no pre-boarding ritual for babies and families with young children; no lines A, B, and C; it's every man and woman for themselves. At this point, it doesn't matter: we're leaving and I'll be on that plane even if they had to strap me to the fuselage.

Our group forms a single line and one by one we try to find the appropriate words of gratitude for Gui Lan. I'm the last in line. After Babe says good-bye, I step up. I place into Gui Lan's hand a card containing a cash tip. No amount of money could ever compensate for what she had done. With tears in my eyes, I say, "I will never forget you. Thank you."

As we hug, she says in a semi-whisper, "Take care of that proud princess."

I board the plane and settle in. Using simple deduction, and based on Lila's exemplary behavior on our previous flight from Nanning to Guangzhou, I optimistically reason we are in for another smooth plane ride on our three-hour flight from Guangzhou back to Beijing. I've been wrong about things in the past, but I rate this one right up there with that afternoon in October 1978, as I watched the Red Sox-Yankees playoff game, I declared, "good, Bucky Dent's up, we're out of the inning."

Lila fusses as we enter the plane and fidgets as we try to get her secured into her seat. Any effort I can muster to entertain, distract, quiet, or even quell her discomfort is an abject failure. Babe cuddles and rocks Lila then offers a soothing, "shhhhh, it's okay."

I'm sure if Lila could somehow put reasonable thoughts together and form a sentence, her response would have sounded something like this: "Okay, my foot! My eardrums are the size of early peas and now you and fatso are dragging me onto another plane to test my ability to withstand cabin pressure at the ripe old age of fourteen months. Well, I've got news for you: I liked the air conditioned hotel room a whole lot better. Get me off this thing. Waaaaaaaaaaa." (Just for the record, she did manage to communicate the "waaaaaaaa" part of this hypothetical sentence).

Lila continues to cry until we reach cruising altitude. As soon as the seatbelt light is extinguished, Babe scoops Lila from the seat and paces up and down the aisle, the only thing that will quiet her.

For strategic reasons, Babe is in the aisle seat to accommodate easy-in and easy-out. I'm stuffed in the middle seat like ten pounds of crap in a five-gallon hat. A young Chinese gentleman sits in the window seat to my left. For the sake of the story, let's give him the name Young Gai. It seems Mr. Gai has two physical problems, both of which affect his head—which unfortunately is located in close proximity to mine. His first problem is a nervous twitch that causes him to jerk his head sharply in my direction every thirty seconds, as if trying to steal quick glances at my book or use body language to communicate: meet me over there, in the aisle. The head movements are as jerky as a squirrel's tail.

But the unnerving twitch is no match for his ferocious sinus infection which causes Mr. Gai to snort, chortle, and rattle phlegm non-stop. It sounds as if he's gargling thumb tacks.

Babe returns but as soon as she settles into her seat Lila starts up again. Meanwhile, Young Gai snorts and snaps his head in my direction over and over while other passengers cast evil glances in our direction. It's insanity at 30,000 feet.

I've never been one to be compassionate about crying babies. Now that I have one, however, I'm defensive and annoyed at the deep sighs slung hatefully in my direction like poison darts.

We deal with Lila's crying and discomfort as best we can—with no luck. Toys placed in Lila's sight are routinely swatted aside like planes being spanked by King Kong. The only thing that keeps me sane is the thought of our flight home. I say to myself: *it's almost over; this isn't going to last forever; deal with it.*

Babe and I barely speak, unable to exchange more than a sentence between the tours up and down the aisles in our collective efforts to quiet Lila.

The flight lasts three hours. It feels like thirty. The plane lands and taxis to the terminal. The moment it comes to a stop every passenger stands up and hastily gathers their belongings then crowds the aisles to deboard. As with boarding, in China there is no common courtesy for deboarding. Travelers simply push straight ahead as though trying to escape a soccer riot.

Babe and I wait for an opportunity to step into the cramped line, an opportunity that never arrives. We exit the plane last—followed by Young Gai.

* * *

With the flight behind us, another hurdle is in our rear view mirror. Once in the terminal, the babies fuss, baby carriages are sorted and erected confusingly, and hundreds of Chinese shout indecipherable instructions all around us. Some members of our group scramble to gather pushcarts and others wait by the luggage conveyer to pull luggage off. At the same time, George locates our new tour guide, a short, thin Chinese gentleman with the English-speaking skills of a mynah bird.

The spring in my step has wilted. I tiredly drag my big feet, swollen ankles, and fat ass from plane to baggage check, then from baggage check to the curbside adjacent to the airport access road. It's early evening and the air is considerably cooler in Beijing than it was when we left Guangzhou earlier. An antiquated bus, about half the size of the busses we had previously traveled in, chugs noisily to the curb.

We collectively gaze at our guide—and one another—as if to say: *this* is our *bus*?

"We're not all going to fit on that," I predict to our guide.

He clearly doesn't understand a word. He smiles uncomfortably, nods his head, points toward the bus, and says, "Yes, yes. Please sit."

His command of English is on par with mine of Chinese, and after a while we give up trying. Tensions are now running high. Each member of our group is exhausted and few of us reason we can comfortably cram our entire group plus luggage into the undersized bus.

"Maybe we can make two trips," someone suggests, a comment that produces a flutter of desperation in my gut as though someone had just asked me, "Fred, where's your wallet?"

"This is bullshit," Rob decrees assertively. "We're all going to fit on this bus, luggage and all, and make *one* trip."

The senior member of our group has spoken and his suggestion goes unchallenged. We cram our luggage onto the bus, then one by one we squeeze into every square inch: a claustrophobic's nightmare. For a person my size, breathing is now a physical challenge. As we inch away from the curb, our group resembles the phone booth crammers of the 1960's.

The only silver lining to the cramped bus is its capacity to deflect our attention from the flight we just endured.

"How far is the hotel?" someone calls from behind me in the dark bus.

"Five miles, that's what Gui Lan said before we left," says another voice.

The bus chugs along at a speed somewhere between .25 and .30 miles per hour. At this rate, I calculate the five mile journey will take a little more than three hours. My forecast is revised pessimistically when we attempt to drive over a speed bump and actually roll *backwards*. I want to laugh to prevent myself from crying; only I'm too exhausted to laugh.

"I hope you're filming this Fred," Tom says.

I don't even know where the camera is at this point, and any ability I have to move a muscle is spent breathing, digesting food, or performing any of the several other involuntary bodily functions keeping me alive.

The bus backfires and chugs and never reaches a speed of more than four or five miles an hour. On several occasions, pedestrians bicycle pass our windows and gaze curiously at the overstuffed contents of our bus as they cruise by. At any moment, I expect Alan Funt to appear from under a peasant hat and scream, "Smile, you're on Candid Camera!" With a mix of disbelief and exhaustion, my mind eventually goes blank.

The five-mile journey takes forty-five minutes, with *no* traffic, and at long last our four-wheeled scrap heap comes to a tired halt in front of our hotel. The only thing missing from the absurd ride is a simultaneous flattening of all four tires and a series of staccato backfires followed by a shrill hiss as we come to a stop.

After a late check-in, we disperse to our rooms and find it adequate: two beds, a TV, and a bathroom. The bathroom is cramped, the mattresses are saggy, and the most intriguing thing on television is a ping-pong match. And none of it matters. The following day we will leave China. The mere thought of our flight home makes my stomach tickle.

* * *

The following morning, after a mostly uninterrupted sleep, we have a hearty buffet breakfast (with a return visit from Mr. Bacon), followed by a short visit to the hotel's pool area. We play with Lila on a swing set and prance about the sandbox. Her disposition has taken a full 180 degree turn during our short tenure as a family. She still prefers Mommy most of the time and the sad memories of her lost foster family still haunt her at various intervals throughout the day. Often times, her eyes become distant as though she is stuck in a confused memory from her past. But the moments tend to be fleeting and ultimately we have made great progress. Babe is wonderful. The unexpected by-product of our visit to China is my freshly discovered level of admiration for her. She rocks, carries, holds, hugs, kisses, and plays with Lila virtually every waking second.

A few hours later, we are packed and ready. We meet the others in the lobby. To our delight, we watch a large bus pull up to the doors adjacent to the hotel lobby. We have officially been upgraded and won't need to endure another rumble in our broken down—and claustrophobic—jalopy. We arrive at the airport and pass through customs without incident.

It seems like years ago we landed in China, fresh and eager for the unknown possibilities of parenthood, anxious and excited to finally see, hold, and interact with Lila. Just two weeks later, Babe and I are both exhausted, emotionally spent, mentally incapable of more than one simple thought at a time, and filled with dread for the upcoming flight.

As my mind struggles with the mix of elation and dread, Babe and I leave behind our odyssey—and Lila, the only place she's ever known—and walk through the transport tube from the airport terminal onto the plane that will carry us home.

So long China. It's been a little slice of Heaven.

Chapter 9
THE THOUSAND MILE JOURNEY ENDS

May 19, 2004. The plane is filled to capacity, not a good thing as Babe and I decided not to purchase an additional ticket for Lila when we booked the flight months ago. How difficult would it be, we reasoned at the time, to keep a little baby on our lap, taking turns bouncing her cheerfully on our knee as we play Pat-A-Cake to pass the time. I suppose we can't be faulted for lack of insight. The only person who raised any objections about no getting the extra seat was my mother, who cautioned me months ago how heavy a baby becomes when held for hours. Having given birth to five children between June 1958 and November 1963, Mom was somewhat of an expert in these matters.

As we drag ourselves wearily onto the plane to begin the last leg of our thousand mile journey, I am a changed person from the one who stepped foot on China soil for the first time two weeks ago. The changes are rooted deep in my character and I find them confusing and weighty. The most obvious of my life's changes is cradled in Babe's arms; a human being with tiny hands, beautiful eyes, and a gigantic legacy. The only thing more overwhelming than Lila's past is her enormous spirit; indomitable, strong-willed, and (suddenly, temporarily) shaken.

The flight, which was booked to capacity months ago, miraculously yields one no-show: the seat directly between me and Babe! Every other seat is warmly covered by a passenger's fanny. By default, Lila has her own seat and Mommy and Daddy have collectively lightened their loads by about nineteen pounds. I attribute the not-so-little-miracle of the empty seat to my mother's faithful prayers.

With two flights already under her belt, Lila is rapidly—albeit unwillingly—approaching frequent flyer status. The first flight was uneventful; the other a three-hour torture fest. With a half-day flight in front of us, I feel more dread than a waiting-room full of patients at a dentist office. We strap in, and the residual effect of two weeks of Chinese food has taken its toll. I take a deep breath and with some difficulty manage to secure my seatbelt. A few minutes later, we are airborne.

The take-off is uneventful, with Lila content to chomp on her butter cookies and explore the unfamiliar objects of her surroundings: magazines, food tray, seat belts, and arm rests. When she gets restless, bored, or worse, Babe or I hold her, rock her, or walk up and down the aisles of the plane. The seconds drip by like hours, the hours like days; our wits dulled by the ordeal of our trip, our minds weary from sleep deprivation. I glance at my watch dozens of times in the first few hours alone, always disappointed time seems to be advancing so slowly. Time's funny that way; dripping when I'm filled with impatience and flying by when I'm having fun.

We do all we can to keep Lila amused: the fake-sneeze-and-falling-cap routine, books, toys, and funny faces. For the most part, she is well behaved, though extremely fidgety. Babe uses Air China pillows and blankets to convert Lila's chair into a makeshift bed. Occasionally Lila nods off for a nap. The few minutes Lila sleeps are heavenly—and usually of short duration.

To complicate the process of getting Lila to sleep, four Chinese adults in the seats directly behind us are raucously engaged in a game of cards. In general, card games are not typically categorized as "contact sports." But the racket they generate, with intermittent screams of delight mixed with smashes on the back of our seats, not only seems like a scaled-down version of rugby, but threatens the cherished and much needed sleep our daughter has fallen into. I resist confrontation as long as possible and reason—quite incorrectly—the card game will eventually end. To my dismay, the noise level gradually increases.

At one point, all four scream simultaneously and I receive a hard shove from the back of my seat's headrest, inspiring two distinct and non-negotiable words in my mind: *that's it.*

I unbuckle my seatbelt, rise slowly from my seat, and turn to face the suddenly petrified—and eerily silent—faces of the participants of the card game. The freeze frame I stare at could be used with great effect as a promotional poster for a horror movie.

"My daughter is trying to sleep. I need you to keep it down," I announce resolutely.

In the movie version of my short speech Arnold Schwarzenegger would deliver the line in the deadpan manner of his Terminator character.

It is neither an appeal nor an ultimatum, just a desperate statement of fact. My tone and fractured face can be easily interpreted in any language. A male Chinese flight attendant overhears my comments and makes a quick assessment. He appears in the aisle immediately after my brief announcement and offers some additional comments—in Chinese—to the card players. I don't understand a word he says, but interpret it to be: *Godzilla is angry; game over.*

I hear nothing more from these four, with the exception of drink orders. Mission accomplished.

* * *

At one point, as Lila fusses and Babe is on the verge of falling asleep, I pick Lila up and transport her to the rear of the plane where I join Danny and his daughter Cecily. Lila rests on my shoulder as I rock her gently to sleep.

"I'm so tired," Danny whispers.

"I've never been this tired in my life," I say. "Just think, only ten more hours we'll be home."

He shakes his head as we both contemplate the lifestyle changes that await us in New York.

The physical demands of rocking and carrying a baby are far more strenuous than I ever expected. Lila's first choice is always Mommy, so Babe is doing far more than I am. During our odyssey, I have discovered an appreciation for the physical demands of mothers everywhere. How did my mother manage with five babies born in little more than six years? For my entire life, I've casually observed women half my size toting babies through malls, amusement parks, along beaches; just about everywhere. I never gave it a second thought. Within days of having Lila, my sense of awe for mothers worldwide has gone from zero to infinity and beyond (to borrow a phrase).

After a short nap, Lila awakens and begins crying. I hastily ramble to my seat to find Babe in deep sleep. As I cautiously slip past her to my seat, I unintentionally nudge her and her eyelids pop open. Having been deprived of sleep for more than a week, her waking state is one of shock and her eyes fill with peril: Where am I? What day is it? Where's Lila? She sits up quickly and regains her temporary loss of senses and says, almost apologetically, "Oh my gosh, I fell sound asleep."

Gee, I wonder why.

I glance at my watch every ten minutes. I curse it as though somehow the watch is somehow to blame that more time hasn't elapsed since my last check. I quell the impatience in any way I can think of: eat a snack, read for a few minutes, pray for the baby to sleep, get up and walk around, whatever distraction that comes to mind. I feel like a caged inmate.

Danny and Karen are seated across the aisle from us with Emily and their baby Cecily, who cries loudly for extended periods of time. Sympathy from fellow passengers is virtually non-existent, except from fellow adopters.

* * *

Whereas the flight to China lasted nearly fourteen hours, the return flight is accomplished in little more than twelve. I'm surprised, therefore, when the seemingly premature announcement is broadcast over the public address system: "Ladies and gentlemen, we are beginning our descent into New York's JFK Airport."

We left Beijing at approximately 12:45 p.m. on Wednesday and we are about to land in the United States at....12:55 p.m. on Wednesday! As I contemplate that oddity of world travel, I conclude this plane ride has, by quite a margin, been the longest ten minutes of my life.

As the plane's wheels touch down and screech noisily atop the runway of JFK International Airport on May 19, 2004, I grab Babe's hand and squeeze it tightly. A flood of tears escape my eyes and streak down my face and I turn away from Babe and Lila to gather my composure.

We are home at last.

We deboard and we can't wait to see Babe's family and introduce them to Lila. Our anticipation of this meeting results in the surge of energy we need. Babe carries Lila and a carry-on bag and I lug the rest: baby carriage, camera bag, assortment of toys, books, and gifts.

We shuffle through the transport tube from the plane to the terminal and I feel like an astronaut who just returned to Earth after a three month trip to the moon.

As we near the turnstiles, dozens of people stand in line awaiting their chance to get through Customs. We eventually reach the front of the line and find ourselves face to face with a lazy-eyed female official who is lethargically slouched forward on her stool, seemingly bored to tears by the flood of bedraggled, triumphant families anxious to reach the finish line. The disinterested frown pasted on her puss rivals that of a church-goer suffering through a 40-minute homily. She ineffectually requests our IDs and paperwork then scrutinizes it. Suddenly her bored expression morphs into a painful grimace—as though she just bit into a piece of Whitman's chocolate and discovered it was filled with anchovy paste.

"This paperwork is wrong," she announces matter of factly.

"What do you mean?" I ask.

She points at two documents with conflicting information on Lila's identity. "The paperwork doesn't match."

With one hand, she extends the paperwork back in my direction. With the other hand, she points to a security office to the side of the turnstiles. She never looks in my direction, opting instead to direct her disinterested gaze toward the rear of the line as she says ineffectually, "Take your paperwork over there and someone will assist you."

My shoulders slump as if someone just informed me that my house had been repossessed. "These are the papers we received in China," I plead.

She refuses to glance my way as she repeats robotically, "Someone will assist you in that office."

I'm frozen and staring at her stupidly and angrily; speechless with frustration when she finally looks my way and our eyes meet for the first time. She celebrates our exchange by calling out in a throaty baritone, "Next!"

Welcome to New York

I step helplessly aside to allow the group behind me to step up and I'm fighting mightily to remain calm. The other couples breeze through customs without incident and wait for us beyond the security bars. A major mood swing has arrived.

"Go ahead to baggage claim. There's something wrong with our paperwork," I say to the others through the security bars. As the words leave my mouth I feel I've just announced my resignation to a meeting of dear co-workers.

Lila is indifferent to our plight and overwhelmed by the frantic activity of the airport. We stride to the small office and enter. The office, a trailer-sized police precinct, consists of a service desk and waiting area. The desk sergeant, a short obese woman with a small beady eyes and a frightening scowl pasted to her mug like cheap make-up, never glances up as we enter and take a seat in one of the five chairs bolted to the floor to the right of the entrance door. As we wait, she reads a document on her desk, which I instinctively assume is a menu from the local Chinese take-out restaurant.

Several minutes later, she looks up and makes an inaudible comment to the other uniformed officer behind the desk, who busies herself on a computer. She glances our way briefly, winces, and makes an expression of disgust to indicate the mere thought of dealing with us is causing her stabs of pain.

"Be with you in a minute," dribbles out of her mouth.

Her peevishness seems to cling to her like a sweaty t-shirt. And what's worse, she seems perfectly content to carry herself in such a fashion. Eventually, she puts her paper down, straightens up her posture to prepare for duty, and peers over her bifocals in my direction as she nods her head once in my direction to signal: and *you* losers, what the hell do *you* want?

I rise from my chair and approach gingerly, braced for a fight, determined to get through this and somehow remain calm and respectful. My Irish temper, however, is slowly rolling to a boil.

"Good afternoon. When we tried to get through Customs, we were told there's something wrong with the paperwork," I say respectfully as though announcing my desire to exchange an unwanted gift for another item in the store. "This is the same paperwork we got through China customs with and I don't quite understand what the problem is."

She carefully reads our documents and asks fiercely, "Is your daughter named Sophia?"

That's Kitty and Rob's daughter, I think to myself. "No, that's the name of another baby we were with in China. In fact, our daughter has the same birth date as Sophia."

163

"That's what happened, they flip-flopped the two documents," she says.
Then how did Kitty and Rob get through Customs?

To my relief and delight, the officer merely shakes her head as if to say:
Boy, those Chinese people are always screwing things up. She grabs a
stamp and stabs an official seal loudly onto several pages of the document.

"You're good to go. Take this back to the line," she says and points in the
direction we came from. Her eyes avert mine, apparently a prerequisite for
employment at this miserable place. Although I was sure this little episode
could have been avoided altogether, I am nonetheless grateful that the delay
had only cost us a few minutes.

"Thank you," I manage through tight lips. And we're off.

* * *

We catch up to the others, who have unanimously agreed to wait for us
near the baggage claim area. In our absence, they grabbed our luggage from
the conveyer belt and loaded it onto a push cart. It was the latest in a long
line of generous deeds our group did for one another on this long journey. We
are a family, now and forever more.

Good-byes are bittersweet. I hug each of them and vow to stay in touch
as I wish them well. I will never forget them.

We walk triumphantly from the baggage claim toward the waiting area.
I am tempted to bend down and kiss the ground.

As we walk, my eyes and ears are assaulted by smiling American faces,
laughter, and occasional shrieks of joy. We scan the landscape of expectant
faces, blended together into one jubilant blur. Eventually, Babe spots her
family and I power up the video camera to film the reunion. Predictably, Lila
becomes overwhelmed and frightened. She is dazzled by the flood of new
faces, all smiling as they gawk to get a closer look at the new princess of the
family. Lila assumes her favorite position, her head buried in Babe's bosom
with an occasional sideways glance toward her new family members. I lag
behind intentionally as I videotape the family reunion from several feet away
before I rejoin my family.

Shortly thereafter, we exit the airport. To our surprise and delight, we are
led to a white, stretch limousine. I am barely able to express my elation, with
my legs rubbery, my mind spent, and my head filled with the cobwebs of

sleeplessness from a half-day flight. As I take my seat at the rear of the limo, my brother-in-law Ben extends a cold Heineken in my direction. I feel as though an Olympics official just handed me the gold medal. I lustily devour the contents in two sips, separated by a belch that registers on the Richter Scale.

As we inch our way home through the misty rain and rush-hour traffic of the Southern State Parkway, my body eases comfortably into a temporary state of relaxation as the question and answer period begins. The one theme that returns to my mind over and over is exhaustion.

"More than anything else, I'm exhausted," I admit to my in-laws. "Someone ought to invent a word for this type of exhaustion—it's beyond anything I've ever felt. I never cried so much in a two-week period in my life."

The stories flow in concert with the Heinekens. I drink four in the first half of our sixty-mile journey home as I swallow large gulps between stories. I savor every sip as if I just stumbled upon the elixir of life.

We stop once, to pee in the woods off the shoulder of the parkway. Lila is asleep and thankfully remains that way for the rest of our ride. We reach our home town of Bellport and I feel as though I have just returned from a war, as if Bellport had been frozen on the day we left for China and has now begun a lengthy thaw for our return. As we travel down our street, the limo driver noisily blares his horn in the tune of *Here Comes The Bride* over and over.

The rain has stopped and the clouds have yielded to a blue sky, bathing our house in the warmth of the late afternoon sun. As we pull to the curb in front of our house, I notice a huge banner: Welcome Home Lila, Babe, and Freddie. Decorations are draped everywhere: streamers, balloons, and a big stork poster with the words "It's a Girl." Between the limo ride and the decorations, I am overwhelmed with emotion and gratitude toward Babe's family.

We exit the limo and I grab the video camera to record the momentous occasion when Babe carries Lila into the house for the first time. Someone opens the door and our dog Daisy scurries frantically outside and begins a delirious sniff and seek routine. I'm hit with a wave of temporary compassion for Daisy; she has no way of knowing her days as princess are officially over. I pat her briefly then videotape as Babe carries Lila through the front doors.

The few tears I hadn't yet cried escape my eyes and roll down my cheeks.

Once inside, we are treated to a buffet of food: sandwiches, chips, cake, soda, and beer. It is a tradition in Nikki's family that homemade chicken soup is prepared for the mother of the newborn baby upon her return from the hospital. Babe had skipped the labor and the first fourteen months of parenting Lila, but the chicken soup tradition continues all the same. Babe gets emotional as she gobbles up Nikki's homemade soup; the same soup Babe once feared she might never taste.

The house is filled with noise and confusion, causing Lila to wake up. Eventually, Babe carries her to her bedroom and gets her into her pajamas and then into the crib. From the kitchen, we watch Babe on the little monitor as it relays the signal from Lila's bedroom.

After an hour of socializing with Babe's relatives in our big kitchen, the multiple conversations in the room—and the residual effects of six beers on my tired mind—cause me to feel dizzy. I am overcome with an even deeper exhaustion than before. I motion with my head to get Babe into the adjoining room and huddle with her.

"I have an appraisal scheduled in Long Island City tomorrow morning. I have to get to bed. I can't keep my eyes open," I say apologetically.

"Should I ask everyone to leave?" she asks.

"No," I say firmly. "Let them stay as long as they want." I kiss Babe and go upstairs.

We have returned triumphantly from China. Lila Rose has come home at last. Before I can contemplate another second of our lives together, before I can look into the future to hope, plan, dream of our first Christmas, I need to do one thing more than anything else. I crawl into my familiar bed, in my suddenly transformed home, close my eyes, and with nothing left to give my wife or my baby, I fall into the deepest sleep I have ever experienced.

ACT III-
THE GIFT

Chapter 10
POST-ADOPTION BLUES SYNDROME

We have Lila, we're safely home from China, the painful years of infertility are a distant memory, our hearts are filled to overflowing, and now everything is right with the world. Right?

Well, not exactly.

In the first few weeks of our return to the daily grind of life, both Babe and I suffer a lethal dose of post-adoption blues syndrome. The euphoria has evaporated. Jet lag and exhaustion have turned my legs into lead weights and robbed me of a sizable portion of my sanity. And Lila's nightly crying fits ensure sleep deprivation will be a constant battle for our wits. The feel-good moments are nowhere in sight.

We've clearly overlooked one key aspect of the adoption process. Our adoption of Lila is official. But Lila has not yet adopted us. That day will come; maybe soon—maybe not. Every baby is different. A new variation of patience will be needed to get to through this initial phase of settling in.

On the first morning home, I awake to a room filled with darkness to Lila's loud cries. In my waking state, I can't decipher whether it's morning or night. The minute-to-minute challenges of our new life together have begun. As with many other aspects of this process, the adjustments are more difficult than expected.

I leave in the morning to drive to Long Island City and my legs are rubbery, my head filled with cobwebs. I haven't thought about work for two weeks and now that it's upon me I have no interest. But I'm self-employed; I don't have the luxury of two weeks paid vacation. It's time to get busy.

Traffic is brutal and an hour on the road is all it takes to lasso me back into the rat race. I get to Long Island City and there's not a parking spot to be found. I circle the block in the industrial park of the building I'm scheduled to appraise and eventually settle for a curbside space a few blocks away. I power walk to the property, inspect the interior of the building, go over some paperwork with the owner, and I'm on my way. I don't feel well.

I get back to where I parked my car and—no car. I look around stupidly as the blood drains from my face and visions of a robbery in broad daylight invade my mind.

Four hours later, I've cancelled all my credit cards (wallet was in the car), reported the stolen car to the local police precinct, found out the car wasn't stolen (towed by NY City's finest), hitch-hiked a ride to the impound beneath the Brooklyn-Queens Expressway, and waited in line to pay both the towing fee and $150 fine to retrieve my car. A half-day's work is down the drain. And with the car back in my possession, I have to rejoin a traffic jam and make my way back to my suddenly unfamiliar home and a life turned upside down by a baby that doesn't like me. And just think: I get to do this all over again tomorrow—less the car towing.

There's a silver lining here somewhere...

* * *

Lila's sleeping habits don't improve. She never sleeps more than a few hours at a time. As a result, both Babe and I spend the first few months of our new life in a perpetual state of sleep deprivation.

Babe is virtually incapacitated as Lila clings to her morning, noon, and night. Housework is pushed to the back burner, meal preparation becomes a constant struggle, and the quality time spent with our dog Daisy is non-existent. In fact, Daisy is more nuisance than dog. She interferes with playtime, constantly sticks her snout into Lila's food, and reverts to old habits of peeing on the floor. This side-show is soon enhanced with pooping and puking. Our love for both Lila and Daisy is unconditional, but the terms of endearment for Daisy have, quite simply, changed.

I continue to work long hours in my two businesses as real estate appraiser and videographer. The two jobs require the one thing I don't have: time. Work is the easy part of the day. When I come home to join Babe for the tasks of parenting, the difficult part of the day begins.

On Friday of our first week home, I steer my car into the driveway of our suddenly unfamiliar home. This task would normally inspire an enticing anticipation of the weekend; relief from work and thoughts of stress-relieving cocktails or a night out at one of our favorite restaurants. For the time being, Friday is just another day. As I pull to a stop inside my garage, dread overtakes me.

Babe's mother Dorothy is a Godsend in the first few weeks. She visits frequently and provides Babe with much needed support. At the same time, she is able to bond with Lila and gradually Lila develops a sense of comfort around her.

One day, Dorothy grabs Lila's attention by placing a silly hat on her head and singing, "I'm Popeye the Sailor man—beep beep!"

Every time she sings "beep beep" Lila laughs giddily. Dorothy repeats her performance over and over with similar results. It quickly earns her the nickname "Grandma Beep-beep." In order to be equitable with the nicknames, we dub my mother "Grandma Amen" as she is most well known for her devout and faithful service to God and the church. Her prayers were felt throughout the adoption process, particularly when we found the only empty seat in our packed flight home was the one in our aisle.

* * *

I'm listening to a Randy Newman CD one night as I work in my office while Babe gives Lila her bath. As the song *Memo to My Son* cascades over the stereo speakers, I think: *what a perfect song from a parent to a baby.* I stop working and bring the portable CD player upstairs to play the song for Babe.

As I climb the stairs I hear Lila's hysterical laugh floating through the closed door of the bathroom. When I open the door, I see her smiling and playing with her toys in the tub, covered with soap suds. When I first envisioned Lila's baths, this is precisely the scene I had in mind.

"She's come a million miles from the baths in Nanning," I say warmly. My announcement startles both Babe and Lila, who were both pre-occupied in their tender Hallmark moment.

Babe turns to me, smiles, and says through an astonished grin, "Do you believe it? I can't get her out of the tub."

I bend down to play and Lila swats at the soapy water and unintentionally splashes me in the face. Shock registers on my face as I wipe soapy water from my eye. Lila stops laughing and freezes, her face briefly turned serious. I smile and then Lila smiles, followed by laughter, and another splash.

"I have a song I want you to listen to," I say to Babe.

"Which one?"

"It's a Randy Newman song. It's called *A Memo to My Son*."

I select the appropriate track, press PLAY on the CD player, and the song begins—piano notes followed by the first few lyrics: *What have you done to the mirror? What have you done to the floor? Can't I go no place without you? Can't I leave you alone any more? Can't I leave you alone any more?*

Babe instantly begins to cry—more intensely than I expected she would. I hug her and Lila doesn't quite understand what's just happened.

* * *

Lila's speech comes along quickly. She learns to say "dada" and "mama" and also picks up some short phrases. One day, we sit at the dining room table and eat dinner as Daisy approaches to gluttonously reconnoiter food scraps from the floor. Lila turns to Daisy and shouts, "Lie down!"

Babe and I laugh long and hard. Seeing our reaction, Lila repeats her newly learned phrase over and over then tosses her head back in hearty laughter as she mimics me. It's hilarious.

Eating is another story altogether. Lila continues to exhibit poor eating habits. She never seems hungry and habitually resists our attempts to feed her. As a result, she is in the lower percentile of the weight range for a baby of similar age. When we got Lila in China, she weighed 19 pounds. By the time of her first visit to the pediatrician she has lost nearly 2 pounds.

With the first visit to the pediatrician scheduled, Babe asks, "Do you have time to go with us?"

"I really don't," I say apologetically. "I have two properties to inspect in the Hamptons."

Babe is disappointed but, as always, she understands.

In hindsight, if I had one decision to make over again in the adoption process it would be my decision to put work ahead of that first visit to the pediatrician.

Babe arrives at the doctor after a drive of nearly an hour. Lila fusses and cries as the doctor busily checks her ears, eyes, and heartbeat, reminding Babe of Lila's physical exam in Guangzhou. After the weigh-in, the doctor offers his chilling opinion.

"Your daughter is not thriving," he says somberly.

"What do you mean?" Babe asks through tears.

"I mean her survival is in danger."

The news causes Babe an unhealthy dose of guilt and anguish. Shortly thereafter, the doctor and nurses strap Lila's arms to her sides and administer a series of shots. The screams emitted from Lila are so terrifying they sound inhuman, as Babe looks on in helpless horror.

After she endures the monumental devastation of the doctor visit, Babe has to fight both tears and exhaustion on her drive home in rush hour traffic. Her occasional glances in the rear view mirror reveal a stressed and nearly passed out Lila as she sits exhausted in the rear baby seat. Her tiny eyelids fight to stay open, her energy and passion for life drained by the steady flow of unnerving, unfamiliar, and unceasing changes in her young life.

I get home before Babe and when she arrives, her facial expression tells the whole story: she is devastated. Her face is etched with emotional pain as though she just witnessed her entire family being blindfolded and executed. She sobs long and deep for minutes, then on and off for nearly two hours as she explains what a horrible experience she endured. At times, she hyperventilates through tears while she fights to remain composed for Lila's sake. Words of comfort elude me. I feel sadness for Babe and Lila—and shame that I placed career in front of this important doctor visit.

* * *

It's August 15, 2004, the day of Lila's baptism. When I was baptized more than forty-four years ago my mother was not allowed to be at the church due to an inexplicable Catholic Church rule. The mother was supposed to stay home and "rest"; which means she was cooking. The father was supposed to stay home and help; which means he was resting. Many years later—as she recalled the baptism—Mom admitted to being inconsolably sad that she couldn't be at the church to witness the baptism of her own child.

By the time of Lila's baptism, however, a new day has dawned in the Catholic Church; baptisms have blossomed into a huge event for which the parents are very much involved. My mom, dad, and siblings are due for a visit from New England and I'm anxious and emotional about introducing them to Lila. The introduction I've rehearsed in my mind about a hundred times is upon me.

The day will start at the church, after which we plan to celebrate with a catered lunch in our back yard. We expect about 100 guests, including all the couples we traveled to China with.

Early on the morning of the baptism, I peer anxiously through the front window of my house and watch my parents pull up to the curb along with my sisters Jeanne, Lorraine, and Alison, and my brother Tommy and his three boys Sean, Keith, and Bobby. I take some deep breaths to suppress my emotions.

With Lila cradled cozily in her right arm, Babe walks to the front door and greets everyone cordially as I stand back and wait for everyone to filter past. This event I dreamed about so many times turns into merely another opportunity for Lila to become shy and frightened by new faces. She refuses kisses and shows a casual indifference—which could easily be interpreted as a modest disgust—toward all her new relatives.

I hope my disappointment doesn't register as I say, "Well, that's pretty much how she reacted to me. Hi everyone."

After a brief stay and dozens of wary glances from Lila, they leave to get breakfast.

"I'll see you at the church," I say and wave bye. When I close the door, my disappointment registers. Lila stares at me defiantly. What can I say? She's only a baby and she has no clue how special and dear these relatives are. How could she? To Lila, they're just another threat to grab her and drag her unwittingly to a hotel room as Babe and I had. Distrust—however temporary—clings to her personality like a Band-Aid.

An hour later, as the setup crew hurriedly sets up the tent, seats, and barbecue pit in my back yard, I hear the doorbell. It's my Uncle Jackie and Aunt Denise, who've stopped by to see Lila.

"How ah ya?" Jackie says in his thick Boston accent, as he and Denise enter the foyer.

We exchange small talk and I ask about the ferry ride. Our conversation is suddenly interrupted as I hear Babe's voice boom from upstairs, "Hon, can you come up here for a minute?"

"Excuse me a second," I say and sprint up the stairs.

As I scurry toward Lila's room, my mind is pre-occupied with dozens of things at once: my family, the caterer, the church, and so on. My mind races until I reach Lila's room. As I enter and see Lila in her white dress and shoes, however, every other thought evaporates. Lila has been transformed into a little angel. I drop to one knee and smile to hide my tears. Babe makes no such attempt and we hold hands as we admire our beautiful Lila, just minutes before the Holy Spirit is called upon to make things official.

"She's a little angel," I say, stating the obvious.

Babe wipes a tear from her eye. "Isn't she beautiful?" she says.

"She's come so far." I stare at her in admiration. "We all have," Babe says. Seconds later, we gather for a group hug: the warmest hug I've ever experienced.

The baptism is held at St. Joseph the Worker Church in East Patchogue, the same church where Babe and I exchanged marriage vows twelve years earlier. Lila cries like crazy when the water is poured on her head. No surprise there.

After the ceremony, we entertain the throng of guests, family, neighbors, and Lila's China cousins. Round tables and folding chairs are placed throughout the rear yard, some resting coolly beneath the big tent. Several workers diligently prepare food as smoke rises from the sizable grill and music plays over the outdoor speakers, mixed with laughter and conversations filling the warm summer air. Coolers of cold water, soda, and beer are sprinkled throughout the yard. The keg of Budweiser rests in a tub of ice to the side of the deck and attracts the loitering presence of many of my beer-swilling friends.

Midway through the party, I set up a small karaoke machine amplifier on the deck and crank the audio loud enough to reach everyone.

"Excuse me," I say into the microphone. It takes several more excuse mes—and a symphony of shhhhs from others—to get everyone's attention. When everyone becomes quiet I begin my speech.

"I just want to thank everyone for coming today. I have a letter from Lila that she asked me to read," I explain as I unfold a single page to read from.

I had written the letter earlier in the week and got Babe's approval to read it to our guests.

"The letter is titled 'What I Know so Far' and I'm happy to read it on Lila's behalf," I say.

I look down at the typed letter and read aloud into the microphone, "My name is Lila. I am seventeen months old and so far I've lived in two countries, taken three plane rides, and I'm having a documentary of my life being produced by a famous local filmmaker."

Some mild applause mixes with a few laughs, as I continue.

"Because I'm so young and haven't been on the earth for too long, I don't know much. But, I *do* know a few things. So on this gathering of family, friends, and neighbors I'd like to tell you about the top ten things I know so far."

I glance to my left. Lila stands on a round, glass-surfaced table as she plays with the big umbrella that protrudes through the table's center hole and extends skyward beyond Lila's reach. Aunt Karen has both hands around Lila's waist to ensure her baptism day doesn't end in a trip to the emergency room.

"Number ten, I am very lucky. When I was in China, Daddy told me I had hit the parent lottery. I don't quite know what that means and besides Daddy stole that line from a friend of his. But I do know I'm lucky to have parents, relatives, and friends who love me and will love me forever."

Polite applause breaks out.

"Number nine: at thirty-six years old, when I'm allowed to start dating," I pause for some brief laughter, "my daddy will turn into something called a chaperone. This I know because Daddy tells me every day."

As I glance down at the page toward number eight, I brace myself. This one will be tough to read without causing deep emotion, so I'll need to reach deep for some resolve.

"Number eight: my Mommy is the best."

I have to stop as loud applause explodes from the guests. I look up and find Babe standing next to Nikki. Unlike me, she doesn't care for the limelight; but she smiles and enjoys the applause.

I continue, "From day one she was sweet, loving, and smart. She is my role model. I love Daddy too. He's kind of funny."

I pause and look over at Lila, who now stares at me curiously. I intentionally allow a frown to come to my face, and then continue reading, "Come to think of it: he's really funny."

I nod pleasingly and smile.

"And he's a great Daddy. He says that one day we'll dance to a song called *Daddy's Little Girl* at my wedding. Considering he won't allow dating until I'm 36, that's a good way off."

More laughter.

"Number seven: I should always appreciate what I have. Both Mommy and Daddy tell me that often. They also tell me I should show my appreciation. And so I thank all of you for taking time from your busy summer to share this special day with me and my family. I thank Nikki, Lance, Nicholas, and Lancie for all they did for me, picking me up in a limo at the airport, and throwing a shower for Mommy, and decorating our house for my arrival, and making chicken soup for Mommy. I'm told that's a ritual, which is a word I'll learn later. I thank Grandma Amen, Papa, and the rest of Daddy's side of the family for traveling so far to be with me. I thank Grandma Beep Beep, Grandpa, Ben, and Brianne for meeting me at the airport and for visiting all the time. And for all the rest of Mommy and Daddy's friends and family, I thank you for your gifts and cards and prayers. We will never forget your kindness and thoughtfulness."

Polite applause is sprinkled through the gathered crowd.

"Number six: the Red Sox will never win the World Series."

A loud and mixed reaction erupts from the gathered guests; applause from the Yankees fans, laughter from others, hearty boos from my New England relatives. It's a reaction I expected.

When the racket subsides, I continue, "During the summer, Daddy has repeated that sentence every time the Red Sox do anything wrong, which is often."

More laughter.

"Number five: there's no place like home. And though I was very sad and confused when I first got here, I can't think of any place on earth I'd rather be than here."

More applause.

"Number four: in my new home, there's way too many things to bump my head on. So far I've found seventy-eight. I hope that's it. But stay tuned."

A murmur of empathy ripples furtively among the parents in the crowd.

"Number three: whenever I have questions about things that happened to me in the past, I'll have what Daddy calls a 'virtual instant replay' because of the constant presence of the video camera."

"Number two- I should always remember the Golden Rule. That's what Mommy and Daddy tell me. I'm not quite sure what that means, but everything they've told me so far is pretty good, so I think I'll find out about this Golden Rule."

"Number one: God is good. He has a perfect plan for my life and today he welcomed me into His family. Way before Mommy and Daddy came to China to get me He was making plans to bring me to this earthly home. When I'm old enough to understand everything, I will thank God every day for that. In the meantime, I'll leave that up to Mommy and Daddy. Thank God for them and thank God for all of you. I hope you enjoy my party."

As I end the speech, I fold the piece of paper neatly and insert it in my shirt pocket. While the crowd applauds, I grab Lila, pick her up and place her atop my left shoulder. The applause briefly gets louder—and then dies off. Then the fuzzy little moment dissolves into reality. Hours later, the party is over. The following day my relatives and friends leave for their drive home.

And life goes on…

* * *

Lila's favorite movie becomes *Mary Poppins,* one of my favorite movies as a child. She especially loves the end when the cast sings *Let's Go Fly a Kite.* Babe takes one of Lila's hands and I take the other. In rhythm with the lyrics we swing Lila high in the air: *Let's* go fly a kite…and Lila squeals her giddy approval. She incessantly implores us to do it over and over as she grabs our hands and flashes a huge grin with her little teeth.

I hope one day her favorite movie will be *Lila Rose Comes Home at Last.* I haven't begun working on it but several ideas have accumulated in my mind and a now clawing desperately to get loose. One of those ideas—at Babe's request—is to use *At Last* in some sort of music montage, but to date

I haven't settled on the appropriate sequence of video.

As our first summer with Lila ends, my beloved Red Sox are positioned to qualify for the post-season. This will provide them ample opportunity to cruelly trample my expectant heart yet again. Their success or failure seems trivial this year. Somehow, Lila's presence in my life puts all other things in a different perspective. Nevertheless, I still follow them closely.

The Yankees, as always, are in the midst of things, and they finish in first place in the East Division for about the hundredth year in a row. The Sox are second fiddle, and they settle for the wild card. The playoffs will be difficult to watch, given Lila's propensity to wake up screaming every night several times.

Each night, Babe and I sit up late and watch the games while we endure Lila's crying fits. The Red Sox beat the Angels in the first round and then beat the Yankees in Game 7 at Yankees Stadium in the American League Championship Series and it's on to the World Series.

It's Game 4 of the Series and the Red Sox are within a game of their first World Series Championship since dinosaurs roamed the earth.

Early in the game, Babe gets Lila to sleep and joins me in the living room to watch the game. We place the monitor to the left of the television set so we can keep an eye on Lila as the game progresses.

A few hours later, the Sox are one out away and I am literally perched on the edge of my seat. And then, the moment I was certain I would never witness in my lifetime: Keith Foulke stabs Edgar Renteria's ground ball and flips underhand to first for the final out. The Red Sox have won their first World Series Championship since 1918. In one ecstatic moment, years of bitter Red Sox losses are washed away for millions of Red Sox fans. At long last, we can sprinkle our stories of misery and heartache with glorious recollections of the year we finally won it all.

At the precise moment the ball lands in the first baseman's mitt, Lila sits up, screams, then quickly lies back down on the bed. The timing of her waking is eerie—as if on cue.

Babe scampers upstairs to tend to Lila. Several minutes later, she rejoins me as I revel in the post-game interviews, award ceremonies, champagne-spraying, and highlights.

"Do you believe that?" I ask Babe when she returns.

"She sat up the second the game ended," Babe says with a face of astonishment. She continues, "What's going on now?"

"Interviews and post-game stuff," I tell Babe distractedly, as I wear out the batteries on the TV remote flipping the channels back and forth between Fox and ESPN.

At the very end of the Fox broadcast, play-by-play announcers Joe Buck and Tim McCarver offer their post-game commentary, after which a highlight reel—consisting of a series of music videos—is broadcast. The video footage begins with the divisional playoff series against Anaheim, followed by the American League Championship series against the New York Yankees. As the highlights are shown, short sections of appropriately suited songs provide the background audio.

After the highlights of the Yankees series, some highlights of the first three games of the World Series are shown, followed by a video clip that chills my spine: Red Sox catcher Jason Varitek running to the mound to embrace Keith Foulke after the final out is made in Game 4. As the footage is shown in slow motion, the accompanying song begins: Etta James' *At Last*!

I turn to Babe wearing a look of astonishment on my face as though someone on TV had just announced we were the winners of the Publisher's Clearinghouse.

I watch the highlights through tear-filled eyes; Lila, *At Last*, and my beloved Red Sox assembled miraculously in a moment I couldn't have conjured up in the most far-fetched fairy tale. There could not have been a more satisfying triumph over the futility and frustration I've endured as both a Red Sox fan and prospective parent.

"I will never forget this moment," I say to Babe. We hug for minutes thereafter.

* * *

I continue to keep the videotape handy for many of the magical moments: the holidays, the trips to the beach, and the unexpected, priceless moments like Lila's frequent recitals on her miniature piano. She bangs the keys loudly for several minutes and then stops, rises to her feet, and takes a bow like Liberace.

In the first half-year with Lila, I can't bring myself to work on the documentary; the special gift I will one day present to Lila. I want to edit the movie while the China trip is still fresh in mind, yet angst and stress chain me to survival mode. Besides, when I view the raw footage even for a brief moment, the emotional scars from China re-open and the feelings flood my soul like the enduring memories of a bitter romance.

Lila's first Halloween is uneventful. We dress her as Pebbles Flintstone and I dress as Fred (Flintstone, that is). Lila is unfazed. She becomes annoyed as we travel door to door in search of candy she doesn't seem to care given to her by neighbors she cares even less for. She seems confused why her Daddy walks around in bare feet.

Thanksgiving arrives quickly thereafter and we enjoy the usual feast, though relatively quiet by our standards. We typically spend the holiday with Babe's brother Lance and sister-in-law Nikki with their kids and other family and friends. But on Lila's first Thanksgiving, Lance and family travel to upstate New York to visit Nikki's sister Celeste. So our celebration is held at our house, with Grandma Beep beep, Uncle Ben and his fiancé Brianne. In many ways, it's easier for Lila to cope with a smaller number of relatives. As a result it is a quiet but nonetheless enjoyable holiday.

A major test comes shortly after Thanksgiving. Babe is invited to dinner by her friend Debbie. It has taken a lot of effort and experimentation, but Lila is finally to a point where she'll sit with me alone for an hour or more. The timing couldn't be better because Babe is in dire need of some adult conversation and a night out.

Babe leaves around 6:00. Lila and I wave bye from the garage as Babe drives off. Lila loves to play in the car. She pretends to drive and turns all the knobs. So before we go back into the house, I hoist her delicately into the driver's seat of our Honda Pilot and then sit in the passenger's seat. She stands up, her palms on the steering wheel when suddenly one of the hands slips and she lurches forward. Her forehead thumps the steering wheel. I catch her before she falls, but the damage is done.

Seconds later, as the shock and pain register on her face—and fear spreads quickly on mine—she mumbles, "Mom-my."

Paralysis grips me as Lila breaks into a loud crying fit. I pick her up and cradle her delicately against my chest, get her inside, and then go to the couch where I rock her and sing to her. She cries for the next hour straight. I'm not even tempted to call Babe's cell phone; Lila could cry for the next week and I will resist. This is one of those moments I'll just have to endure as best I can as I reassure myself things are going to get better. Eventually, as a throbbing headache takes aim at my sanity, Lila cries herself out and falls asleep.

Meanwhile, Babe sits distractedly through dinner afflicted with an unfortunate case of self-imposed guilt. When she returns, one glimpse at my face tells the whole story.

"What happened?" she asks, her face alarmed with panic.

"She banged her head on the steering wheel right after you left and cried for an hour," I admit sadly.

The sailing will become smoother, but nights like this leave an unfortunate hangover on our hopes—and an assurance that Babe's self-imposed guilt will continue.

* * *

We're outside church with Lila after Sunday mass when we run into a casual friend we haven't seen in a while.

"Who's this?" he smiles and points to Lila.

Lila casts "the look" in his direction and snuggles up to her favorite place near Mommy's breast (come to think of, one of my favorite places as well).

"This is Lila," I say, "She's our adopted daughter."

"Our *daughter*," Babe says, offering a subtle correction.

Babe's point, subtle as it is, carries a powerful message: Lila is our daughter—period. There is no need to qualify the description with "adopted" or any other disclaimer: biological, brown-eyed, or dark-haired. Imagine the look on people's faces if I said, "I'd like you to meet my non-biological, two-legged daughter Lila." From that moment on, I refer to Lila as our daughter. It's a simple yet important transition.

The fact Lila is not our biological child is completely lost in our everyday interaction. The love is unconditional. The commitment to love is not diluted by a lack of shared gene pools. I love and cherish Lila as my daughter and can't imagine having a greater love for a child; biological or otherwise.

In one of the workshops at New Beginnings, Cathy Dinowski warned us about the likelihood of ignorance and prejudice we should expect from some members of the general public. Perhaps because Babe's eyes are more Asian-looking than Lila's, and owing to the fact Babe and Lila bear some resemblance to one another, we haven't experienced any discernable prejudice.

One day, Babe and I discuss the baby girl of a friend of ours.

"Her baby looks more like the father than the mother," Babe says. Almost as an afterthought, she adds, "When people see me and Lila together, they *always* recognize me as the mother."

As Babe finishes her sentence, I gaze at her curiously, not sure if she is serious.

"Are you serious?" I ask.

"What do you mean?" she says, a bit taken aback.

I lean forward wearing one of those you-have-to-be-kidding-me smirks on my face and say, "Uh, this just in: you're not Lila's biological mother."

A look of astonishment overtakes Babe's face as though she just realized it was Christmas and she'd forgotten to buy presents.

"I can't believe I just said that," Babe says.

She has bonded with Lila so completely she momentarily lost sight of the fact Lila is not her biological child.

* * *

Lila's first Christmas approaches and she's more comfortable with us than ever. Her personality blossoms. One day in early December I arrive home from work and Lila screams, "Daddy!" and then runs into my arms. It's a moment I've seen in movies and TV shows, one that I've witnessed firsthand with other parents. Based on the rocky road Lila and I have stumbled across as daughter and father, however, it's a moment between us that often seemed unattainable. Our hug lasts several seconds.

Lila is wonderfully funny and imaginative and she has conjured up several imaginary playmates: Mimi, Candy, and Nobody, to name a few. Nightly conversations often digress into a variation of Abbott and Costello's *Who's on First*.

"So who'd you play with today, Lila?" I ask.

"Nobody."

"How come, didn't any of your friends come over?"

"Nobody did."

"I know. Why?"

"Because she wanted to."

"Who wanted to?"

"Nobody."

She often blames her bad behavior on any of these various figments of her imagination, like Flip Wilson declaring, "The Devil made me do it."

Though Lila's sleeping habits barely improve, she makes significant progress in virtually every other area. Her eating habits improve appreciably. Her ability to travel in the car, at one time an impossibility, becomes easier with more frequent trips—like the visits to see my family in New Hampshire.

But sleeping is, pardon the pun, a non-stop nightmare. Whether it's night terrors, bad memories of China, or just a vivid imagination, Lila wakes up in the middle of each night crying and screaming as if in deep pain. Ironically, one of Lila's nightly crying fits resulted in a life-changing purchase of an audio book.

It is a weeknight and Lila has woken up several times. Between each interruption, Babe and I manage to steal a half hour of sleep at a time—not exactly the type of restful slumber we need to rejuvenate. The fifth (or so) interruption awakens Babe and by the time she gets Lila back to sleep she finds it impossible to think about going back to bed. Frustrated, she quietly slips downstairs to the living room and flips on the television.

As Babe channel-surfs, repelled by the tawdry offerings of cable TV at 3:30 a.m., she eventually comes across a show featuring Pastor Joel Osteen. She stops her channel-surfing and focuses on Osteen's sermon in front of hundreds packed into his Lakewood congregation. An hour later, she's punching an 800-number on the phone to order the audio book titled *Your Best Life Now*. The messages contained on those five CDs will eventually transform our lives. Had Babe not been awoken in the middle of the night several times, she may well have missed the inspiration and opportunity to hear Osteen preach. Talk about a blessing in disguise.

* * *

Babe is unable to continue to work. When we left for China, she envisioned a scenario whereby she could work from home as a graphic artist and eventually return to the job in a full-time capacity. That scenario failed to transpire. Babe is busy with Lila virtually every waking hour and the night hours continue to be an endurance test. Her energy is sapped and any attempt to do work on her computer at night is futile. A full night's sleep becomes a distant memory of years gone by. Holding down a job at this point is just not in the cards.

With the loss of her job comes the loss of our health benefits. As a result, I reluctantly leave the private sector and my real estate appraisal business and take a supervisory job with the Suffolk County Division of Real Estate. The benefits of this civil service job are tremendous and Babe and I figure we can compensate for the cut in salary with the money we earn in the videography business. Nothing comes easy any more.

With Christmas upon us, we look forward to introducing Lila to all the wonders of the season: the decorations, toys, Santa Claus, crowded malls, and of course the nativity sets and her first introduction to the real reason we celebrate Christmas. We know Lila will understand little of it and will be overwhelmed by the flurry of activity, but we are excited nonetheless.

I also look forward to all the Christmas specials on television: *Rudolph, Frosty, Charlie Brown*, and my personal favorite *The Little Drummer Boy*. As a boy, I became inspired when the Little Drummer Boy used his one possession (a drum) to provide a gift for the newborn king. I always got goose bumps as the song ended:

I played my drum for him, pa-rump-a-pum-pum

I played my best for him, par-rump-a-pum-pum, rump-a-pum-pum, rump-a-pum-pum,

Then He smiled at me, pa-rump-a-pum-pum, me and my drum.

Little Drummer Boy remains one of my favorite Christmas carols—particularly the version sung by the Vienna Boys Choir (no disrespect intended to David Bowie and Bing Crosby).

During that first holiday season with Lila, I listen over and over to Joel Osteen's *Your Best Life Now* audio book as I drive to and from work; about a half-hour. I derive strength in the messages. I become inspired to take the focus off my own difficulties and re-direct my focus toward helping others and being thankful for my blessings. In addition, Osteen introduces me to a concept he calls "favor of God" and insists believers in God can expect preferential treatment as a result of being one of God's children. All believers should live with faith and expectancy that God supernaturally grants favor to all His followers. By living favor-minded, Osteen insists, believers realize more of the abundance God has planned for their lives.

Living favor-minded is a foreign concept to me, not something often preached about in the Catholic Church. Initially the concept strikes me as selfish. Eventually, however, I embrace the concept and attempt to put it into practical use—with some great results. There is one incident in particular where I felt God's favor in a big way, an affirmation from God that Babe and I were on the right path.

It is mid-December. The drastic changes in our careers have resulted in some serious cash flow issues. Despite our sudden financial difficulties, Babe and I need a night out. So we arrange to have Grandma Beep-Beep babysit for Lila and we visit the restaurant closest to our house, and one of our favorite restaurants at the time: Meritage Restaurant in Bellport.

Meritage is a beautifully decorated restaurant that offers an eclectic—and somewhat pricey—menu. We arrive on time and the restaurant is filled with patrons. Christmas wreaths, lights, and poinsettias add to the already ornate and tasteful décor. The restaurant buzzes noisily with laughter and loud conversation mixed with light instrumental holiday music floating from the speakers.

Our reservation is for 7:00 and we are seated right away. We decide to splurge and throw financial caution to the wind and order cocktails, appetizers, and expensive entrees, even a bottle of wine. During the meal, Babe and I discuss our financial situation in positive terms as we take stock of our lives and thank God for all we have.

"We'll find a way out of this," I say confidently, referring to the temporary financial hole we've dug. "We just need to keep trusting God and expecting His favor in our finances and every other aspect of our lives. And we need to be grateful for what we have right now; no room for self-pity, just gratitude."

"Remember when we kept wondering when He'd finally bring a baby to us?" Babe says.

"And now look, I can't imagine our lives without her."

"Me either," she says dreamily.

"We're going to be OK. Just keep expecting God's favor and miracles. Say it aloud every day: I have the favor of God. *All* things work for the good for those who believe."

It is a wonderful and much-needed evening out. Our loving discussion drowns the festive noise all around us and I feel all alone with Babe. It's the most intimacy we've enjoyed in a long time.

After dessert I politely wave to our waitress and make the universal "check" signal and shortly thereafter she visits our table and drops off the billfold. I don't care to look at the final tally as I expect it to be more than $200. I slip my credit card into the appropriate slot near the top of the billfold and then wave a second time to the waitress. She arrives wearing a puzzled look on her face.

"This is all set," I say and attempt to hand the billfold to her.

She flashes a mischievous grin and says, "I don't think you read your check," and then turns and walks away from our table.

My first thought is: *oh no, they don't take credit cards here any more.*

I cautiously open the billfold as if trying to prevent the springy snake from rocketing out of a box of trick candy. Once the billfold is open, I peer at our check, which reads: *Merry Christmas and thanks for your business over the years. Love, Keith.*

The entire meal—drinks, wine, and all—is on the house. It is the first and only time that ever happened to us at Meritage. I have to imagine Keith (co-owner) received a sudden inspiration to do something for us. In my head, I hear the triumphant voice of Joel Osteen: *that, my friends, is the favor of God at work.*

Babe and I exit the restaurant practically in tears. Everything we just spoke about at the dinner table has been soundly validated. And if that wasn't enough, God has one more trick up his sleevel.

We drive the short distance from the restaurant to our home and barely speak, both of us stunned at the fortunate turn of events. The radio is tuned to WALK-FM, which plays non-stop holiday music this time of year. Minutes after we leave the restaurant, I pull up the driveway of our house and bring the car to a stop. A second before I remove the ignition key, the car's speakers broadcast the first notes to a Christmas song.

"Brrrrrum, Brrrrrum, Brrrrrum"—the angelic voices of the Vienna Boys Choir singing *The Little Drummer Boy*. I glance at Babe and shake my head in disbelief as a pool of joyful tears forms in both eyes. Babe and I hug wordlessly for a long time and allow the wonderful Christmas carol an opportunity to wrap itself around us.

* * *

In preparation for Christmas, I take the video tapes from the China trip and assemble several clips into an edited three-minute "Preview of Coming Attraction" video of the soon-to-be-edited *Lila Rose Comes Home at Last*. I give the DVD to Babe as a stocking stuffer. When Lila watches the footage, her happy disposition abandons her and she turns melancholy and silent, her eyes fixed in one of those far away gazes that suggest she has unwittingly traveled back in time to China and the loving foster family she was ripped from. I haven't seen this gaze in months.

We decide we won't show the footage to her again for a long, long time.

On Christmas Eve, we introduce Lila to Santa Claus via Babe's Uncle Whitey and his well worn—and loosely fitting—Santa outfit. He drops by unexpectedly and Lila is overwhelmed. When she sees Santa, her first reaction is to scurry over to the Christmas tree, grab a cookie from the opened box that sits under the tree, and hand the cookie to Santa. Fortunately, I have the video camera at the ready and capture the priceless moment on tape.

Christmas morning, Babe carries Lila downstairs from her bedroom to the living room, where dozens of gifts have miraculously appeared overnight. Lila's eyes bulge wide—the same way mine did when I saw the food in the White Swan buffet. Our first Christmas with Lila is one that both Babe and I hold as the dearest in our twelve year marriage.

* * *

After the New Year and our annual trip to New Hampshire to see my family, the post-adoption blues have officially begun to recede. Our lives are turned upside down, but that's no different from any other parent. Whether adopted or biological, children change your life. Actually, children don't change your life; they *become* your life.

188

After the holiday season, I begin the journey to make Lila's movie. My solitary goal is to make the best movie I can, to give my whole heart and imagination to the process and produce a special gift for my little miracle, something she will cherish and pass down to future generations of our family.

My method of making movies involves several stages. I liken the process to a gourmet chef preparing a special feast. First, I view all the raw footage. This is akin to the chef taking inventory of the ingredients. Then I view the raw footage a second time as I record audio notes onto a hand-held tape recorder. This allows me to prepare the ingredients: chop, separate, and trim the fat. The final step of the initial stage of the movie–production involves transcribing my audio notes onto a detailed video clip log: finalizing the recipe and getting it down on paper.

Once the raw footage is viewed and logged, scenes begin to formulate on their own, as the various clips busily jostle for position in my subconscious mind, each begging to be recognized, like a classroom full of second-graders frantically waving their hands at the teacher because they know the right answer.

For Lila's movie, the viewing of the raw footage is more difficult than usual, for two reasons: (1) I had accumulated more than four hours of footage and had little time on my hands to view it, and (2) some of the footage is difficult to watch, particularly the first day we got Lila and a lot of the footage from the four or five days thereafter when Lila did little else except cry or appear traumatized. The ill feelings still assail me; I simply haven't recuperated sufficiently to watch the footage and assemble it into an edited movie. So the project stalls in January.

When I re-commence, I attack the next stage: song selection. I had previously decided on several songs (*Into the Mystic, Here Comes the Sun, At Last*), and after I view the footage I select several others. I play the songs over and over as I sit in my studio or drive around Long Island. I envision the edited video as I play affiliated songs on my car CD player. I use this technique frequently and find it helpful to crystallize the vision for the movie. Even when played at a low volume beneath a voiceover, music has a significant impact on movies. It can help drive the story, or create a mood, or accentuate a clip with a related song lyric. Good music converts movie-making problems into evocative solutions.

I had learned from my mistakes and, therefore, wisely decide not to set a deadline for completion of the movie. I will progress at whatever pace my schedule will permit. As originally planned, I will complete the movie in time for the one-year anniversary of our adoption day (May 10), a date commonly referred to by adoptive parents as Gotcha Day. I plan to invite the other couples we traveled to China with over to the house to view the movie. But the invitations will not be mailed until the movie is complete.

As I view the raw footage and record my preliminary notes, something strange happens: The movie begins to formulate scenes on its own. Ideas mysteriously pop into my head like Lottery balls in their wind-blown Plexiglas bin. As I drive, I'll hear a song on the radio and—WHAM—I'll suddenly recognize it as a perfect song for a section of my movie. Edited sections of the movie suddenly burst into my imagination. It's as if the edited movie is being communicated to me telepathically—or should I say supernaturally—one scene at a time.

In early March, Babe phones New Beginnings to let them know I'm editing the movie and to find out if they'd like a copy when I'm done. Justine from New Beginnings answers the phone and she and Babe speak for several minutes, during which time it gets suggested that perhaps the movie would appeal to an audience of prospective adoptive parents in a workshop-type setting. By the end of the phone conversation, tentative plans have been made to hold a fund-raiser to benefit The Tomorrow Plan (more on that later) in conjunction with the movie's premiere. Justine says she will begin advertising the event as soon as we have a date and place picked out. Just like that, in the span of five minutes, my future gift for Lila is a Big Event.

With sections of the movie occupying space in my creative subconscience, I write the script. With my notes from the raw footage in hand, I visit the local library on several occasions and get all my thoughts onto the page, including the voiceover narration, song selections, and special editing notes. I can't yet figure out how to effectively incorporate the song *At Last* into the movie. But I have eliminated one possibility from my mind. Originally, I considered using the song to accompany the footage of the day we got Lila, a montage of video played at half-speed. As I watch the footage of Adoption Day over and over, however, I decide to leave the raw footage in tact. The footage—and the anarchy of the affiliated audio—possesses honesty, courage, and deep emotion. To gloss over it with *At Last* would rob the story of its candor. It doesn't need nor deserve the Hollywood treatment. It has to be replayed just as it occurred, complete with crying, sadness, tears, emotion, and confusion.

With the script on paper, I settle in front of my computer to commence the last stage of the production: editing. The best ingredients have been selected and prepared, the recipe has been carefully written, and now it is time to prepare the video feast: the movie born to my heart the moment I decided to adopt; the movie I will use the best of my creative imagination for in order to produce a special gift for Lila; the movie that has suddenly sprung to life in ways I never intended or dreamed of; the movie inspired by God Himself.

I'm confident the editing will be completed within a few months. Inspired by the exciting prospect of reaching the finish line, I begin my search for a suitable venue to hold the Premiere of the movie I have yet to finish.

My instinct tells me: something special is happening here...

Chapter 11
THE PREMIERE OF "LILA ROSE COMES HOME AT LAST"

The adoption agency phones several times during the editing phase and I teasingly dangle enticing details of the movie. In the meantime, I contact the corporate office for the Farmingdale Multiplex to make arrangements to rent one of their auditoriums for a private showing of the movie.

I book the theater reservation by phone with the woman responsible for coordinating group events from the corporate office in Texas. After the August 4 date is secure, I ask "Would it be possible to speak to the projectionist prior to the event?"

"I would *strongly* suggest you meet with him," she says.

Her answer alarms me. It carries the same foreboding urgency as a leather-clad biker saying: *You have three seconds to step away from that Harley.*

She provides the cell phone number of the projectionist and then curtly rushes me off the phone.

In the weeks to follow, I complete the editing. It is a joyful yet difficult process that forces me to relive the stressful trip to China and the torturous years of infertility. After most editing sessions, I walk from my studio (above my garage) downstairs to the living room and see Lila. Her beautiful face and playful disposition rejuvenate me each time; her daily presence keeps me inspired and focused, mindful of how miraculously we have overcome our trauma.

I edit one section at a time and end up with ten short movies which I will eventually assemble as one project on my computer. Eleven weeks into the process, I complete the final section of the movie (the Credits) and then create one master file, stringing together each of the ten short movies. After the assemblage is successfully completed, I watch the entire movie from start to finish. As I view the movie in its entirety for the first time, I search for sections that might need of additional editing, explanation, or voiceover. I watch it by myself and by movie's end—as expected—a monster of emotion tramples me and I cry my eyes out.

In the aftermath, I sense there's something special about the movie. God brought a great story and a wonderful baby to me and Babe. At the same time, He blessed me with imagination and a passion to make movies. The combination of faith, passion, and imagination has resulted in a movie I'm sure will touch Lila's heart when she's old enough to watch it. I find it difficult to objectively judge my own work; but as I sit in my studio and wipe tears from my eyes after the first viewing, my instincts tell me the movie is unique. It evokes a range of emotions and presents the adoption story in an uncompromisingly honest way. Unlike other family movies I've produced, I feel Lila's movie could possibly be of interest to those outside the immediate circle of my family and friends.

When I show the movie to Babe, she too is moved to tears.

"That's the best movie you've ever done; it's wonderful," she sniffles as her crumpled and soiled Kleenex works overtime.

I'm tempted to dismiss her compliment as biased. But deep down I think it's good. The day after the viewing with Babe, I phone the adoption agency and bring Justine up to date.

"The theater is booked for Thursday August 4. We'll have use of it from seven to nine p.m.," I say.

"How's the movie?" she asks excitedly. From day one, she's been excited about the movie and I appreciate her enthusiasm.

"It's a little more than an hour long, and I really think you're going to like it," I say assuredly.

"Sound great Fred, we'll start advertising on our web site and sending invitations," she says.

The big night has begun to build steam.

* * *

I visit the Multiplex on two occasions prior to the event to meet with the projectionist, whose physique suggests he either runs marathons or is malnourished. In addition to his wiry frame, he wears a patchy beard, the type the owner decides to grow and then, for all intents and purposes, forgets about. The dark rims of his eyeglasses frame thick lenses, magnifying his piercing, intense eyes. In every way, his physical appearance tells me he is a technological genius.

Both meetings with the projectionist take place in the vast projection room of the multiplex. Based on portrayals from movies and TV shows I had previously viewed, I imagined the projectionist area as a small booth; a seedy place of solitary confinement and lustful yearnings—like the one in *Cinema Paradiso*. I am amazed to find out how wrong I am.

The projection room is a large open room with a low ceiling, concrete floor, and concrete block walls. The room is about twenty-five feet wide by several hundred feet deep, essentially a catwalk for the multiplex, with several large projectors in place. Near each projection station, the movie title and playing times are posted on a white sheet of paper. The projectors are much larger than anything I've ever seen, about the size of a commercial furnace, next to huge computers the size of a foot locker that provide professional audio for the auditorium. Movie reels are placed flat atop large spools, with the film extending from the reel to the projector.

On our first meeting, the projectionist provides a full tour. Perhaps his ulterior motive is to impress me with his technical knowledge. It works. As I gawk enviously at the equipment, I instantly realize this is a scene I'll replay in my mind forever.

Later, we turn our attention to my movie. He intensely sizes up my digital playback machine and spouts, "Nice unit."

I feel like a young boy whose tricycle has just been complimented by Lance Armstrong.

He hooks up my machine to his state of the art projector and minutes later the projector's lamp has warmed sufficiently for a test run. I press the PLAY button and the movie begins. Unfortunately, the projector is set to a different aspect ratio than my playback machine. In lay terms, this means everyone on the screen appears short and squatty—like Barney Rubble. As a result of the incompatible settings, I watch the first few minutes of the movie as if viewing it through a fun house mirror. In addition to displeasure over the flawed video signal, the projectionist isn't thrilled with the audio. Despite the glitches, I am overjoyed to view my little movie projected onto the screen of a multiplex.

"Give me a few days to work on the aspect ration and the audio. Let's plan on meeting one more time before the night of the event," he says.

I agree and shortly thereafter I leave.

As scheduled, I meet the projectionist a week before the premiere. We bypass the small talk and briskly get down to business as he once again attaches my digital playback machine to his projector. When everything is ready to play, he instructs, "Why don't you go downstairs into the auditorium. Pick out a seat anywhere and then give me the thumbs-up when you're ready. Then, as the movie plays, walk around and sit in different sections to test the audio. We have plenty of time before the matinees start so I'll let her run as long as you need."

I scurry down the stairs from the projection room, through the emergency exit door and into the main section of the multiplex. I follow a wide, carpeted hallway the color of a throat lozenge to Theater 12, the largest in the complex with a seating capacity of 350. I settle into an aisle seat ten rows from the screen, turn to the rear of the theater, and issue a thumbs-up to the projectionist. Shortly thereafter the auditorium lights begin to dim.

As the movie—in its correct aspect ratio—fills the huge movie screen, I am overtaken by a surge of joy, pride, and wonder never before realized in my life. A stream of tears runs down my face as I watch the movie all by myself in the middle of a theater of 350 empty seats. I honestly believe, perhaps selfishly, that God Himself has arranged for this short matinee viewing. The movie I had toiled over in my little studio is suddenly larger than life. In the catalog of life's experiences, this moment has its own page—its own *chapter*! It is completely awesome. Frederick Ford Copolla has left kindergarten and advanced directly to college.

I swiftly move about the theater and sit in various locations, mesmerized. At one point I walk to the front of the theater and turn to view 350 empty seats, above which a stream of flickering light carries my movie to the screen. In that brief moment, I feel like Rocky Balboa standing in the boxing ring the night before his big fight with Apollo Creed. I am filled with fright and excitement.

Eventually, I conclude the audio is acceptable in every corner of the theater, so I return to the projection room and give the projectionist my favorable assessment. We're good to go.

I make one final appointment to do a dry run an hour or so before the actual showing of the movie on August 4, then I leave. As I walk out of the projection room and back to my car in the nearly abandoned parking lot of the multiplex, I'm walking on air.

The first thing I do is call Babe.

"Hon, it's unbelievable," I say excitedly into my cell phone and then describe the entire experience. I'm shaking as if I were the only audience member at a private concert by The Beatles. She is thrilled, mostly for me as she knows how hard I had worked and how much of my heart I put into the editing.

"Catherine Zeta Jones has nothing on you," I bubble boastfully.

"It looks good?"

"It looks *great*."

As I drive and speak on the phone, I am in another world. I repeat how amazing it was for me to watch the movie on the big screen all by myself, like a favorite dream that magically came to life.

Later that day, I phone Justine at the adoption agency and frantically deliver the good news. "It really looks great Justine. What a treat to watch the movie on a screen at the multiplex. It was unbelievable."

"I'm so excited," she sings, "We've received about eighty RSVPs."

"Really? Between them and the people I invited we might be looking at a hundred, maybe a hundred and a quarter."

As I contemplate the fast-approaching premiere, the thoughts send nervous butterflies into my stomach. From now until the night of the premiere, I will have to deal with a blend of uncontrollable fear and nervous anticipation that looms intimidatingly overhead like a ravenous buzzard.

We'd love to have Lila attend the Premiere, but her first reaction to the footage was so gloomy we don't intend to risk further harm. She'll view the movie when she's ready.

In the meantime, she makes great strides in every area—except the sleeping. She's brilliantly smart and she has a strong memory. In addition, she picks up sentences and makes some perceptive associations.

One night, for example, we are seated in Howard's Café, a casual pub/restaurant we've visited many times in the past. A plate of fried mozzarella sticks sits in front of Lila. There's two left and they rest horizontally on the plate a few inches apart. Lila points to the two mozzarella sticks and says something that sounds to me like, "Pod but."

"What honey?" I ask.

"Pause but," she repeats. Her message just got clearer but I still can't decipher its meaning. Babe can.

"Do you know what she's saying?" Babe asks, her eyes wide in amazement.

"No, what?"

"Pause button," Babe says slowly and points to the two mozzarella sticks, which resemble the symbol for the pause button on our TV remote.

I'm flabbergasted.

A minute or so later, the owner of the restaurant (John Norton) comes over to our table to say hello. John has a son about the same age as Lila. John and his wife Denise have been friends of ours for years and they experienced similar infertility issues during the same years we experienced ours.

During the conversation, he offers, "You guys really did something special. She's such a lucky baby."

It's not the first time someone has praised us for our decision to adopt. The compliment always makes me feel a bit uncomfortable. We really didn't do anything except follow God's lead. To take credit for this seems unnatural and selfish. Lila may be a lucky baby, but I always feel Babe and I are the lucky ones.

* * *

The premiere of Lila's movie is held on a beautiful summer night on Thursday, August 4, 2005. Grandma Beep-Beep agrees to baby-sit so Babe and I can attend together. We're both sorry Lila won't be there, but we feel we have no choice. Before I leave, I pick Lila up and give her a big hug and kiss then say, "You're going to be a big star tonight honey."

As we drive to the multiplex, I feel nervous anxiety.

"How do you feel?" Babe asks.

I take a deep breath. "Nervous. Nervous and excited."

"Everyone's going to love it," she says assuringly. Babe knows I need affirmation more than anything else at this moment.

"I'm not a good judge of my own work. Sometimes in comedy, I'll write something that I *know* will get big laughs, then I do the joke on stage and it bombs. But this movie," I shake my head as I struggle for the right words, "I just think it's special."

"It *is* special. It's going to be special to Lila, that's the main thing," Babe says.

Self-doubt has become the undesired by-product of placing Lila's movie on display to the public. I find it a constant struggle to stay upbeat. Deep down, though, I really feel the movie is good. It is fast-paced, it provides an honest look at the China adoption process, and it's entertaining—even funny in some parts. Maybe because the issue is so personal to me, I can't objectively assess the quality of the movie. I'll just have to wait to see how others react.

We arrive early, at 6:00. Once inside, I proceed to the auditorium and set up a small amplifier with a hand-held microphone at the front of the theater, to the right of the big screen. Pauline from New Beginnings is scheduled to speak about the Tomorrow Plan, the fund that will benefit from the donation money raised by the event. After her speech, she will introduce me and I, in turn, will introduce the movie. I expect more than a hundred guests so I figure a small amplifier is appropriate to reach the back sections of the theater when announcements need to be made.

Babe and two of our neighbors and good friends, John and Debbie, set up a long table at the entrance to the auditorium. On the table, they place several photos of Lila, a copy of the invitation to the movie, a fishbowl for a 50/50 raffle, and a red shoebox with a big slot cut into the top for donations to the Tomorrow Fund. Meanwhile, I scramble frantically to the projection room to visit the projectionist. His first attempt to play the movie for a dry run results in no video or audio signal to the screen. I look at him and observe, with a stab of panic, a furrowed brow and an obvious look of concern on his face. If he was a cartoon, a giant question mark would have appeared above his head.

"Uh-oh," he mutters ominously.

His comment sends an electric current through my body and an instant case of projectile diarrhea surging through my bowels.

"Uh, go ahead down and test your microphone. I'll try a few things to get her running right," he says with a voice strangled by distraction.

"Ok, I'll test the mic and come back up in a few minutes," I say nervously.

I leave and suddenly I'm haunted by a vision of a hundred people sitting in a theater staring at a blank screen. Fear invades my mind. As much as I trust the projectionist and his expertise, we have reached High Noon and there is little time to spare. The doors officially open at 7:00 and the scheduled movie time is 7:20. The projectionist's ominous "uh-oh" was issued at about 6:10. This isn't good.

Babe knows something's wrong as soon as she sees my face. "Something the matter?" she asks.

"No, nothing, he's got a minor glitch," I say. I hope the lie doesn't register on my face. "I'm going to the front of the theater to test the microphone."

I walk into the theater and turn the amplifier to the "ON" position. As I test the microphone, with a series of "test 1, 2, 3s," I am distracted by unsavory thoughts: Will the projectionist fix the problem? Will the Barney Rubble body shapes re-emerge? How many will attend? What will they think of the movie? Will they laugh? Relate to the story? Cry? Self-doubt assails me. And the worst part is: I am helpless to do anything. The movie is done, the projection of the movie is in the projectionist's hands, there is nothing more I can do except...

...alone at the front of the theater, forty-five minutes away from the premiere of the movie and a potential disaster of gargantuan proportions, I stand still and whisper a plea to God that all problems will wash away and the event will go smoothly. The prayer calms me and reinforces my belief that the difference between failure and success is a thin line that is often and easily erased by faith in God.

When I return to the projection room with my heart relocated to its temporary seat next to my Adam's apple, the projectionist is all smiles as he attempts to give me a technical explanation of what went wrong. To be honest, once he says, "I figured her out," nothing else registers in my overheated brain. I heard what I needed to hear and my mind is now at ease. I nod thoughtfully as he sails through his technical explanation. I pretend to understand, offering an occasional "uh-huh" to complete the illusion. When he's done, I issue some last minute instructions.

"The microphone works fine. I'm going to have someone from the adoption agency speak first then I'm going to introduce the movie. When I'm done talking, I'll give you a signal to roll the tape."

We are ready to go. And at that moment, a sense of calm envelopes me like a group hug from a band of angels. In the cradle of that calm, I know the premiere is going to be a huge success. I just know it.

There's a popular saying that's used these days: It's All Good. I'm not sure of its origin, but as I spoke with a friend prior to the event, I used that term to describe my feelings as the movie premiere approached. I explained it was for a good charity, and the movie was a good story with a good ending, it was all about love, family, faith in God, and miracles; and everyone attending was probably in some way attached to the story, either through their own adoption or through their support of me and Babe. There wasn't a single bad thing to think or say about this night.

It's All Good.

When I re-emerge from the projection room, I check in with Babe, who is now seated at the table alongside our friend Debbie in front of the entrance to the auditorium. She instantly recognizes the relief on my face.

"We're good to go," I say confidently as I check my watch.

"What time is it?" she asks.

"About quarter to seven. I'm going to the main lobby to see how many people are waiting to get in," I say, and leave abruptly. My heart is racing.

I stride briskly down the wide, carpeted hallway of the multiplex, past several entrance doors to other theaters as I approach the main lobby. When I arrive at the lobby, I stop in my tracks, shocked. A line of more than *two hundred* is wrapped halfway around the lobby. I recognize a lot of faces but most are strangers. I greet some friends hastily and distractedly with a forced smile. Minutes later, an usher removes the velvet rope and the herd of attendees noisily advances toward Theater Twelve.

I walk with the line and speak to co-worker Peter Belyea and his family, then others; yet I'm unable to settle in to conversations of any substance. My mind is overwhelmed by several thoughts at once.

The donations pour in, by check and cash, for The Tomorrow Plan. I never expected such a big crowd. Many of the attendees responded to New Beginnings' invitation. Most of those I traveled to China with are here: Rob and Kitty with their two daughters; George and Shirley with daughter Jada; Tom and Colleen sans daughter; Danny and Karen with their two daughters Cecily and Emily. All are surprised and disappointed that Lila is not here.

"I tried to show the raw footage to her around Christmas and she got real melancholy," I say regretfully to Karen as I stand with her in line, "I just don't think she's ready to watch it just yet."

By the time 7:00 rolls around, more than 230 guests have poured into the movie theater. The noisy conversations of the auditorium soothe my ears like the warm-up notes of a great orchestra just prior to the concert. Neither my parents nor my siblings are able to free up time in their schedules to attend, as the event is held mid-week and most of my immediate family lives hundreds of miles away in New England. My nephew John and brother in law Jerry (Lorraine's son and husband) traveled from New Jersey and are in attendance. Furthermore, I plan to make a DVD copy of the movie to show the others in a just a few days, as Babe, Lila, and I will be traveling to New Hampshire to attend my nephew Evan's baptism.

My pulse rate quickens uncontrollably as I confer with Pauline to collectively improvise a game plan. Minutes before the scheduled 7:20 show time, we make our way to the front of the auditorium. I power up the amplifier and tap the microphone a few times with my index finger. The noise echoes and bounces loudly around the theater as I hand the microphone to Pauline and step aside.

"Good evening. My name is Pauline Park from New Beginnings Children and Family Services in Mineola. I would like to first thank Fred and Dorothy Ford for sponsoring this unique event. The donations you made on your way into the theater will go to The Tomorrow Plan, a program sponsored by the China Center of Adoption Affairs to assist special needs orphans with emergency medical expenses. The children benefiting from the fund are usually older orphans who have not been assigned a family, many of whom suffer from debilitating diseases and illnesses. I would like to thank you all for your generous contributions. And now I'd like to introduce the producer of the movie, Mr. Fred Ford."

The audience applauds politely as I take the microphone from Pauline.

"Thanks Pauline. The movie you're about to see is the personal journey to adopt as told by me and my wife Dorothy, who many of you know simply as Babe. Before we roll the tape I'd like to thank New Beginnings for their efforts promoting the movie. And I'd like to also thank the projectionist, who is a true professional and has shown a great interest and enthusiasm in this movie event being a success." I look up in the direction of the projection booth and salute. Polite applause ripples though the audience.

"And finally, before we begin I would like to make a dedication."

I steel my resolve. It will take all I have to hold back tears.

"This movie would never have been made if not for the love of a beautiful woman who I have the good fortune of having as a partner in life, a partner in business, and my best friend. She has always inspired the best in me and she is responsible for arousing my passion to make movies. She has given her whole heart to our daughter Lila, who is the fortunate beneficiary of having such a wonderful woman as her role model. And so the premiere of this movie is dedicated, with love, to my beautiful wife Babe."

More polite applause breaks out as I fight tears and cast a loving, misty smile in Babe's direction.

"And now ladies and gentleman, it gives me great pleasure to present *Lila Rose Comes Home at Last*," I announce and motion up to the projection booth. As I make my way from the front to the rear of the auditorium, the lights gradually extinguish. The movie begins with the appearance of the MGM trademark on the big screen; the same one that opens my favorite movie of all time: *The Wizard of Oz*. Through the magic of digital editing, however, I have replaced the lion's face with my own. The audience laughs its approval. The premiere is off to a roaring start—quite literally.

Babe and I watch the movie from the rear of the auditorium, adjacent to the exit door. We opt not to sit, as I am too nervous to begin with, and want to observe the reactions of the audience. The reactions are heart-warming and way beyond anything I imagined. They laugh. They cry. They applaud. When the photo of Lila's first smile is projected onto the screen, the audience issues a loud and collective "Aw-w-w-w-w-w." The reaction touches a chord for both me and Babe.

The seventy-two minutes speed past us like a gush of wind. The audience members have remained in their seats throughout. By the end of movie, a chorus of sniffles filters through the audience.

As the credits roll down the screen to Judy Garland's *Somewhere Over the Rainbow*, I make my way slowly toward the front of the theater with Babe. To end the night, we will pull the winner of the 50/50 raffle out of a fish bowl. By the time we reach the front, the credits have ended and the final photo of Lila is being projected onto the screen, along with the dedication. I reach down and grab the microphone, power up the amplifier, and then turn back to the audience. As I do, I'm overwhelmed to see the entire audience standing and applauding; a tribute that stirs such gratitude I nearly break down. I glance to my left and see Babe, who smiles clumsily at me with tears in her eyes.

Look Ma, I really can fly like Superman.

The movie that had its genesis as a gift to Lila has become—in the span of little more than one hour—much more than simply a gift. As I soak in the unforgettable vision of the audience, with their loud ovation tickling my ears like the Breath of God, I realize with great certainty and pride, my instinct is right: the movie really *is* special.

Approximately 8,000 miles from Lila's birth place, forty years removed from my first visit to the Regent Theater in Arlington, and ten light years beyond the computer frustrations and early failures of my barely noticeable video-editing career, I stand alone in the front of a theater and enjoy the greatest and most unexpected moment I've ever known. For one brief moment, I can call myself a film-maker. All inspired by my precious baby girl from halfway around the world.

Chapter 12
A LIFE OF ITS OWN

I wake up Friday morning after the premiere with the sweetest hangover in recent memory. The audience reaction to the movie clings to my mind like childhood memories of Christmas morning. I can't wait to share the movie with my family in New England.

I'm taking a vacation day today to prepare for our trip north. On Sunday, my nephew Evan is to be baptized and my sister Jeanne asked me to be godfather. We plan to stay in New England from Saturday until Wednesday.

Evan is a miracle baby. His mother, my sister Jeanne, is severely afflicted with rheumatoid arthritis. In addition, she endured a major back operation, had a steel rod surgically inserted into her spine several years ago and had long ago given up hope of having biological children. Suddenly, at the age of forty-two, she got pregnant with her first child. As a result, she was required to stop taking her weekly pain-killing injections and her Motrin. She refused to complain—a trait she inherited from Mom and Dad—despite her indescribable level of discomfort.

At eight months pregnant, Jeanne's OBGYN asked her to consult with a Neonatologist. Their concern was the Morphine Sulphate Contin Jeanne was taking. During the consultation, the doctor somberly suggested Jeanne's baby would probably go through withdrawals once he was born and would likely remain in the hospital for four to six weeks to treat the withdrawals. This piled an unfortunate layer of guilt atop her physical discomfort. Upon hearing the news, Jeanne cried uncontrollably every day for weeks.

Jeanne's son Evan was born on Christmas Eve. Both he and Jeanne left the hospital the day after Christmas; Evan never encountered withdrawals. I look no further than Mom's prayers and the healing power of God—which exceeds all human understanding—when I try to explain such a miracle.

* * *

We leave on Saturday morning. During the drive, I ask Babe, "How much money was raised at the premiere?"

"I didn't get an exact count," says Babe, "but it was more than $3,000."

"That's great," I say. "That's awesome."

We cruise east past the farms and old homesteads and vineyards of Long Island's north fork and then onto the huge ferry at Orient Point and enjoy a smooth sail across Long Island Sound. Lila enjoys the ferry ride, though she gets cranky later in the day during the auto ride through Connecticut and Massachusetts. Hours later, we arrive at the Red Roof Inn in Salem, New Hampshire, about two miles from my parent's house. After we check in and unpack, we head to Mom and Dad's for a visit.

As we pull up to my parent's house, I notice the driveway is crowded with cars, a common sight around the holidays. We climb the stairs on the left side of my parent's white and gray hi ranch—the home I lived in from the time I was ten until I left for college—and enter the side door. I see Mom at the kitchen table. As always, she wears her cheery smile and gives us all a warm greeting, followed by an offer for a cup of coffee and the inevitable questions about the ferry ride. Dad overhears the fuss as he sits in the den watching TV and joins us. Jeanne, her husband Bill, and baby Evan are also there and before long a loud reunion commences.

Once settled, I say, "I want to show you the first part of Lila's movie."

"How long is it, Freddie? I don't think we have time to watch the whole thing," Mom says.

"I just want to show you the first ten seconds."

The unsuspecting audience gathers in the den as I place the DVD in the player and start the movie. The MGM trademark appears, followed by my face instead of the lion's and then my huge lion roars. Everyone laughs.

"Maybe on Monday we can watch the whole thing," I say suggestively.

"Yah, tomorrow's going to be hectic, we're better off waiting until Monday," Jeanne says.

With the Multiplex reaction still fresh in my mind, I'm more excited than ever to show the movie to my family but happy we'll have the extra few days to spend in New England. I don't visit often enough and usually don't have more than a day or so before I have to get back to Long Island to tend to either of my two careers which have—sadly—taken priority over my visits to New Hampshire.

The baptism takes place on Sunday. Before the mass, Jeanne says to me, "Mom is going to be so relieved."

"Yeah? Why?"

"She's just been very anxious about getting Evan baptized. She asked me so many times when we were planning to have it done."

In the eyes of our family, Mom is a living saint. She leads prayer groups for the church and operates a prayer hot line from her home phone. She devotes much of her time to service for the church, Bible studies for the elderly, a Bible study shown on local cable television, and writing her book *A Note of Confidence in God's Word*—a daily devotional. I'm sure her anxiety about Evan's baptism had to do with her concern about the million-to-one shot something might happen to Evan before he gets baptized, which in the Catholic faith carries some dire consequences.

"This worked out perfectly," I say soothingly.

And so it did. The jam-packed church is humid and stifling but the mass is beautiful and all the babies behave. After the mass, my family gathers at a local restaurant for brunch. I sit with Mom and Dad and catch up on small talk. When brunch is done, I say to Mom, "We'll come over tomorrow morning. I was thinking we could go to the amusement park with Lila."

"Yah, I'd love that," Mom responds affably, and smiles.

We leave and drive to our motel room to relax. Later that night, we have dinner and then get to bed early in anticipation of a busy Monday. Lila will have her first visit to an amusement park and we'll get to spend some rare quality time with Mom and Dad. Later in the day, I hope everyone has enough energy and interest to watch my movie.

Lila falls asleep around 8:30. Babe and I punch the clock a few hours later.

At 3:30 a.m. the phone rings in our hotel room. At such an hour, it jostles my brain like a blast from Gabriel's horn. I'm incoherent as I rise from the bed to answer.

"Hello," I mumble into the phone.

"Freddie, it's Cathy, your parent's neighbor across the street."

"Yah, hi."

"Your father needs you at the house. I'm sorry Freddie. Your mom passed away."

Though barely awake, I feel as though someone reached inside me and sliced away part of my soul.

"I'm sorry," she repeats sincerely.

I sit on the edge of the bed stunned.

"Thanks," I say. "I'll be right over."

I hang up and Babe, who's sleeping next to Lila on the other bed, sits up and asks in a concerned half whisper, "Who was that?"

"My parent's neighbor Cathy." I pause a moment and try to make sense of my thoughts and feelings—not an easy task at 3:30 a.m. when you've just been informed that your mother, who you saw yesterday in seemingly perfect health, is dead. I don't know how to tell Babe so I simply say, "My mother died."

"*What*?!"

I get up and rub my temples, unable to filter the flood of thoughts and emotions. "I'm going to the house. My father needs me."

I dress hastily and tell Babe I'll call her later. I leave the hotel room and drive the desolate streets to my parent's house. It's a drive I've made thousands of times over the course of more than thirty years but now seems eerily unfamiliar, as though occurring in a haunted dream. I enter through the same side door I came through just one day earlier and once again the first thing I see is Mom. Only this time she's on the kitchen floor covered by a white sheet. The sight of it sends a wave of unfamiliar sickness through my body. A police officer is in the room waiting for the ambulance and medical examiner.

"Hi," he says somberly as he nods to me. "I'm sorry."

"Thanks," I say and move past Mom and the police officer as quickly as I can. I go into the living room where I see Dad seated in the big chair in the corner. We embrace and both of us begin to cry. It's a surreal moment; one I never want to experience again.

Things will never be the same…

* * *

Our mini-vacation turns into a week of unexpected mourning. The grief is somehow bearable because of the suddenness of Mom's death. More than grief, I feel shock and disbelief. Despite the bad feelings, I am at total peace that Mom is in Heaven. The peace washes through my soul in a continuous flow.

A day before the wake, I'm visiting dad when a group from our church arrives. A man and two women represent the grief committee, who selflessly volunteer to spend time with families and spouses of the recently deceased to help them cope with the grieving process. It has to be a difficult ministry and I appreciate their presence.

"Your mother was a beloved member of our church," one woman says sincerely.

The words barely console my father, who is on the verge of tears during the entire visit.

"It's such a coincidence," I say, "all five of her children were here for Evan's baptism. It was as if my mother planned it—as though she didn't want to inconvenience any of us to have to make separate travel plans in her behalf."

The woman smiles warmly. "You mother didn't believe in coincidence. She often said: coincidence is God's way of remaining anonymous."

I instantly embrace the words as a fossil of truth. It sounds precisely like a thought God would inspire in Mom's heart and mind.

We leave days later with heavy hearts and concern for Dad. He just lost his partner of forty-seven years. Nothing I say carries sufficient consolation.

Parenting takes no holidays and Lila doesn't understand what happened to Grandma Amen so she continues to cry at night and do the things two year olds do. Like any two year old, she is indifferent when I speak about Grandma going to Heaven.

Two days after the funeral, we prepare for our trip back to Long Island, burdened by an emotional load we didn't carry during our drive a few days ago. When we say good-bye to Dad I feel more sadness than any other moment during the ordeal. We visit the cemetery before we get onto the highway for the drive home. As I kneel at Mom's grave site I cry uncontrollably, tears that rise from deep in my soul and nearly choke me as they attempt to rinse the grief from my mind. I've been able to hold back these tears for the sake of staying strong for others; yet as I kneel at Mom's grave they refuse to be held back any longer.

Once back in New York, I go through the motions and life temporarily evolves into a meaningless treadmill. The world seems quite different.

* * *

A few months after we resume our lives, something happens. The little movie I made for Lila, with its unexpected success at the premiere, takes on a life of its own.

While in New England, I had given the movie to each of my siblings. Shortly after she watched it, my youngest sister Alison was inspired to share the movie with her friend Cathy, whose daughter was going through infertility hell. Cathy reluctantly agreed to watch the movie, all the while insisting her daughter Jen probably wouldn't like such a movie; it would only upset her further. Alison starts the movie and within five minutes, Cathy glances toward Alison with tears in her eyes and says, "I need to show this to my daughter. Do you think I could borrow it?"

A few days later, Cathy's daughter Jen receives the movie, watches it with her husband Brandon, and shortly thereafter they decide to adopt. Jen indicates to Alison that the movie "normalized adoption" for them. It put their hearts and minds at ease that average, good-hearted couples like me and Babe experience infertility and adoption all the time. The movie's references to God also influenced them and gave them strength to move forward. In the months to follow, we will hear many similar reactions.

New Beginnings asks us to participate in a second showing of the movie, at the Adoption Annex in Great Neck. I sit in the back of the crowded classroom with Babe and the audience reacts with laughter and tears, applause at the end, and requests for copies of the movie from every participant.

A week later, Pauline asks me for extra copies of the DVD. She has posted an offer for the DVD on the New Beginnings web site and received an unexpectedly strong response, one she can't keep up with. The movie's life has grown. I feel like my child was just accepted at Harvard.

* * *

Dad continues to grieve Mom's death. My sister Jeanne says he has not been feeling well and coughed up blood recently. After numerous unsuccessful attempts, she persuades Dad to visit the doctor.

Days later, I get an email from Jeanne. In it she writes: *Dad has been diagnosed with Stage 3B lung cancer. The condition is terminal.* I stare at the words for thirty seconds as though reading about the assassination of the President. The blood drains from my heart.

The oncologist ultimately recommends chemotherapy. Dad's horizon is suddenly strewn with difficult days and painful uncertainty. Simultaneously, he has to cope with the emotional trauma brought about by Mom's death. This can't be easy.

In one of Jeanne's emails, she writes: *Dad finally watched Lila's movie. Before he put it into the DVD player, he asked me if he was going to be able to get through it. I told him it was emotional but ultimately had a happy ending. He watched the movie and loved it. In the weeks and months to follow, he showed the movie to everyone who visited.*

I feel badly Mom never got to see the movie. I could have justifiably become bitter. Her death just a few days after the premiere—and a day before I planned to show it to her—seems cruel, particularly since Mom always loved her family above all others. As with Mom's death, however, I am somehow at peace when I think about Mom missing out on the movie. I'm neither angry nor bitter. On the contrary, I attribute the life the movie has taken on to my mother's spirit. Her role in the movie's success and its ability to impact others, therefore, goes way beyond spectator.

Weeks prior to Christmas, we attend the New Beginnings Holiday party at the Huntington Townhouse, a large catering hall. Lila is dressed in a red and white dress and she's cuter than a basket full of puppies. As we enter the large room where the event is held, I overhear someone to my right say to their child, "Look, honey, that's Lila Rose."

Babe and I exchange amused glances. Suddenly—and we hope temporarily—Lila has become Shirley Temple. Apparently, the movie has been viewed by more people than we are aware.

"Hello Ford Family," says Pauline warmly. The New Beginnings staff is on hand and they feel like family members.

"Merry New Year," I say.

Lila turns shy. She did the same thing at the agency's summer picnic. When she spends time around the other families we traveled with to China, she becomes withdrawn and somber—regardless of the mood she was in previously.

Pauline grabs my arm lightly and says, "I'm so sorry about your mom."

"Thanks," I say. "It was quite a shock."

"I have to ask: did she see the movie?"

I frown and shake my head slowly. "No. I planned to show it to her on Monday and she died Sunday night."

"That's so sad."

In one sense Pauline is right: it is sad. In a larger sense, a sense that goes beyond logic or fairness or comprehension, there is a reason why the three incidents (movie premiere, Evan's baptism, Mom's death) occurred together. I simply can't shake that notion that the life of the movie and the life of Mom's spirit are linked; one entity capable of supernaturally reaching and touching others.

Most of the others we traveled to China with are in attendance and they are seated at a large table at the far end of the crowded, noisy room. Colleen waves excitedly to us as we talk to Pauline. I wave back and then raise my index finger to suggest we'll be there in a minute. When we're done with Pauline, we make our way through the maze of tables and chairs. As we do, we are stopped three separate times by attendees who want to tell us how much they love the movie. None of the faces are familiar. Of those who stop us, one woman says she and her husband were undecided about adoption but after they saw the movie, they called New Beginnings to get the paperwork and start the process.

"We're so happy to hear that," says Babe sincerely. "Thank you." Babe's humble comment barely describes the level of appreciation we have come to realize when others comment on the movie, particularly when total strangers seek us out, send a letter, or email.

We reach our China family and greet them with hugs, handshakes, and kisses.

"This feels like a reunion of the members of Gilligan's Island," I say jokingly.

Tom smiles and as he shakes my hand he says through gritted teeth, "You're killin' me."

"What do you mean?"

"Ten people have recognized me from your movie," he blushes. Tom is not one for attention and his sudden and involuntary placement under the spotlight has thrust him momentarily and unwittingly into the role of a movie star.

I laugh and hug the man I have come to call my brother.

Lila, on the other hand, doesn't laugh. She doesn't even smile. She won't participate in the games or songs and barely budges when a scrawny version of Santa shows up to give away toys and candy canes. She somberly endures the party while clinging to Babe. A resolute glare is pasted to her face and she demonstrates a total unwillingness to do anything but sulk. The same feeling of dread and confusion I had in Nanning revisits me. I hope the setback is temporary.

* * *

Despite the step backward at the holiday party, Lila continues to make great strides. She speaks well, understands English, and is hysterically funny. Her laugh could cheer up a death row inmate.

Babe and I are mindful that everything we do or say has an impact. We choose our words carefully and try to always set a good example. Despite our good intentions, invariably we fail at times. On one occasion, for example, Grandma Beep Beep is at our house for a memorable—and embarrassing—visit.

We're seated at the kitchen table, when Beep Beep says, "I cut out an article I'd like you to read," and hands the newspaper clipping to me.

I don't have my reading glasses handy and can't decipher a single word so I say, "Lila, can you get Daddy's glasses?"

A minute later, as Beep Beep and I continue to talk, Lila re-appears. She holds two martini glasses, one per hand, and says, "Here Daddy."

The embarrassment is overwhelmed by the avalanche of laughter. Meanwhile, a lesson is learned and a new rule is adopted pertaining to Friday happy hour.

Days later, we travel to New Hampshire to visit Dad for the Christmas holiday. I haven't seen him since his first trip to the hospital months ago. Through emails, Jeanne tells me all his hair—as expected—has fallen out in reaction to the chemotherapy.

We get to the house and enter, as always, through the kitchen door on the left side of the house—an entrance that's now permanently attached to a traumatic memory. Dad is seated at the kitchen table with my sister Lorraine and niece Mary. He greets us with a big smile and tells us how great he's feeling—though we suspect otherwise. Dad has never complained in his life. He's chiseled out of the same granite that sets apart those who belong to the Greatest Generation. Along with Mom, he is the greatest role model of my life. In every sense of the word, he's my hero.

It's a solemn visit, nothing like past Christmas holidays. Throughout our visit, Dad makes light of his loss of hair. He walks around and says, "Etcetera, etcetera," like Yul Brenner in *The King and I*. He faces cancer as he's faced every other aspect of his life: with courage and dignity and humor and integrity and humility.

Lila gradually begins to warm up to Dad, despite his changed appearance. On the first night of our visit, however, Dad's getting ready to go to bed and he leans to Lila for a kiss. She refuses to kiss him.

"Not tonight, huh, OK," Dad says resignedly, "Good night everyone."

He leaves the room, walks downstairs, and I become angry. My face turns red and I grit my teeth.

"She's still just a baby," Babe says.

"She knows better," I mutter angrily.

I feel badly about my anger and later apologize to Babe. It's not Lila's fault; it's no one's fault. It's wrong to raise my voice or show such anger in front of Lila. Yet I have become intensely defensive about any feelings of rejection Dad might feel from Lila. Mom never really had a relationship with Lila; the opportunities to bond were too rare and Lila was always frightened around new faces. I don't want the same thing to happen with Lila and Dad.

Days later, as the holiday ends, we have lunch with Dad and then he walks us to the car. I don't want to leave him. I wish there was more I could do. He gets kisses from everyone and then turns to Lila, who is cradled in Babe's arms. For a second, I am revisited by a Nanning flashback; seconds before we got Lila as she sat in the arms of the woman from the orphanage and wore her familiar scowl. A year and a half later, she wears the same fear-filled scowl of as she glares at my father. Dad leans forward. Lila glances briefly in my direction and detects a look on my face that she's uncomfortable with. Seconds later, she shifts her attention back to Dad, leans to him, and gives me a kiss. I feel a hurricane of relief.

* * *

The list of friends we've promised a DVD copy of the movie to is long and growing. I continue to offer free DVD copies to New Beginnings. I'm flattered they would want copies, and in keeping with the spirit of generosity my mother always taught—and lived by—I think of the free copies as a way of sharing my faith and our adoption story for the benefit of others.

One of the couples we share the movie with is my friend and former co-worker Jimmy and his wife Lynn, who waged their own battle against infertility during the time Babe and I waged ours. Like us, Jimmy and Lynn turned to adoption. I ring the doorbell of their home and Jimmy answers.

"Ho, look at this," he says loudly. And we hug.

I hold up a copy of the DVD case. "As promised," I say.

"This is your adoption movie?"

"My soon to be famous adoption movie."

He invites me in and I say hello to Lynn and their beautiful baby girl Olivia. I don't have much time and we scurry through some random small talk before Jimmy says, "Did you hear about Lynn's mother?"

My heart sinks. "No, what happened?"

"She nearly died. She wasn't feeling good so she checked into a hospital and they did a bunch of tests…"

As he speaks, the words become silent and my mind drifts off to Mom. Apparently, neither Jimmy nor Lynn is aware of my mother's death. When he's done with his description of their ordeal, I ask them to send best wishes and love from me and Babe, and then I say, "I guess you didn't hear about my mom."

A concerned look grips both of their faces. "No, what happened?"

My planned visit of a few minutes extends by several more as I try to get through the story of Mom's sudden death—a story I've painfully repeated too many times during the past four months.

Weeks later, I visit Jimmy's house again, this time to watch the Super Bowl. During a commercial break, Jimmy asks, "Freddie, do you mind if I give your adoption movie to a friend of mine?"

"Not at all. Share it with as many people as you like."

"We showed the movie to my friend Joey and his wife and they both got real emotional. Then Joey asked if he could borrow the movie."

"That's great. If you want I'll send him a copy. I share the movie with anyone who wants to see it."

Three months later, I learn that Jimmy's friend Joey and his wife Nadine decided to adopt from Korea. When I speak to Jimmy about it months after the decision is made, he indicates my movie made a huge difference.

It's the third time I've heard such a comment. It never fails to lift me to a place I never dreamed possible. I recount the story for Babe later in the day.

"I never saw this coming when I made the movie," I say.

* * *

Months later, New Beginnings conducts an adoption workshop. They request my participation.

"We want to show the movie and have you as the host," says Justine.

"Whatever you want," I say. The adoption story is a piece of my heart and the one thing I am most passionate about. Now that I've seen first hand how the movie can affect others, I take every opportunity to share the story.

I arrive the morning of the workshop at Winthrop Hospital in Mineola and see my New Beginnings family at the registration table. I enter through the motion-activated glass doors and blend into the crowd. As I busily exchange handshakes and hellos, a woman gently tugs my arm and introduces herself and says she recently saw my movie.

"As soon as the movie ended, we decided to adopt. I'm planning my entire Mother's Day around a showing of the movie to my parents and in-laws."

Her comment unintentionally opens a floodgate of emotions as I think of Mom. Not more than two minutes into my visit, I'm nearly in tears. Comments like this humble me to the point of embarrassment. They strengthen my belief that God worked through the story of Lila's adoption to create a movie that goes beyond entertainment to touch hearts and affect lives.

"Thank you so much," I say. "I'm flattered. My wife will be so happy to hear what you've said."

During a quiet moment later in the workshop, I sit and chat with New Beginnings Executive Director Tim Sutfin and he asks, "When do you plan to show the movie to Lila?"

Tim is a bright man filled with interesting opinions and lots of adoption experience.

"On her sixteenth birthday."

Tim shakes his head. "She has to grow up watching that movie. By the time she reaches sixteen she'll be the only person in the adoption community who hasn't seen it."

His suggestion causes me to think. I haven't attempted to show Lila any portion of the movie for more than a year, based on her prior reactions. Maybe the time is right to try again.

Meanwhile, the movie lives on. If I'm right about my hunch—that the life of the movie is tied to my mother's spirit—then there's no stopping it.

I keep coming back to the word coincidence. I can't categorize two intersecting and life-altering events—the premiere of the movie and Mom's death—as happenstance. The events happened when they did for a reason.

I find it equally difficult to label the increase in the number of babies available for international adoption and the number of couples who experience infertility as unrelated coincidence. Many adoptive parents go through infertility Hell before they reach a decision to adopt. Among other things, infertility is a humbling experience. Like most personal crises, infertility has the power to inspire either self-pity or prayer. I imagine many of the couples who experience infertility have faith in God. In ways mysterious and incomprehensible to the finite minds of parents worldwide, God brings together separate prayers from thousands of miles apart, across oceans and continents, to create miracles. Not only does the miracle result in a baby for parents tortured by infertility, but it provides hope and a home for one of God's precious creations—and perhaps an answer to the lonely, desperate prayer of a mother forced by societal pressure to abandon the fruit of her own womb.

Lila is living proof—our very own miracle.

I will simply never forget that magical day in May of 2004, when total exhaustion gripped my body, mind, and soul, and the last few tears I held inside escaped my eyes and streamed down my face as I watched Babe through a camera lens as she carried Lila through our front door for the first time. It was a seminal moment in my life and the most significant part of God's miraculous, perfect answer to our prayers. It was the exclamation point to the greatest story of my life; the day that Lila Rose came home at last.

ACKNOWLEDGEMENTS

This book would never have been written if not for the inspiration of three women: my mom, my wife, and my daughter. In no particular order, I thank them for showing me what life and love are all about.

Every good thing I've done in life has been influenced by my father. This book is no exception. Dad is the best role model I could ever hope for and the most dedicated teacher of the English language I know. His red pen was much appreciated and needed as I worked through various revisions of this book. His courage and love inspire not only my writing, but everything I touch. As of the writing of this book, his lung cancer is in remission and he has far surpassed the typical life expectancy of Stage 3B lung cancer patients. The little tree Dad planted to commemorate the death of his father in the early 1960's now towers more than fifty feet into the sky, well above the three story house on Wyman Street, the home of my first memories.

It was my good fortune to grow up in a home with strong, compassionate, and wonderful women. To Lorraine, Jeanne, and Alison: thank you for your support, your encouragement, your input, and your inspiration. I love you all.

To my brother Tommy and my many cousins, aunts, and uncles who have helped shape my life, inspire my endeavors, and support the adoption of Lila Rose, I thank all of you. In particular, I thank my cousin Joanne, who temporarily stepped out of retirment and returned to her career as editor to lend her thoughts and talents to my book.

Grandma Beep Beep provided suggestions for the book that were both appreciated and needed. I am thankful for her generosity of spirit, her kindness, and her willingness to give so much of herself to this project and to our family.

Lance, Nicole, Lancie, Nicholas, Ben, Brianne, and Grandpa gave us a welcome home from China I will always remember with fondness and appreciation. Their presence in Lila's life and the extraordinary welcome home they provided are a big and much appreciated part of this story.

To all those who've already seen Lila's movie, in particular those who offered words of praise, thank you. Your words and kindness lit my path and fueled my passion to write this book and offer the movie to a wider audience.

To Tommy Ansbro, whose big heart and keen insight pertaining to shared memories always kept me moving in the right direction, thanks brother.

Bill Reynolds inspired me to read aloud what I've written; the eye is much more forgiving than the ear. His words served me well, as did his suggestions to cut, cut, cut; eliminate unnecessary words; avoid cliches; write as simply as the subject matter will allow. In the spirit of simplicity: thanks Bill.

To Matt and Laura Balkam, I appreciate your enthusiasm, kind words, and support. The world needs more people like the two of you.

To Uncle Jackie, thanks for letting me use the prom photo. I'll be sure to forward any and all fan mail I receive in your behalf.

To my family at New Beginnings: Tim, Justine, Pauline, and Cathy, thank you hardly seems sufficient to express my gratitude for all you've done. I appreciate your involvement in all aspects of this journey. Tim, thank you for reminding me this is a love story.

In early 2006, Pauline Park from New Beginnings traveled to China to donate $10,000 to the Tomorrow Plan. More than $3,000 of the money was raised at the premiere of Lila's movie. The money is to be used for surgery and rehabilitation of special needs orphans. The donation was made, in part, in the name of my mother Joan Ford. I cannot find adequate words to describe the depth of appreciation I felt when Pauline informed me of this news.

Last, but hardly least, I would like to thank God. He is alive and He listens to our prayer. As you reach the finish line of this book, I'm happy to inform you I have prayed for everyone who took time from their lives to read it. Along with my thanks, take heart that you are blessed.

DVD copies of Fred Ford's *Lila Rose Comes Home at Last*, are available for purchase, with proceeds being donated to The Tomorrow Plan. For more details, please send an email to Fred at effeff15@aol.com or send a letter to Fred Ford, 33 Fairway Drive, Bellport, NY 11713.

LaVergne, TN USA
08 December 2010

207926LV00004B/177/P

9 781606 102923